FOR ANOTHER DAY

● ● ●

ONE STRIKE AWAY BOOK TWO

● ● ●

MARY J. WILLIAMS

<u>ABOUT THE AUTHOR</u>

Writing isn't easy. But I love every second. A blank screen isn't the enemy. It is the opportunity to create new friends and take them on amazing adventures and life-changing journeys. I feel blessed to spend my days weaving tales that are unique—because I made them.

Billionaires. Songwriters. Artists. Actors. Directors. Stuntmen. Football players. They fill the pages and become dear friends I hope you will want to revisit again and again.

Thank you for jumping into my books and coming along for the journey.

<u>HOW TO GET IN TOUCH</u>

Please visit me at these sites, sign up for my newsletter or leave a message.

http://www.maryjwilliams.net/

https://www.facebook.com/maryjwilliamsauthor/?ref=hl

https://twitter.com/maryjwilliams05

https://www.pinterest.com/maryj0675/

https://www.instagram.com/2015romance/

https://www.goodreads.com/author/show/5648619.Mary_J_Willia ms

MORE BOOKS BY MARY J. WILLIAMS

Harper Falls Series
If I Loved You
If Tomorrow Never Comes
If You Only Knew
If I Had You (Christmas in Harper Falls)

Hollywood Legends Series
Dreaming with a Broken Heart
Dreaming with My Eyes Wide Open
Dreaming Again
Dreaming of a White Christmas
(Caleb and Callie's story)
One Pass Away Series
After the Rain
After All These Years
After the Fire
Hart of Rock and Roll
Flowers on the Wall
Flowers and Cages
Flowers are Red
Flowers for Zoe
One Strike Away
For a Little While

WITH ONE MORE LOOK AT YOU

TABLE OF CONTENTS

PROLOGUE

● ≈ ● ≈ ●

NICK SANDERS WAS four years old the first time he died.

He died again just after he turned seven. And once more during his ninth summer.

While each was a bloodless, pain-free death. The kind without a body. No autopsy. And no burial. Inevitably, each experience left an indelible mark.

As Nick sorted through the ratty cardboard box his mother had stuffed into the back of the spacious walk-in closet, he wondered why she would hold onto anything from those days.

Scrambling for work that barely paid the rent on a studio apartment in a building that any day could—should—be condemned. A place where crackheads lay sprawled in the stairwells soaked in their own urine, the remnants of vomit crusted on their chins.

Why would she want to remember a time when they were always hungry? When the only clothes on their backs came from the charity box at the local mission? When she would hold him, thinking he was asleep, and weep in despair?

A situation that forced her to fake her own son's death. Three times.

Nick had cried the first time his mother sent him to stay with her friend on the other side of their Los Angeles neighborhood.

"I'll come back for you," Annie had promised, wiping the tears from his cheeks. She pried his arms from around her neck, kissing his forehead. "I need you here so I can make our lives better. Remember? Another day."

Annie Sanders clung to the idea like a drowning woman clutching at the smallest piece of driftwood, hoping she could stay afloat until help came. Don't worry about a month from now. Or a week. Survive for another day.

1

Annie told the neighborhood church that her little boy had died. She had nobody to lean on and desperately wanted to go home to be with her family. The next day, she had three hundred dollars in her pocket.

Of course, staying in that neighborhood was impossible. Annie collected Nick, moving them to another crappy apartment in another crappy part of town. The scam worked twice more.

The next time, Nick didn't cry. Or the next. A little older. Wise beyond his years. He understood why his mother took money that wasn't rightfully hers. But he made himself a promise. One day, he would take care of her. He would move her to a nicer place. Buy her anything she wanted. She would never again have to lie to put food on the table.

Nick had kept that promise. Baseball—his ability to play the game at a high level—turned out to be their salvation. When he signed his minor-league contract right out of high school, every dime went to his mother.

As Nick's fortunes increased—fast, but never fast enough—he made certain Annie Sanders reaped the benefits. His teammates bought themselves fancy cars and expensive toys.

Gladly, Nick took care of the woman who had taken care of him. Not because he felt obligated or in her debt. Because he loved her.

No matter what, Annie had never missed a game from the first time he laced up a pair of cleats. Though she refused to move north after he received his first big payday—thanks to the Seattle Cyclones—she continued to follow his every at bat.

They had survived. Together. The money was great—Nick enjoyed every perk that being a baseball superstar afforded him. But the best part was the pride in his mother's eyes when he handed her the keys to her new home.

A townhouse in Venice, California.

Annie had protested, but Nick knew she enjoyed decorating every inch of the place. He hired her a housekeeper. Bought her a car. And made certain all the bills were sent to him. Her days of struggle and hardship were over.

Nick's biggest fan, the only thing that could have kept Annie Sanders from watching her son play in his first World Series was the late-stage cancer that ravaged her body.

But the television in her room had been tuned to the games. Every inning. Every pitch. Through sheer will, she lived to watch the Cyclones take the championship. Two days later, she was gone.

The hole left by his mother's passing could never be filled. Nick's only consolation was that he had been there to hold her hand as she took her last breath.

"Why, Mom?" Nick muttered, finding nothing in the box of any value—sentimental or otherwise.

"Maybe she forgot the thing was there," Spencer Kraig said, picking up a pile of clothes earmarked for the Goodwill.

"Makes sense," Travis Forsythe agreed. "I can't tell what's in half the boxes gathering dust in my attic."

Nick shook his head. "Mom never lost track of anything. If she kept something, she had a reason."

"We're through. Do you want to take a few minutes?"

"No. This was Mom's house, not mine. Without her, the place feels like nothing but empty rooms."

Nick didn't know how he would have gotten through the past week without Spencer and Travis. More than his teammates, they were the best friends a man could ask for. The death of his mother hit Nick hard. He knew the day was coming. She had been sick for almost a year, an aggressive form of cancer moving from her breasts, riddling her body.

Treatment after treatment failed until the question was no longer if, but when.

Given a choice, Nick would have forgone any kind of memorial service. But Annie Sanders made some good friends since moving here. A luxury she hadn't allowed herself before.

The women's club made the arrangements. Nick attended out of respect for them. Spencer and Travis at his side. Damn good friends.

His mother made her wishes clear. She didn't want a lot of fuss. And she didn't want to be stuck in a casket six feet under.

"Sprinkle my ashes someplace peaceful," Annie told Nick. "On a hill. Where spring flowers bloom."

Nick would find his mother's hill. Later. When the numbness had worn off.

Except for her most personal items, clearing out his mother's home hadn't been something Nick wanted to do. He left that to some highly recommended professionals. They left her clothing neatly folded on the stripped-down bed. The furniture was headed to auction—proceeds going to a women's shelter.

All that was left was the cardboard box. And memories. So many memories. The good, the bad, and even the ugly. Now that his mother was gone, he wouldn't have parted with a single one.

"I love you, Mom."

With what felt like a fist clenching Nick's heart, he quietly closed the front door.

CHAPTER ONE

● ≈ ● ≈ ●

ONE WEEK LATER

NICK SWIRLED THE ice in the plastic glass, diluting the brown liquid that the stewardess tried to pass off as whiskey. Maybe. If he were desperate.

But Nick wasn't much of a boozer.

In his younger days, he never had the time, money, or inclination to imbibe beyond the occasional beer. During his fast rise through the minor leagues, he stuck mostly to soft drinks.

Nick's first real taste of whiskey came courtesy of Ross Burton. After signing a contract for more money than he ever thought possible, he and the Cyclones' owner sealed the deal with a handshake and a glass of what Ross called *mother's milk*.

After tasting the good stuff—smooth, perfectly aged whiskey the color of deep, rich caramel—how could he be expected to settle for less? Nick spent the first two decades of his life scraping at the bottom of the barrel. Now that he could afford to travel first class, that was exactly what he did. All the way.

Nick frowned at this drink. Too bad first class didn't always live up to the billing.

"We land in about an hour." Not as picky as Nick, Travis drained what was left of the liquid in his glass. Straight tequila. "A night on the town in New York."

"Then you head to South Carolina."

"And you to Maine." Travis stretched his long legs—booze aside, the room in first class was worth the price. "Sure you don't want some company?"

"Because you're worried about me? Or..." Lips quirked, Nick shot his friend an inquiring look. "Are you trying to put off a certain meeting with a certain woman?"

Travis shrugged. "My shit can wait."

"Mine is hardly time sensitive."

"Maybe not. But you don't know what you'll find. You should have taken Spencer up on his offer."

"I don't need Yoda to hold my hand," Nick said with more humor than animosity. "Besides, he had more important things to worry about."

"What worry?" Travis laughed. "He's getting married, not trekking up Mt. Everest."

In Nick's opinion, marriage was the more daunting proposition. But if Spencer was happy—ecstatic was more like it—so was he.

"I'll be fine."

"You look like you haven't slept in days."

Nick had slept. Fitfully. That damn box—or rather what he found inside—preyed on his mind. Deciding to make this trip helped. Or that's what he kept telling himself.

Damn that cryptic letter. Though Nick refused to damn his mother, for one of the few times in his life, he was angry with her. Genuinely pissed. The words on that single page had opened old wounds he had thought long healed and forgotten.

Leo,

I used to put dear before your name but finally realized my mistake. You don't care about me. You never did. Lies. One after another. Repeated over and over again. Young and foolish, I desperately wanted to believe. Older and wiser, I now know better.

But you and I are no longer important. Please. I can't tell you what needs to be said in a letter. Call me. I'm barely hanging on, Leo. I don't know how much longer I can live this way. You're my last hope.

Annie

Nick had read the letter over and over, the words burned into his brain. His mother had enclosed her current phone number and address. He recognized the location. They lived there for about six months the year he turned eight.

The envelope, never opened, was stamped with a big, red *RETURN TO SENDER*. But Nick could easily read his mother's handwriting.

Leonard Cartwright. Jasper, Maine.

Question piled upon question. Who was this Leonard Cartwright? Could he be Nick's father? How many times had she written him? What had he said? Or had all the letters come back unopened?

Nick's mother wasn't here to provide him with answers. Another jarring reminder that Annie Sanders was gone. Forever.

"Promise me one thing," Travis said. "Call if you need me. For any reason."

Nick nodded. "That goes both ways."

"I'm headed to redneck territory." Travis grimaced, a trace of a long left behind Southern accent sneaking into his voice. "A place I had hoped to never see again. In and out with as little fuss as necessary."

Sounded like a good plan. Nick was looking for some answers. The less time he spent in Jasper, Maine, the better.

"Bermuda is just a skip and a jump away."

Travis perked up. "Warm sandy beaches. Cold drinks."

"And hot women in tiny bikinis. A cabana on the water. Three days. Four at the most." Nick smiled, fist bumping Travis. Finally, something to look forward to. "I'll meet you in paradise."

CHAPTER TWO

● ≈ ● ≈ ●

A CITY KID through and through, Nick had spent some time in small towns during his minor-league days. However, back then, he was always passing through, not settling in to stay. Eyes focused on taking the next step toward the big time, he socialized with his teammates but made few lasting connections with the town's residents.

The women were plentiful. Though a trifle desperate and less polished than the ones Nick ran with these days. Like the players they sought out, the ladies of the minor leagues looked for an upgrade. Latching onto a professional athlete was their way of moving up the ladder and a better life.

Nick had his fun, but he made sure *fun* was as far as things went. When he left town, the only baggage he carried was the kind he could sling over one shoulder. Drama free. Woman free. And most important, disease free.

Crazy in this day and age, but Nick knew of many a young man who let a good time get in the way of common sense. *No glove, no love.* Words to live by.

As Nick drove past the sign welcoming him to Jasper, Maine—Home of the State Champion Soaring Eagles—he wondered what he would find. *Peyton Place, Pleasantville,* or something in between?

Parking the rented SUV, Nick looked up and down the row of sidewalk-fronted businesses. Nice, he thought. Neat and clean. Not exactly bustling, but at just a little after nine, the hour was still early.

Sliding from the driver's seat, Nick zipped up his jacket. November in Maine was a damn sight colder than Seattle, though not as cold as he had expected. Reaching into the cab, he flipped open the glove compartment. *What do you know?* He chuckled. *Gloves.*

"There you are!"

Out of the corner of his eye, Nick caught a flash of blond hair covered by a dark knit hat. Though bundled in a thick, shapeless, cable-knit sweater, he had no problem determining the whirlwind to be of the female variety. A flash of bright blue eyes rimmed by dark lashes and full lips naturally the color of ripe raspberries.

Not pretty, Nick's radar took note. Pretty was forgettable. Something about this woman made him look twice. Then, look again. She, on the other hand, didn't show the slightest personal interest. Grabbing Nick by the wrist, she tried to tug him toward...?

Nick had no idea of her intended destination. Though she had a surprisingly strong grip, he easily resisted her efforts.

"Come on!" Huffing, she pulled with all her might—to no avail. "Damn it. Do you need a tip just to move your ass off the sidewalk? What is this world coming to? Fine. Wait here."

Amused—add curious—Nick leaned against the side of his vehicle and did as she commanded. He waited. Perhaps he could mine a little pleasure from this trip after all.

Bursting from the storefront, as fast on her feet as when she entered, Nick cocked his head to the side, imagining the curves he would find under that all-encompassing sweater. The hem hit her about mid-thigh of a pair of long, shapely legs. Encouraging.

"Here." Taking Nick's hand, she slapped a bill into his palm. "If that isn't enough, too bad. Get your ass in there and unclog the sink."

A twenty? Not bad. Nick wasn't so far removed from poverty that he scoffed at money no matter the amount.

"Well?" Hands on hips, the blonde waited, obviously at the end of her patience. "I can kick you in the ass if that will get you moving."

Nick had no doubt she would try. The heavy work boots that covered her feet looked as though they had seen plenty of action. Kicking butts and so forth.

What the hell? Nick used to be quite the handyman. A clogged sink should be a cinch. Twenty bucks and a little time to get to know the interesting blonde? Sounded like a win-win situation.

The sign above the door read, *Murielle's Muffins and Stuff.* Nick breathed in the scent of baking bread and cinnamon. He took in the long glass-front case filled with mouthwatering pastries. Much more than muffins, they still made up the majority of choices. The blueberry streusel looked particularly tempting.

"Back this way." The blonde motioned for Nick to follow.

Through a swinging door, Nick found the kitchen where all the amazing scents emanated. He knew nothing about baking—or bakers—but the set-up looked professional to his untrained eyes.

Clean—always a plus. Organized. The only blotch on the otherwise sparkling room were the soggy towels lining the floor by the sink.

"You didn't bring your tools?"

Before Blondie could blow a gasket, Nick pointed to the wrench on the counter.

"That's all I need."

At least Nick hoped, taking off his jacket. If the job proved bigger than his limited ability, he would spring for the plumber.

"Fine." For the first time since she accosted him on the street, her face relaxed. "If you need anything, holler. I have to get some scones into the oven before the lunch rush."

The clog turned out to be a one, two, three fix.

One, unscrew the pipes.

Two, remove the disgusting buildup of gunk that consisted of slime, a spoon, three pennies, a long, dangerous-looking needle, and a ring. The diamond wasn't big, but Nick wondered how it could go missing without somebody noticing.

Three, reattach the pipes. Some minor clean-up, and voila, job done.

Turning the tap on full force, Nick felt a sense of pride as the water disappeared in a steady, even flow.

"Done? Thank you so much."

Hands covered in chunky bits of flour, the blonde gave Nick an awkward but enthusiastic hug. She had removed the knit cap and bulky sweater. Her hair was held back by a clip at the base of her neck. And the curves he imagined? Jeans and a plain, light-green t-shirt showed them off very nicely.

Before Nick could do more than perk up over how the brush of her body felt against his, she broke away. Expertly, she used her elbow, squirting soap from a nearby dispenser into her palms.

"I usually take care of minor problems. But Murielle had a dental emergency."

"You aren't Murielle?"

Over her shoulder, she sent him a surprised look.

"You must be new in town."

Not one to share his business with strangers, Nick simply nodded.

"Mm. That explains the mistake. Everybody knows Murielle. Anyway, I'm on my own this morning because of an owner with a broken crown and an assistant baker/waitress who woke up to three sick kids and a lot of projectile vomiting."

"Nice image." All of a sudden the gooey buns cooling on a rack didn't look quite as appetizing.

"I know." With a sigh, she dried her hands. "Sorry about earlier. I probably came off—"

"Wild-eyed? Crazed? Looney?"

"All of the above."

When she laughed, her eyes sparkled, sending a zing of desire through Nick's blood. An interestingly beautiful face, excellent figure, an agile brain, *and* a sense of humor? She wasn't just a home run. She was a freaking grand slam.

"Should I pay you now? Or will Erikson send a bill?"

"Erikson?"

She opened one of the ovens, removing something flaky and golden brown. Nick recognized the modified biscuit from the trip he took to Dublin three years ago. From the looks of them, these scones could rival Ireland's best.

"Erikson. You must be new if you can't remember the name of your employer."

"About that—"

A bell sounded, drawing her attention.

"Hold on a second. Customer. Would you like a cup of coffee?"

"Sure."

"Come on." Once they were in the restaurant area, she handed him a mug from under the counter. "Help yourself."

"Rowan." A woman with big red hair, wrapped in a long, red coat, and sporting bright red lipstick smiled a toothy smile. "This is an unexpected surprise."

Unexpected? But not in a good way? Nick gave the woman a closer look. Her demeanor seemed pleasant. But her smile didn't reach her eyes. Rowan—nice name—didn't seem to notice the undercurrent of dislike emanating from her customer.

Or perhaps she simply didn't give a flying leap.

Nick smiled at the thought. The woman's appeal kept growing. By leaps and bounds.

"Hello." Her smile turning predatory, the woman's attention landed on Nick. Holding out her hand, red nail polish—what else—glistened on her long, manicured nails. The scent of musk warring—and unfortunately—winning the battle against cinnamon and sugar. "I don't believe we've met. My name is Patrice. Who are you?"

"He's the plumber," Rowan announced unceremoniously.

Patrice snatched back her hand as if worried she might catch something. *Plumber cooties?* The idea amused him. And if her smile was any indication, Rowan felt the same.

"One dozen croissants." Rowan handed Patrice a white box tied with a red ribbon.

12

"Mm." Patrice swiped her credit card. Taking the receipt, she gave Nick a lingering look before exiting the shop.

"Croissants every morning. The woman has no imagination."

"She's very..." Nick searched for the right word. "Red."

Sometimes only the obvious would do.

Rowan chuckled. "Patrice Dandridge. The town's self-proclaimed fashion plate. Red Thursday. Blue Friday. And so on."

"You're joking. A different color every day?"

Who had that kind of time or energy?

"Except her hair. She settled on that shade of red around our junior year of high school. She was Patty in those days. Funny what marrying money does to some people."

Rowan and Patrice went to school together? Nick wasn't great at guessing ages, but he never would have pegged the women as contemporaries.

Fresh and natural, Rowan looked years younger. Twenty-five? Maybe? Patrice, with her heavy makeup and pinched mouth, appeared to be well-preserved and pushing forty.

Wisely—if he ever ran into the woman again—Nick planned on keeping his opinion to himself.

"At last. The cavalry has arrived."

Rowan rushed around the counter as three women walked through the door greeting each as if they were a long lost friend.

"You should have called sooner." A tall, angular woman with a shock of white hair shook her head. "As usual, you try to take care of everything and everyone."

"I was fine until the sink backed up. Luckily, Erikson sent—" Rowan frowned. "In the rush, I forgot to ask your name."

"Nick," he said, stepping forward.

"Well, hello, tall, dark, and sexy." The second woman, around five feet tall with a well-rounded figure, met Nick halfway, her hand taking his. She batted her false eyelashes. "Handsome goes without saying."

"For the love of Pete, Mona. The boy is young enough to be your grandson." The angular woman shook her head. "*Great* goes without saying." She sighed when Mona simply rolled her eyes without taking them from Nick.

"Ignore my friends. I'm Delta. This is Rae," she said, introducing the third woman. "And Mona, let go of Nick's hand." Grinning, Mona shrugged. But she did as Delta instructed. "The lunch prep won't get done by itself."

Hello, alpha dog. Nick chuckled to himself at the thought. Rae and Mona didn't question Delta's authority, heading for the kitchen with only a backward glance or two.

"If any of you ladies lost a pretty diamond, it's sitting by the sink."

Mona gasped, glancing at her empty ring finger.

"Why didn't I notice?" she asked, hustling through the swinging door.

"She never does," Delta smiled a mix of exasperation and affection. "Was her ring the clog culprit?"

"Among other things."

"She never learns."

"All part of Mona's charm," Rowan pointed out as she checked the till.

"Hm." Delta didn't sound convinced. Frowning, she looked at Nick. "There is something very familiar about you. Around the eyes."

Nick waited as Delta turned her head. Right, then left. He had inherited the dark-brown color of his irises from his mother. Is that what this woman saw? Had Delta known Annie Sanders?

The question reminded Nick why he came to Maine. To find answers. Not play the plumber or get his flirt on with the local baker. Not that he couldn't do all three. Multitasking was one of his specialties.

The logical move would be to simply ask. Did you know my mother? Nick wasn't sure why he held back. Some instinct. The need for self-preservation. Against what, he didn't know. But for now—until he had a better lay of the land—his would play his cards close to the vest.

"I haven't been in Jasper very long."

"No?" Delta paused as if the answer was just within reach. But whatever she was searching for didn't come. "A plumber? I imagine we'll see more of you now that you're on our radar."

"I hope so. But I'm not—"

"You."

As Delta pointed at Rowan, Nick sighed. He kept trying to tell somebody—anybody—that he wasn't a plumber. Setting the record straight wasn't easy. These women shifted gears faster than a race car driver on a hairpin turn.

"Me?" Rowan asked, shutting the till with a resounding snap.

"Rae can handle the food. Mona and I are more than capable of waitressing." Delta pointed to the door. "Go."

"You don't work here?" Nick asked.

"I used to. After school. Now, I help out in a pinch."

"Well, the pinch is over," Delta said. "Murielle should be back this afternoon before closing time. We'll be fine. And take this one with you. Maybe buy him a cup of coffee."

Rowan met Nick's gaze, her lips twitching at Delta's attempt at matchmaking.

"Murielle's serves the best coffee in town."

"Then buy him a drink." Delta raised an eyebrow at Nick. "You like beer?"

"I've been known to throw one back now and then. But not at," Nick glanced at his watch. "Ten forty-five in the morning."

Delta rolled her eyes. "Subtlety is lost on the young. Rowan is a single, attractive woman. Are you?"

"An attractive young woman?"

So, shoot him. Delta had lobbed one right over the plate. Nick couldn't resist taking a swing.

"Smart ass." In spite of herself, Delta chuckled. "Are you single? Unattached? Fiancée? Girlfriend?"

"No to all of the above."

"Boyfriend?"

The last question came from Rowan. Smart woman. Never take anything for granted.

"I'm straight," he told her.

With a satisfied nod, Delta left them alone.

"Good to know." Rowan took her sweater and hat from behind the counter. "I'll pass the word along to the single—equally straight—women of Jasper. A man with your skills isn't easy to come by."

"My *skills*?" Nick waggled his eyebrows.

"As a plumber." Rowan shoved Nick's jacket at him. "Why does a man's brain automatically land on sex?"

"Because we're men." Nick held the door for Rowan.

"So simple. So sad." Rowan took a deep breath of the brisk fall air. "And so true."

"In our defense, men have certain hormones that—"

"Rule a certain appendage?"

Nick chuckled. "Like most men, I have a certain fondness for my… appendage."

"Stop." Rowan held up her glove-covered hands. "This conversation turned weird—fast. Thank you for helping in my hour of need. I'll make sure Murielle sends the bill to your employer. Along with a stellar job evaluation."

"I'm not a plumber," Nick blurted out the truth. He couldn't take another round of hemming and hawing.

"Excuse me?"

Under Rowan's sharp, blue gaze, Nick suddenly felt like a little boy caught with his hand in the cookie jar. Resentment shot through him. Damn it, he hadn't done anything wrong.

"You grabbed me," Nick reminded her. "FYI? When you're wound up, getting a word in edgewise is impossible."

"How hard are four words?" Rowan paced. Not back and forth, but in a circle. Nick judiciously refrained from pointing out that she was, quite literally, winding herself up. "You just said them with little trouble. *I'm not a plumber*. End of story. Instead, you fixed Murielle's sink under false pretenses?"

"I unclogged a pipe. Now, if I had attempted to unclog an artery, I wouldn't blame you for chewing me out."

"Clever. That tongue of yours is very glib." Rowan crossed her arms. "Are you a lawyer?"

"Are you asking, or accusing? And why are we having this conversation in the middle of the sidewalk?"

"Answering a question with another question. Typical lawyer maneuver," Rowan muttered. "Where do you suggest we talk?"

"Dinner. Tonight." That shut her up. "Since you know the town, I'll leave the choice of restaurant up to you."

Judging by the stormy expression on Rowan's face, Nick expected a resounding no. Happily, she surprised him.

"Will you tell me who you are? What you do? And why you spent your morning masquerading as a plumber?"

"Will you admit that a good chunk of the guilt falls on you?"

"Deal." Rowan shook Nick's hand. "But first. I need a name. Nick...?"

"Sanders." Turnabout was fair play. "Rowan...?"

"Cartwright."

Nick felt a chill race up his spine, thinking of the letter in his pocket.

"Cartwright?" he asked, his mouth suddenly dry. "Are you any relation to Leonard Cartwright?"

"Do you know my father?"

Nick shook his head trying to process this new information.

"He's a friend of a friend."

Close enough. And all Rowan needed to know at the moment.

Rowan accepted Nick's explanation with a nod.

"*Pie in the Sky* is the best place in town for a quiet, leisurely meal," she said. "May I have your phone?"

17

On autopilot, Nick did as Rowan asked, using his password to give her access.

"There," she said, typing quickly. "My number and address. Pick me up at seven thirty?"

Nick nodded, watching as Rowan disappeared around the corner. Climbing into his SUV, he thought about his next move. He wanted to talk to somebody. Spencer or Travis. But what would he say that wouldn't sound crazy? And really, really twisted.

If Nick could believe what he'd gleaned from the letter? The one he found in his mother's belongings? He had just made a date with his sister.

CHAPTER THREE

● ≈ ● ≈ ●

"MOVE THE BIG shrub to the end of the driveway, Josie. Get Maris to give you a hand. I marked where to dig the hole. If you have any questions, don't hesitate to ask."

Rowan double checked her color-coded chart—just to be safe. On big jobs like the Frederick's remodel, she made extra-certain the right plants went in the right place. Mistakes could be fixed, but she and her crew were working a tight timeframe.

If they maintained their current pace, they would finish two days ahead of schedule. Which meant a bonus to be split evenly between her employees. And for Rowan, the satisfaction of silencing the doubters who hadn't believed an all-woman crew could do the job.

From day one, *RTC Landscaping* had plenty of skeptics. Rowan had worked hard learning the craft. She started small with only a dream. Hiring nothing but women hadn't been part of the plan, just something that happened organically over time.

How many times had she heard the refrain that women didn't have the muscles or stamina to work long hours in the sun. Lifting. Digging. Planting pretty posies in a row was one thing. But what about building walls? Or clearing out overgrown backyards?

Big landscaping jobs should be left to men because women—according to Rowan's male detractors—weren't built to handle the wear and tear.

Three years later, Rowan had proven them wrong time and time again.

"Rowan?" Josie hesitated. "What's the name of the shrub we're putting in? The kind of plant?"

Rowan lowered her clipboard. Through the lenses of her dark sunglasses, she observed the eager expression on the young woman's face. Most of the time, she didn't bother with specific names. Most of the time, her crew didn't care. They were plants. Flowers. Trees.

However, every so often, when somebody expressed interest, Rowan gladly took the time to pass on what she knew. She encouraged the thirst for knowledge. Maybe someday, Josie would want to open her own business. A florist shop. Or a greenhouse.

Or, Rowan sighed as she considered the possibility, a rival landscaping company. Having a competitor could be a good way to stay on her toes. Though not so great when she had been responsible for training them.

However, the day Josie became her rival—*if* that day ever came—was years in the future. For now, Rowan was happy to satisfy the young woman's curiosity.

"Maplewood Viburnum," Rowan said. She doubted Josie cared about the Latin name, *viburnum acerfoilium*. "I chose the plant because the height will top off at six feet, matching the wall and gated entry. Plus, that variety prefers partial shade and can tolerate drier soil. Our client is conservation conscious. She specified a garden that needs as little water as possible."

"How do you remember all that?" Josie asked, her eyes wide.

"Years of study. And," Rowan lowered her voice to a conspiratorial tone. "A huge computer database. My own personal cheat sheet."

Josie laughed. With a wave, she went back to work.

Marsha Frederick exited the patio doors. Closer to sixty than she liked to admit, she had covered her thin frame in a long, flowing caftan that seemed more appropriate for lounging in Hawaii than Maine in November.

In each hand, Marsha carried a cup of steaming coffee. Grateful, Rowan removed her gloves, wrapping her hands around the hot ceramic.

"Looks like the weather is going to cooperate," Marsha said, scanning her almost completed backyard.

"I can't tell. Are you happy or disappointed?"

"What a silly question. I hired you to finish by the middle of November."

"But if for any reason we don't. Hard-freeze. Blizzard. You will still have your redesigned backyard. Admittedly, a few months late. But you won't have to pay the bonus."

"I do love saving money." The idea brought a smile to Marsha's lips. She may have inherited her millions from her father. But she held onto the fortune—expanding her wealth ten-fold—by using her brains and innate frugality.

"That said, I want you to succeed. Every other landscaper told me they couldn't possibly finish before next spring. Most refused to begin until late April. But not you."

"I hesitated," Rowan shrugged.

"For about ten seconds. I knew you wouldn't turn away from a challenge. Especially one your male counterparts said couldn't be done."

Rowan had wondered if this job—and hiring her—was Marsha's way of thumbing her nose at the old-boys club that still existed in Jasper. Women weren't held back by a glass ceiling. The barrier was made of thick, galvanized steel. Money gave Marsha an advantage. Her acid tongue had taken care of the rest.

When possible—and earned—Marsha pulled other women through the crack she had created.

"You gave me my first job when nobody else would."

"Including your father?"

Rowan shrugged. Complicated didn't begin to describe her relationship with Leonard Cartwright. He wasn't easy to know—or love. But the respect she felt prevented her from speaking ill of the man who had married her mother and provided a home for Rowan and her brother.

Marsha shivered, letting the well-worn subject slide. "Come in the house. We can turn this coffee Irish."

"Not me." Rowan closed the door behind her. "I still have three hours of work on site. There's a smaller job I need to check in on. Plus another hour of paperwork."

"Will that give you time to pretty up for your date? Not that you need much help in that category." Marsha sighed as she poured a generous dollop of whiskey into her cup. "You work in the sun and wind day after day. How do you keep your skin so clear and smooth?"

"Diligence and good genes." Rowan's mother just celebrated her fiftieth birthday yet barely looked thirty. She frowned. "How do you know about my date?"

"Then Delta was right." Marsha looked delighted. "The hunk asked you out."

"Maybe I did the asking."

"Did you?" the older woman asked, raising a cosmetically darkened brow.

"No. But if he hadn't, I would have."

"Really?"

Marsha's surprise was understandable. There wasn't a resident of Jasper who didn't know the circumstances that led to Rowan's broken engagement.

She caught her fiancé cheating with his secretary. On the couch in his office. In the middle of the day.

Locks were put on doors for a reason. In his arrogance, Wilton Jacobs believed he was above such precautions. Who would dare enter his domain without warning?

The woman he was set to marry in less than a week. That's who.

Juicy didn't begin to describe the gossip that dominated Jasper for the next few months. A scandal concerning two of the most prominent families—not just in the town but in the state—was bound to have legs.

Two years later, Rowan still heard the whispers.

What the gossips didn't understand—what Rowan had only shared with her best friend—was that Wilton hadn't broken her heart. He did her a favor. The only emotion she felt, other than a bit of embarrassment, was relief.

Rowan had dodged a very big bullet.

Since then, she had concentrated on building a successful business, dating rarely. By choice. However, word at the daily coffee klatches was that Rowan Cartwright was still hung up on her ex.

"Good for you." One of the best things about Martha. She never let a question dangle uncomfortably for long. "Nick? Is that his name? Delta claims he's quite the dish."

"He's the best-looking man I've ever seen."

"In person?" Martha asked.

"In person. On the cover of a magazine. In a movie. Nick Sanders is gorgeous. Period."

"Wow." Grinning, Martha fanned herself with her hand.

Wow, indeed. Frazzled, Rowan had grabbed Nick off the street. He should have told her to go to hell. Instead, he took pity on the mad woman and fixed her sink.

What a sweetheart! Well before she had paused long enough to take a close look at his face, Nick had already built up a surplus of brownie points.

In the middle of brushing an egg wash onto the scones, she glanced Nick's way. Boom! Something happened she hadn't thought possible even before her fiancé disaster.

A man took Rowan's breath away.

"Earth to Rowan." Laughing, Martha snapped her fingers in front of Rowan's eyes.

"Thanks for the coffee. I better get back to work," Rowan said as she grabbed her gloves and headed outside.

"I need to get a look at the man who put the bloom in Rowan Cartwright's cheeks," Martha called out, laughing with delight.

Rowan stood on the patio, giving herself a mental shake. What was wrong with her? She never let a man muddle her brain. Work came first.

Maybe that was her problem. Whittling her social life down to almost nothing was great for the bottom line. But Rowan had become a dull girl.

Nick Sanders couldn't be as good looking as she remembered. Could he? Chances were good that she had let her hormones cloud her judgment. He would arrive for their date and turn out to be an attractive, leaning toward average, man.

Average was good. In the long run, Rowan would be better off with average. What would she do with a drop-dead gorgeous man? Other than enjoy a mindless, no strings attached, one-night stand.

Rowan jogged down the path they had recently lined with cobalt blue pavers. She wasn't the one-night stand type. But she had to admit, the idea intrigued her. A step out of her comfort zone.

Laughing at herself, Rowan hefted a bag of mulch over her shoulder. If—and she had her doubts—Nick turned out half as good looking as she built him up to be, she might consider a lusty good night kiss. But sex on the first date? With a virtual stranger? With no plans on ever going out with him again?

"Sorry, Nick. No man has that much sex appeal."

"MAYBE I WAS wrong."

"Wrong about what?" Nick asked as he helped Rowan into the SUV.

"I wondered if I had imagined how good looking you were." Clear-blue, guileless eyes looked into his. "The truth? You aren't a figment of my imagination."

"Thank you?" Nick answered, not sure if Rowan meant her words as a compliment or not.

Rowan shrugged. "I don't know how I feel."

Join the club, Nick thought as he walked to the driver's side.

The woman smelled good. And looked even better. Rowan had left her long, blond hair loose, flowing well below her shoulders. The moon caught the silky strands turning them a glowing silver that—

Whoa, fella. Nick never waxed poetic. Never. Yet here he was, thinking about Rowan's hair in the moonlight when only a few hours go, he thought she was his sister.

24

Thank the Lord for the internet. After checking into his hotel room, Nick had cleared the question of their mutual paternity with surprising ease. With a few clicks on his laptop, he discovered Leonard Cartwright wasn't Rowan's biological father. He became her stepfather when she was four years old.

Though nothing had happened, Nick was relieved to know he hadn't lusted after his sister.

However, Rowan thought of Cartwright as her father. If Nick kissed her—which at this point seemed like a foregone conclusion. If the kiss led to more? In good conscience, he had to make a confession first.

Nick had come to Jasper for one reason. To find out if Leonard Cartwright was his father. Not because he wanted some big, emotional reunion. He wanted to know why a man would abandon the mother of his child. Forcing her to live in abject poverty

Nick could do the math. Annie Sanders was fifteen when she found out she was pregnant. Leonard Cartwright was in his mid-twenties. And married to his first wife. That bit of information alone made Nick want to punch the bastard's lights out.

Clutching the steering wheel, Nick stared straight ahead, his mind racing. He jumped when Rowan laid a hand on his arm.

"What's wrong?"

"I need to tell you something."

"As I recall, you promised to tell me several things."

Rowan's touch—the way she gently rubbed his arm—soothed Nick. At the same time, she stirred something in him. A primal need to satisfy his desires.

The feelings she evoked were surprisingly intense considering their short acquaintance. But the truth couldn't be denied. Nick wanted Rowan more than he had wanted any woman in a very long time.

"Leonard Cartwright is my father. Maybe. Probably."

"Okay. Not exactly what I expected." Rowan dropped her hand, her warm gaze turning cool. "So, we aren't on a regular date.

You want what? Information? An introduction? Do you want me to make your path easier?"

"When I asked you to dinner, I didn't know who you were."

"Right. Our meeting was a coincidence."

Rowan sounded skeptical, and Nick couldn't blame her. But he resented the need to defend himself.

"You grabbed me, remember?"

"Yet, you were waiting right outside the shop." Rowan's quick brain saw the flaw in her argument before Nick could correct her. "I wasn't supposed to be there. Which means you weren't looking for me."

"I didn't know you existed. Coming to Jasper was a spur of the moment decision. I googled Leonard Cartwright, but only to find out if he was still alive and living in the same place."

"Then hopped on a plane—or were you close enough to drive?" Rowan sighed. "I'm confused. Your story didn't begin this morning."

"No. But it did begin here in Jasper. Almost twenty-nine years ago. I can only tell you what I know. Which isn't much."

"Why not ask your mother?"

"She died. I found a letter when I was cleaning out her house. The letter led me here."

"I'm so sorry, Nick."

"Mom was sick for some time. But knowing the end was coming and the reality were two different things."

"Why are we having this conversation here?" Rowan shivered.

"What was I thinking? Let me start the engine."

"Let's go inside." Rowan took her keys from her purse. "I have a very good bottle of wine. Unless…"

"Unless what?"

"I know for a fact my…? Your…? I don't know what to call him. *Our* father?"

"Jesus. Don't." Nick shuddered, his face showing his disgust. "I thought you were my sister for less than an hour. Too long in my book. We aren't related."

"By marriage—"

"By nothing. If we were, I couldn't do this."

Nick wrapped his hand around Rowan's neck. He didn't pull, he coaxed her closer. He wanted her to understand what was about to happen. A kiss. *State your objections now or forever hold your peace.*

"What are you waiting for?" Rowan taunted lightly.

"That smart mouth of yours is going to get you in trouble."

Rowan smiled, showing him she wasn't the least concerned. Winding her arms around his waist, she asked, "Are you trouble, Nick?"

"I guess we're going to find out."

Nick didn't waste any time. He took Rowan's mouth, eager to discover her taste. Her sigh brushed against his lips. Sweet. Hot. Running his tongue along hers, he threaded his fingers through her hair. Soft. Intoxicating. He couldn't stop.

Changing angles, Nick deepened the kiss. The windows carried a fine layer of steam, the heat they generated making the cold a distant memory.

"We should go inside," Rowan gasped as Nick's teeth bit into the side of her neck.

"Lead the way."

"To talk," she clarified.

Breathing deeply, Nick looked into Rowan's eyes. What he saw made him smile. She wanted him. As much as he wanted her.

"I could persuade you to change your mind.

"Probably. But please don't."

Honesty was high on Nick's list of prized qualities. Rowan could have shrugged off his claim, denying the overwhelming attraction between them. Instead, she told him the truth.

Rowan's willingness to show a touch of vulnerability only made him want her more. And guaranteed Nick would keep his hands to himself. For the time being.

The walkway to the house was lit by twin lampposts casting a warm glow over the dark cobblestones. The front yard wound around the house, the grass neatly trimmed. Manicured shrubs provided a nice border, lending some privacy from the street and sidewalk.

"This is nice," Nick said as they walked up the front steps. "The upkeep must take some time."

"I enjoy the work."

Nick heard Rowan's chuckle as she unlocked the door.

"Did I miss the joke?"

"I make my living prettying up other people's yards. Wouldn't it be ironic if my place was a mess?"

"From what I can see, you must be good at your job. I'd hire you."

"Would you?" Rowan seemed pleased. She turned on the hall light.

"If I didn't live on the other side of the country.."

"Finally. A of piece to the Nick Sanders puzzle." She hung his jacket in the closet next to her own. "Where across the country?"

"Seattle. And I already told you about my possible paternity. Seems like a pretty big puzzle piece to me."

"But the small pieces are the ones that make you who you are. Where you live. What you do." She raised an eyebrow. "We've established that you aren't a plumber. What *do* you do for a living?"

"Baseball."

"You manufacture them?"

Nick laughed. "No. I play the game. Second base."

"Huh." Seemingly satisfied with his explanation, Rowan continued, not missing a beat. "A professional athlete. The Seattle...? Sorry, I'm not up on team names.""

28

"Cyclones."

"There you go." Rowan slipped off her shoes. Barefoot, she padded down the hall, stopping in the kitchen. "Wine?"

"I'd prefer beer. If you have some."

"Another piece falls into place."

"Beer over wine." Nick took the bottle from her, twisting off the cap. "What does that say about me?"

"Nothing. But when I add the things I already know. You're kind," Rowan sipped her wine. "Thoughtful."

"How do you know?"

"You unclogged a sink without question or request for compensation. Though I did tip you." Rowan's eyes sparkled with humor.

"I didn't keep the twenty."

"But—"

"I slipped the bill into your wallet when you were busy counting the till."

Frowning, Rowan retrieved her purse. "Well, I'll be..." She held up the money. "I wanted you to keep this."

"I enjoyed playing plumber. When I was a kid, calling for help wasn't an option. Either I fixed the clog, the leak, whatever. Or we lived with a clog, a leak, whatever."

Nick realized he had just given Rowan another puzzle piece. His childhood wasn't a happy topic.

"You're easy to talk to," Nick rubbed the back of his neck. "I don't know how that makes me feel."

"While you decide, I'll order a pizza. Or would you prefer something else?"

"Pizza is fine. Any topping but anchovies or pineapple."

Nodding, Rowan made the call.

Keeping his beer, Nick moved around the open space. The kitchen flowed seamlessly into the living room. Hardwood floors. Tall windows. The furniture was minimal, the surfaces free of the little doodads some people found charming. Nick found them annoying. What purpose did they serve except to gather dust?

Rowan kept a few pictures in silver frames along the fireplace mantle. Family and friends, he supposed. Curious, he picked the photo featuring a man and woman.

"That's my mother. And Leonard Cartwright."

Nick had seen Cartwright's picture during his research. He was handsome. In good shape and aging well. However, he never smiled. Not in one single picture—including this one—did the man look as though he wanted to be there. Impatient was the word that seemed to fit.

"Are they happy?"

"They suit," Rowan said, her arm brushing Nick's. "They entertain a lot for business. Mom loves playing hostess. When she's organizing, she's in her element."

"And Cartwright?"

"Wheeling and dealing. He's been good to us, Nick." Rowan frowned. "I don't know why I feel the need to defend him. Leo is—"

"You say he's your father yet, you don't call him Dad?"

"He's Leo." Rowan shrugged. She moved to the sofa. Sitting, she tucked her feet under her legs. "He never asked me to call him anything else. But my brother Geoff and I took his last name. He's the only father I remember. So..."

Nick took the seat opposite Rowan. A comfortable overstuffed chair, he sank in, his expression thoughtful.

"I didn't spend a lot of time wondering about who my father was." Absently, Nick used his thumb to pick at the edge of the bottle's label. "My questions made my mother sad. She had enough weighing her down without me adding to her problems."

"You took care of her."

"We took care of each other."

Nick didn't elaborate, his thoughts turning dark. While his mother struggled to survive, Leonard Cartwright was enjoying his fat-cat lifestyle. Where was the justice?

30

"Tell me about your mother," Rowan urged as if sensing the turmoil inside Nick. "You obviously adored her."

"You know those stories where a woman finds the superhuman strength to lift a car off her trapped child?"

"Yes."

"That was my mother. But not just once. Every day of my childhood. Looking back, I don't know how she managed."

Once he began, the story flowed from Nick with surprising ease. Few people knew what his life had been like. Travis and Spencer were aware. His best friends were the only people he trusted enough to tell that part of his life.

But this was the first time Nick shared the details from start to finish. Something about Rowan made opening old wounds easier than he would have imagined.

Her kind eyes. The instant connection like nothing he had ever felt before. The way she sat and listened without commenting while clearly fully invested in what he said.

All these qualities combined to make recounting the most intimate details of his childhood, if not easy, a little less painful.

Nick found himself relaxing. He had never been a big proponent of the notion that to lessen his burden, he needed to share the load. But the longer he spoke, the more he wondered if there was something to the theory—given the right time, the right place. And most of all, the right person.

"I think she sold her body."

Nick had never spoken of his suspicions. Not to his friends. And certainly not to his mother.

Rowan gasped, the first sound she had made since he began. Not words. Just that one cry of distress.

"I can't say for sure. And I never asked because I knew how the thought made me feel. Sick. Powerless. I can't imagine what she would have done if she thought I suspected."

"She did what she had to do."

Relieved that Rowan understood, Nick met her gaze, grateful for the tears that hung on her lashes. Tears he had long ago lost the ability to cry for himself—or his mother.

"We survived. That may not sound like much. But—"

"You're wrong. Survival," Rowan swallowed a sob. "Survival is everything."

"Hey." Skirting the coffee table, Nick sat next to Rowan, taking her in his arms. "A few tears is one thing. Don't make yourself sick." He smoothed back her hair as he kissed her forehead. "My story isn't a tragedy."

Rowan nodded, hiccupping. "Your mother took care of you. Then you took care of her. A perfect happy ending. Except..."

"The heroine died."

Fresh pain shot through Nick's body. Progress. A week ago he felt numb, unable to choke the words past what felt like a permanent lump in his throat.

"Life isn't fair." Tears streamed freely down Rowan's cheeks. "Annie deserved more time. Years and years."

"Who are you?" Amazed, Nick lifted Rowan's chin. Her glistening eyes cut his emotions to the bone. "I feel like you crawled inside my head. Not a great place to be most of the time."

"I wish I could take the bad memories away." Rowan touched Nick's face, her warm, soft hand like a soothing balm. "But they helped make you the man you are today. And there is nothing I would change about who you are."

"You don't know me. I can be a real asshole."

"You mean you aren't perfect?" Her eyes widened dramatically. "Shocking."

In spite of the heavy subject matter, Nick had to smile.

"Far from perfect. Do you want me to run down a list of my faults?"

"What would be the point? Some of the things you consider faults, I might see as virtues. And what you think of as a virtue—"

"Might be a fault in your book." Nick shook his head. "The way your brain works is something else."

"Fault or virtue?" Taking a tissue from a nearby box, Rowan wiped her eyes.

"Virtue."

Nick kissed her temple. Then the end of her nose. Her lips were a natural progression. One he couldn't resist.

"The pizza will be here any second," Rowan said breathlessly between increasingly intense kisses.

"I'd rather feast on you."

The second the words were out of his mouth, Nick wanted to groan. Not his style and corny to the extreme, he wondered where the thought had come from.

"Did you just say that?"

Rowan's laugh caused a domino effect. Nick snorted, breaking out in the best laugh he'd experienced in weeks. Collapsing onto the sofa cushion, he took Rowan with him, her unrestrained mirth vibrating up and down his arms.

"I could leave the money on the porch. With a big tip."

"I do like cold pizza," Rowan sighed, smiling.

"Is that a yes?" Nick reached for his wallet.

"Tempting, but no."

"I could—"

"I know. You could change my mind." The doorbell rang. "You're awfully confident of your sex appeal."

"Fault or virtue?" Nick inquired, handing Rowan a twenty.

"What do you think?"

"I pick virtue."

"Surprise, surprise."

Enjoying the sound of Rowan's chuckle as she left to answer the door, Nick picked up the empty beer bottle and wine glass, heading for the kitchen.

"An eight-dollar tip for a twelve-dollar pizza. Brock Todd was over the moon."

"What does Brock usually get for his trouble?"

"I have no idea. Three bucks is my average. Depends if he hustles his backside or stops to flirt with his girlfriend. She lives two houses down, so depending on the direction of his arrival, my luck is pretty hit and miss."

Good, bad, or somewhere in between, there was no way to ruin the scent of a freshly baked pizza. Steam rose as Rowan opened the box.

"Looks like Brock swung around from the north tonight. About now, he's knocking on Charmaine's door."

"Letting somebody else's pizza get cold."

"Young love." Rowan handed Nick a plate. "Most of the people on my block are pretty tolerant."

"I suffered from a lot of teenage lust. Never love."

"I'll bet you didn't suffer long."

Smiling, Nick bit into a slice, the burst of spices hitting the back of his tongue in a perfectly composed symphony of flavor.

"This may be the best pizza I've ever eaten," he declared, taking another bite, his eyes closing as he let himself savor the amazing flavors.

"*Angela's Trattoria*. The best Italian food period," Rowan declared with pride. "Angie and I have been best friends since preschool."

"You don't have to sell me." Nick took two more pieces before sitting at the counter.

"Nick."

"Something wrong with your pizza?" he asked, noticing that Rowan had only eaten one bite. "I'll be happy to take whatever you don't want."

"The food is fine."

"Hey." Taking her hand, Nick waited until Rowan met his gaze. "I pretty much spilled my guts all over your living room floor."

"A nice image."

Nick chuckled. "Talk to me, Rowan."

"I like you. And I believe what you've told me. But…"

"You've known me less than a day." Nick frowned. "Seems like longer."

"I know." Rowan squeezed his hand."

"However, despite this—connection—Leonard Cartwright is family."

Rowan nodded, visibly relieved that Nick understood.

"Leo isn't always the easiest man to deal with. He's used to having his own way."

"I can identify."

Rowan's lips quirked. "There's no way to anticipate how Leo will react when you meet him. He might welcome you with open arms. Or toss you out on your backside."

"He could try." Nick's eyes narrowed, almost enjoying the idea. "He wouldn't succeed."

Seeing the worry in Rowan's eyes, Nick grimaced.

"I don't know if Leonard Cartwright is my biological father. But if he is, that means he had sex with a fifteen-year-old girl. For my mother's sake, that makes me sick to my stomach." Nick pushed away his uneaten pizza. "But I'd be pretty pissed no matter who the girl was. *Girl*, Rowan. Not woman."

"I can't defend him. I wouldn't try."

Nick had hardened his heart against Leonard Cartwright. But Rowan was another matter. Her obvious distress made him wish he could make all of this go away.

"Cartwright might be innocent."

"Thank you," Rowan kissed Nick's cheek. With a sigh, she walked to the refrigerator, removing a bottle of wine. "Would you like another beer?"

"No. One is usually my limit."

"We both know that Leo is your father. I can see the resemblance. So can you."

"Maybe."

"You don't want to look like him?"

"No." Why beat around the bush? "I have my mother's eyes. That makes me happy."

"Will you listen to Leonard's side of the story with an open mind?"

"If he talks, I'll listen. The rest?" Nick shrugged. "I should probably go. Unless...?"

"Tempting. You have no idea *how* tempting."

"Yes. I do."

Nick held Rowan's hand as she walked him to the door. A sweet gesture that didn't feel out of place. The feel of her fingers twined with his felt... right.

"No sex for you tonight." Rowan sent him a sideways glance. "Unless..."

"You're the only person I know in this town. Except for the ladies I met at Murielle's. And the guy who checked me in at the Jasper Inn." Cupping her cheek, Nick smiled. "I don't pick women up in bars. Only in front of the occasional bakery."

"You're funny. I like funny."

Rowan wound her arms around Nick's neck. She smelled so good. Like taking in that first fresh breath of air after a cool, mid-summer rain.

"Better than sexy?" Nick asked, brushing his lips across hers.

"Funny *is* sexy. But you? Well, you're the whole package. I know there has to be something wrong with you."

"*So* many things."

"You say that with such pride."

Rowan's laugh turned to a sigh as his lips moved to the side of her neck.

"Isn't that a sin? Pride?" Nick looked into Rowan's deep blue eyes, patiently waiting for her answer.

"Absolutely," Rowan nodded. "And lust."

"That's one of my favorites." Nick smiled. "How about you? Should we stop?"

Rowan stood on her tiptoes, the added height bringing her gaze level with his mouth.

"Absolutely not. Sin away."

What could a man do when a woman—so warm and soft and sexy—invited him to sin?

The kiss was carnal. Hot beyond belief. On and on and on. Taking Rowan into her bedroom—into her bed—was so damn tempting. But Nick knew she wasn't ready.

Cursing his sense of fair play, Nick stepped back. Rowan's eyes remained closed, her mouth wet and slightly parted. He deserved a medal for the act of self-control needed to walk away.

Or a thorough head examination.

"Am I crazy to send you away?" Rowan asked.

"If you are, so am I."

Resolute, Nick grabbed the doorknob. The brisk night air washed over him, cooling his ardor—but not much.

"Wait. You forgot your jacket."

"I wouldn't get far without these," Nick said, taking his keys from the pocket. "You scrambled my brain, Rowan."

"I'd say that's only fair. Since you do the same to me." Rowan stood, so tempting, holding the door. "I was going to invite you to join me for breakfast. But I get an early start."

"How early?"

"Seven. I have to be on the job by eight at the latest."

"I'll get my morning run in then meet you. *Murielle's Muffins*?"

Rowan nodded.

Waiting until she closed the door and he heard the locks click in place, Nick walked to the SUV. Tomorrow would be an interesting day. He hoped to meet with Leonard Cartwright. Or at the very least, set up an appointment.

Nick couldn't imagine how he would feel if a grown man showed up claiming to be his son. He had no proof. Only an old letter.

The answers Nick sought were here in Jasper. He was certain. And he wasn't leaving until he had what he came for.

CHAPTER FOUR

● ≈ ● ≈ ●

"WHAT IS THERE about a sweaty man?" Mona asked with a flirty wink. Setting the cups on the table, she ignored Rowan, concentrating on Nick. "Not too sweaty. Just enough to bring out the yummy factor."

"I love Mona," Rowan said as the waitress left, her hips swinging. "She'll be flirting as she takes her last breath. Then start again with St. Peter as soon as she reaches the pearly gates."

Rowan sipped her coffee. She wasn't one of those people who needed a shot of caffeine to get her morning motor running. Since she was a little girl, she woke full of energy no matter how much sleep she had the night before.

A major plus for a woman in her business.

"Should I have taken a shower?" Nick lifted the edge of his hoodie, taking a sniff. "My run took me right by here, and I didn't want to be late."

"You're fine."

To prove her point, Rowan did her own test. She leaned close to Nick, breathing deeply. He smelled of warm, clean, healthy male. And something uniquely him. A little heady for so early in the morning.

"Not too offensive?" Nick asked.

"As long as you shower in the next hour or so, no problem."

Great, Rowan thought. Now she had the picture of a wet, soap-slickened Nick in her head. Though she hadn't seen him naked, she had touched him through his clothes. His body was rock hard. Muscled in all the right places.

Rowan felt her blood heat. For a woman who liked sex but wasn't concerned about going without for long periods of time, the path her brain kept taking was disconcerting. Her libido wasn't underdeveloped. She had simply needed the right man to get her motor running.

Apparently, Nick Sanders was the man. Rowan wasn't sure how she felt about that.

Nick was a virtual stranger. Yes, they'd made an instant connection. He shared intimate and painful details about his childhood. Maybe she was crazy to believe every word he said. To trust his motives. But Rowan's instincts told her this man was exactly who and what he seemed to be.

Time would tell if she was wrong. Until then, she would give Nick the benefit of the doubt. Partly because that was who she was. But honestly? The main reason was simple.

Good looks, charm, and the overwhelming attraction aside, Rowan liked Nick Sanders.

"Here you go. Fresh orange rolls, a fruit plate, two croissants, and freshly made citrus butter." Mona smiled at Nick, fluffing her teased-out bouffant hairdo. "Enjoy. Your two dozen sticky buns will be ready to go when you are, Rowan."

"Interesting breakfast," Nick said. But the skepticism in his voice didn't stop him from taking a croissant—and two orange rolls.

"Most mornings I grab a carton of yogurt from the fridge. Once a week, I splurge. For my crew and me."

"How did you end up with all women employees?"

Nick had done most of the talking the night before. But Rowan had dropped a bit of her history.

"Pretty simple. The men who applied for the jobs didn't want to work for a woman. Honestly? Some of the women weren't that thrilled to start. But I weeded the lollygaggers out quick enough."

"Weeded. A landscaping joke?"

Rowan nodded.

"Good one." Nick popped the last piece of roll into his mouth. "Any of those men regret not taking the job?"

"I've had a few reapply. But my crew is loyal, and turnover is minimal."

The fact that Rowan paid top dollar, offered an excellent health plan, and frequently awarded bonuses didn't hurt.

"Well, there's my girl." A big man wearing a crisp white apron dusted liberally with flour, lifted Rowan into a bear hug. "I didn't get a chance to thank you for saving my butt yesterday."

"Anytime." Rowan laughed, squeezing tight.

"Who do we have here? A new boyfriend? About time."

"A *friend*," she qualified.

Rowan didn't want anybody getting the wrong idea. Massive attraction was one thing. She and Nick were a long way from anything bestowing a title on what they felt.

"You didn't tell me *Murielle* was Walter *Bone Crusher* Murielle." Nick lightly chastised Rowan.

"Nick Sanders." Murielle held out one of his massive hands. "What the hell are you doing in Jasper?"

"I was about to ask you the same question."

Looking from one grinning man to the other, Rowan frowned.

"You know each other?"

"Nick Sanders. Damn, son." Ignoring Rowan, Murielle shook his head. "The way you play second base is a pleasure to behold. Congrats on the championship. I hope you're enjoying the moment. They don't come along very often."

"I'm still processing. But I'll never forget or take the moment for granted."

"Good man. I never got back to the big game. Makes me wish I had taken some time to savor the win. Unfortunately, I spent the four months in a party haze. Then back to work worrying about the next season."

"You won the World Series?" Rowan asked, trying to keep up.

Chuckling, Nick shrugged. "I had some help."

"Honey," Murielle sent Rowan an exasperated look. "You and this young man looked mighty cozy ever since you arrived." His narrowed gaze moved to Nick. "Should I take that to mean you didn't tell my girl who you are?"

41

"I told her I play baseball."

Rowan had the good grace to flush. "I don't follow the game."

"Or any other. How long did you work for me before you figured out what this ring on my finger meant?"

Murielle held up his right hand. The behemoth gold band was about as subtle as fireworks on the Fourth of July. The championship year was emblazoned in diamonds along with the name of his former team.

"Who has time to follow sports?"

Rowan didn't know why she felt the need to defend herself. As a busy woman with a business to run, the best she could do was support the local high school teams. Professional sports had never caught her interest.

"Slickest second baseman in the game," Murielle said, ignoring Rowan's muttered excuse. "That play you made in game six of the series? Damn, son. Saved the game."

"Where's your ring?" Rowan asked after Murielle left to check something in the kitchen.

"We get them at the home opener next season."

The way Nick's lips twitched, Rowan expected him to burst out laughing at any second.

"You think my lack of baseball knowledge is funny, don't you?"

"Not at all," Nick assured her. "However, your obvious discomfort? Sort of tickles my funny bone."

Rowan frowned, not certain what to say. Had she misread Nick? Was he one of those men who—no matter how much success he achieved—needed his ego stroked every hour on the hour? She had been engaged to a man like that. And had avoided getting mixed up with another ever since—like the plague.

She would hate to add Nick to that list.

"Don't look so serious." Nick chuckled, his dark eyes filled with good humor. "I don't care if you follow baseball or not. As for not knowing who I am? Join the club. Other than Murielle, I doubt another person in this room would know my name."

Spying three teenage boys huddled together at a table across the room sharing earnest whispers as they sent furtive glances Nick's way, Rowan had to laugh.

"Want to bet?"

Before Nick could figure out what she meant, one of the boys—pushed by his buddies—worked up the nerve to nervously shuffle across the room.

Trey Paulson. Tall and gangly, his face covered in freckles that matched the bright red hair that flopped over his eyes, Rowan recognized him as one of the high school jocks who often hung out at Murielle's.

"Mr. Sanders?" Trey squeaked out. Clearing his throat, he wiped his hands on his jeans. "Could I get your autograph?"

"Sure," Nick said with an affable smile. "Do you have a pen and paper?"

"I..." Trey's eyes grew wide with panic before a dejected look came over his face. "No, sir."

Taking pity on the boy who looked as though he might jump out of his skin at any moment, Rowan reached into her bag, pulling out a pad. Digging deeper, she found a pen emblazoned with her company logo.

Taking her offering, Nick winked.

"Would your friends like one of these, too?"

"Yes, sir." Flushed with excitement, Trey motioned the other boys over, his arms flapping like an awkward bird about to take flight.

Rowan watched as Nick handled the star-struck young men with ease. Kind was the word that first popped into her head. He spoke to them as equals. Getting their names, he made the inscriptions personal, not simply jotting down his name in illegible script.

And the questions. After finding his voice, Trey began spewing anything and everything that popped into his head. His friends were just as enthusiastic.

Entertained beyond words, Rowan was sorry she had to leave. But work came before pleasure.

"I have to go." Standing, she slipped on her heavy jacket, taking the ever-present knit cap from the pocket.

The boys made themselves at home, taking seats at the table.

"Give me a minute, guys."

At the counter, he picked up the waiting box of pastries.

"Put this on my bill, Mona."

Not seeing Rowan's frown, he walked with her to her truck.

"That is the last time you pay my way," Rowan warned. "The pizza last night was one thing, but those rolls are for my crew."

"Tell you what," Nick said, depositing the box on the seat. "You can buy me lunch, and we'll call it even."

"Dinner last night. Breakfast this morning? Followed by lunch?" Hiding her pleased smile, Rowan put on her gloves. "You might get sick of me."

"Unlikely."

"I'm flattered that you want to spend so much time together." Rowan lowered her voice, not wanting to air Nick's business on the streets of Jasper. "Don't you have something else to do? Something more important?"

"Important?" Nick looked skeptical.

"Cold feet?" Rowan asked as she grabbed the steering wheel, pulling herself onto the seat.

Leaning against the open passenger-side door, Nick shrugged.

"More like lukewarm."

"If you need a gentle push, I can set up a meeting."

Truthfully, Rowan worried. Leo wasn't an easy man at the best of times. Nick was so easygoing and kind. She didn't want him shredded by her stepfather's brusque—sometimes deliberately cruel—manner.

"No." Nick sounded adamant. "There's no need for you to get in the middle. Though I'm afraid I already put you there."

"You didn't." Rowan had given Nick and his situation a lot of thought in the wee hours of last night. "You haven't asked anything of me. Leo will understand."

Honestly, Rowan wasn't sure she spoke the truth. As if sensing her thoughts, Nick met her gaze, raising a questioning eyebrow.

"I don't care what the man thinks about me." He shrugged. "I came for answers, not to bond with my long-lost father. However, if my actions cause you any trouble, I'll stop."

Rowan felt a warm glow settle near her heart. Gorgeous, sexy, *and* a thoughtful gentleman. His mother would be proud of the man he had become.

"Three questions? Did you come to Jasper to harm Leonard Cartwright?"

"No," Nick frowned, obviously annoyed that she would bring up the idea.

"Are you after his money? A free ride? A big payday?" Rowan asked, tempering her unsavory words with a smile.

Nick sighed, his lips curving slightly as he caught on to where she was headed.

"Again, no." Nick raised an eyebrow. "And that's *four* questions."

"Wrong. Number two was the main question with a part A and B."

"Okay. I'll give you a pass. Though technically, I'm right and you're wrong."

Rowan laughed. Every second she spent with Nick reinforced her initial attraction. Adding layers. Good thing he wasn't staying in Jasper long or she would be in big trouble. She could handle a flirtation. Maybe even a steamy night or two.

Despite an engagement that ended badly, Rowan wasn't blocked off to the idea of falling in love. With the right man. Something told her that man wasn't Nick Sanders. Not long term. Not forever.

"Hey," Nick placed a hand on Rowan's arm. "Why the pensive look?"

"Work." A small lie was a lot easier than trying to explain where her thoughts had wandered. Rowan started the engine. "I really need to get going."

"You didn't ask your third question."

"Lunch. I have sandwiches and hot soup delivered around noon. Want to join my crew and me? The setting isn't elegant but the food is good and the view spectacular."

"Text me the directions. I'll be there."

"Are you always so affable?"

"No."

Without any elaboration, Nick shut the truck door. With a wave, he returned to Murielle's. As Rowan pulled from her parking spot, she had plenty to think about on the drive to work.

Last night, Rowan had seen many emotions flash through Nick's eyes. Sadness over the loss of his mother. The helplessness of a childhood filled with more hardship than she could imagine.

When he teased or flirted, his dark irises were sprinkled with flecks of gold. When he became aroused, they heated to molten chocolate.

But when Nick stepped back from her truck, Rowan had her first glimpse of a different man. The one who hadn't let his start in life stop him from getting what he wanted.

Rowan didn't know what would happen when Nick met with Leo. Her stepfather was used to getting everything his own way.

Something told her she didn't have to worry about Nick. Maybe a hunch. Or the glint in Nick's eyes. This time, Leo may have met his match.

CHAPTER FIVE

● ≈ ● ≈ ●

NICK CONSIDERED HIMSELF to be a patient man. At least professionally.

Baseball was all about waiting. Waiting on the bench for his time at bat. Waiting for the pitcher to throw the ball. Waiting to make a play when more often than not, the action took place on a different part of the field.

If Nick lost concentration for even a second, he could cost his team the game.

In his profession—during the marathon of a one hundred and sixty-two game season—patience wasn't just a virtue, but a vital necessity.

Perhaps Nick's ability to focus on the trivial things for nine innings—day after day—was why away from the ballpark, he could smell a stall job a mile away. Bullshit, was bullshit. Even when presented in the dulcet tones of a British accent.

Away from the game, the length of Nick's impatience fuse was much shorter. And burned a damn sight faster.

"The name is Nick Sanders," Nick said with a barely controlled growl. Instead of kicking a hole in his hotel room door, he stopped pacing and took a seat on the bed. "I would like to make an appointment to see Leonard Cartwright."

Four times he'd given the information. To four different people. Nick didn't know if he was moving up the food chain or getting shuttled laterally from minion to minion. Either way, the method seemed like a bad way to do business.

And a great way to piss off Nick. The woman on the other end of the phone couldn't know the mistake she made. But his close friends would have told her. Poke him once, okay. Poke him four times? Big mistake.

"Mr. Cartwright is out of the office all this week. If you like, I can transfer you to his assistant. She can tell you when he'll be back."

Taking a deep breath, Nick reminded himself to keep cool. Blowing up at a voice on the phone—tempting as the thought may be—wouldn't solve anything.

"I spoke with his assistant three transfers ago. She said Cartwright was in a meeting. After that, the word was that he's out to lunch. Somebody on this merry-go-round claimed he had stepped out for a few minutes."

"Mr. ...?"

"Sanders. Nick Sanders. I'll give you props for originality. But you should consider coordinating your answers. Is Leonard Cartwright in or isn't he? Ms.—?"

"Havisham."

Seriously? As in *Great Expectations*? Nick wondered how a woman with a posh English accent handled the unavoidable jokes her name must generate. His guess? A cool, withering stare.

"Either way, Mr. Sanders," the woman's tone grew clipped with annoyance. "A meeting with Mr. Cartwright is out of the question."

"Aren't you at least going to ask why I want to see him?"

Silence met Nick's question as Ms. Havisham mulled over her answer. Or was she consulting somebody before getting back to him? Anger settling into a simmering boil, he wondered—not for the first time—if he should have gone to Cartwright's office instead of calling.

Nick doubted his physical presence would have moved matters along any faster. However, he always found it an advantage when he could look into his opponent's eyes. Like facing a pitcher with the bases loaded and nobody out. One glimpse of panic—no matter how fleeting—and Nick knew he was in control. He was about to bring one or more of those baserunners home.

The talent for reading an adversary carried over into Nick's personal life. Not that he could always spot a liar. But he watched

48

their eyes. One flicker. A twitch. And he knew the lies were about to flow.

Unfortunately, Nick hadn't anticipated that his morning would turn into a marathon session of phone tag.

"If you would like to see Mr. Cartwright, he has an opening on Wednesday morning."

Nick knew something was off, but he couldn't figure out what. Why the sudden turnaround?

One thing he knew for certain. The whiff of rotten that filtered through the phone wasn't his imagination. Because? Simple. The instinct he trusted and rarely ignored.

On the less logical side? Way too many James Bond movies.

"Ms. Havisham." Breathing deeply, Nick hoped his voice sounded more reasonable than he felt. "My business with Mr. Cartwright won't take long. A few minutes. Surely he can fit me in sooner."

"Wednesday, Mr. Sanders. Take it or leave it."

"I'll get back to you."

"But—"

Hanging up, Nick collapsed onto the mattress, his phone clutched tightly in his hand.

Nick had a trump card to play. One that might have gotten him a meeting that very day. If Cartwright was his father, the name Annie Sanders was bound to get a reaction. But when Nick dropped his little bombshell, he wanted to be there to witness the fallout.

Wednesday. Nick hadn't planned to stay that long. In and out. Wasn't that what he told Travis? Bermuda beckoned. However, the call of warm beaches and bikini-clad women wasn't quite as strong as when he crossed the city limits.

Just over twenty-four hours ago Nick had never stepped foot in Jasper, Maine. Though nice enough, he wasn't sticking around at Leonard Cartwright's convenience. Perhaps the man would fill in the gaps in Nick's past. More than likely, he would spout nothing but excuses and lies.

If he hadn't promised himself that he would find the answers he sought, Nick would have packed his bag and headed out of town without a backward glance. For the life of him, he couldn't think of a reason to waste another minute of his time in this town.

As his phone buzzed, Nick checked the screen. What he saw brought a slow smile to his lips. The text was short, sweet, and to the point.

Are we still on for lunch?

Proof he wasn't always right. Rowan was all the reason any man would need to stick around. Closing his eyes, Nick pictured her smile. The situation might be complicated, but the feelings she stirred in him weren't.

Nick enjoyed Rowan's company. Throw in a healthy dose of old-fashioned lust and what was there to think about? Wednesday wasn't that far off. Besides, only a fool would turn his back on the chance to see a lot more of the beautiful blonde.

Thumbs nimbly running over the keys, he answered Rowan's text. Short, sweet, and to the point.

Yes. Please.

Before he could stand, she answered.

So polite. A definite virtue. See you soon.

Polite was good. Saying please and thank you came easily to Nick. But that didn't mean he couldn't be ruthless when necessary.

Nick would get his information. If Leonard Cartwright gave him a fight, all the better.

And he would get Rowan. *She wasn't anybody's pushover,* Nick thought with a smile. But the heat between them was undeniable. Winning his way into her bed would be worth the effort.

No. Not effort. Pure, unadulterated pleasure.

STARTING A BUSINESS is never an easy undertaking. No matter how well prepared, there are always unexpected twists and turns.

Rowan hadn't jumped blindly into the world of landscaping. Besides her education, she compiled reams of research. She contacted the most experienced people she could find. Hours of time spent bending ears and reading emails. If she had a question, she asked. Then followed up with a dozen more.

Determined, Rowan refused to proceed until she was as prepared as humanly possible.

Using her own money saved from summer and after-school jobs, Rowan started small while still in college. She built a customer base of people who knew they could count on her to do the job well, on time, and at a fair—often below-market—price.

Back in those days, Rowan was mostly a one-woman crew. If she needed help now and then, she would hire a local kid to pick up the slack.

When Rowan was ready to expand, she took out a small business loan—her hand shaking as she signed the papers. A big step she hadn't taken lightly.

Thank God for Rebecca Gibson. Pretty. Young. The single mother needed a job with flexible hours. Efficient, capable, and— most important—trustworthy. Rebecca quickly became Rowan's right-hand woman. She was able to take on more than one job at once, knowing she had somebody she could count on to keep the work on track.

In less than two years, Rowan paid off her loan. Instead of putting every penny back into the business—as she had for so long—she started to allow herself the occasional luxury. Like a new set of tires or a trip to the beauty parlor

After trimming her own hair for so long, having a professional take care of the shaping and styling was a luxury indeed.

"One more week." Rebecca shook her head, surveying the almost-finished project. "I wondered if you were crazy when you took this job."

"Join the club," Rowan laughed as she lifted a bag of compost from the back of Rebecca's truck.

"If I didn't know you so well, I never would have guessed you had any doubts. What's the saying? Never let them see you sweat? That's you to a T."

"I sweat all the time," Rowan said, emptying the bag into a wheelbarrow.

"You know what I mean. When most people would be chewing their nails to the quick, you're cool as the proverbial cucumber. I've always envied that quality."

Rowan appreciated the compliment. However, just because she had a great poker face didn't mean she hadn't spent plenty of anxiety-riddled nights tossing and turning.

For a long time, Rowan's business survived from job to job. Once that changed, the wise move would have been to stay on the same sure and steady course. Instead, she grabbed at a job that was out of her company's comfort zone.

Bigger than anything *RTC Landscaping* had ever tackled, the Frederick job could have turned into a disaster. Not monetarily. But a lot of Rowan's business came word of mouth. If her reputation took a major hit, it might never recover.

Go big, or go home. How many times had she reminded herself of that little idiom? When a risk paid off, the reward was worth the sick stomachs and sleepless nights. When the risk failed...? Luckily, Rowan thought with a slight shudder, she wouldn't find out.

Straightening, hands on hips, Rowan sighed with satisfaction.

"The last of the plants will be in by Tuesday. After that? A little clean-up and a bit of polish."

"You did it," Rebecca said.

"*We* did it. You. The crew. You've worked your asses off keeping on schedule."

"My ass was just fine before, thank you very much." Rebecca patted her shapely, jean-covered backside. "I would tell you to keep that in mind for the next time. But why waste my breath?"

Rowan didn't mention the job she had an eye on. One she might have hesitated over a few months ago. Now? Her confidence in herself and the women who worked for her was at an all-time high.

"I have to get to the Jenkins place." Rebecca gave Rowan a hug.

"We're about to break for lunch. Why don't you stay?" Rowan smiled. "Unless you already have plans."

Rebecca kept company with Darren Stratham. The romance had started slowly—Rebecca's choice, not Darren's. She had two children and a full-time job. Plus the still raw memories of a failed marriage. Finding time for romance was hardly a priority.

And a banker? Not Rebecca's usual style. She had always gone for the bad boys. Motorcycles and tattoos. Irresponsible and easily lured by big cleavage. What was she supposed to do with a nice, down-to-earth guy?

Darren's charm, persistence, and the fact that her kids adored him finally won Rebecca over. The tattoo on his right shoulder—a badass leprechaun no less—didn't hurt.

To Rebecca's surprise—and delight—there was nothing boring or staid about her banker. Reliable plus just the right amount of edge equaled just right in her book.

"Darren is out of town until Sunday." Rebecca fluffed her cap of short, dark hair before putting on her gloves. Lowering her voice, her dark eyes sparkled as she looked at Rowan. "I think he's going to propose."

"What?" *Finally*, Rowan added to herself. "How do you know?"

"A feeling." Shrugging, Rebecca tried her best to contain her grin, failing miserably. "The little hints have been getting bigger. And, Darren is taking me out to dinner on Sunday. Without the kids. To *Pie in the Sky*."

"Why didn't you say so?" The fanciest restaurant in town was *the* place for 'spontaneous' marriage proposals. "Book the hall."

"We aren't there yet."

Seeing Rebecca's frown, Rowan placed a hand on her friend's arm.

"I know you love him. Silla and Shirley love him." An understatement. Rebecca's daughters thought the sun rose and set on Darren Statham. "What's the problem?"

"I want to spend the rest of my life with Darren."

The absolute conviction in Rebecca's voice brought a smile to Rowan's lips. The touch of envy she felt wasn't unexpected. While not looking for the love of her life, she wouldn't complain if he dropped in unexpectedly.

"Marriage scares me. What we have—Darren, the girls, and I—is so right. What if—?"

"Stop right there." Rowan knew the dangers of what if. The words were an endless circle without an answer. Rebecca was better off if she never jumped on that particular train. "What happened during your first marriage won't happen again. Not with Darren."

"But—"

"He's a different man. And you're different this time around."

"I am." Rebecca perked up. "That silly girl who followed an idiot—and her hormones—to the altar no longer exists. I grew up not just because I had to for the girl's sake. But for my own."

"You have a good man. The right man." Rowan confirmed what her friend already knew.

"I do." Chuckling, Rebecca nodded. "Listen to me. I guess I'm ready for the big day."

"There you go."

"Oh, God. What if after all this angst, Darren doesn't pop the question?"

"Then *you* ask *him*."

Rebecca seemed to like the idea, her face lighting up.

"I can do that. Hooray for the twenty-first-century woman."

"Hooray for women, period," Rowan countered, nodding toward her hardworking crew.

"Truer words were never spoken. Oh, my God." Wide-eyed, Rebecca's mouth hung open. "Who is that? Yummy. I wonder if

54

Darren would mind if I licked him? Just to see if he tastes half as good as he looks."

Rowan could tell before she turned who had put the look of awe on Rebecca's face. Hadn't she reacted in a similar fashion the first time she took a good gander at Nick Sanders? And the second time. And the third.

Rowan watched as Nick walked toward them. Yummy didn't begin to describe him. From the top of his dark hair that she knew from personal experience was unbelievably thick and soft to the touch. To that face that made her believe that miracles do happen.

What other explanation was there? The man took her breath away. Pure and simple.

And Rowan wasn't alone. The women on her crew stopped what they were doing as he walked by. She could almost hear their collective sighs.

"Good morning, Rowan." Nick checked his watch. "Yup. Still morning with five minutes to spare."

Even the sound of his voice sent a shiver down Rowan's spine. She would have bet her favorite set of gardening tools—the high-end ones she bought herself for her last birthday—that Nick hadn't noticed the attention he garnered from every woman within gazing distance.

His focus completely on her as if they were the only two people in the world didn't hurt. A fact that wasn't lost on Rebecca.

"How long has this been going on?" her friend said under her breath as if whispering the words would magically render Nick temporarily deaf. "And why didn't you tell me?"

Rowan ignored the questions, settling on an introduction instead.

"Rebecca Gibson, meet Nick Sanders."

"The baseball player?" If possible, Rebecca's face lit up even more. "My boyfriend is a huge fan. He wheedled me into watching the World Series. Surprisingly, I wasn't the least bit bored."

"What a relief." Charming as always, Nick's tone was tinged with irony. "We do our best not to put too many people to sleep."

"And you succeeded," Rebecca assured him.

"You know who Nick is?" Once again, Rowan seemed to be the only person outside the baseball loop.

Going on as if she hadn't heard Rowan's question, Rebecca's eyes didn't waver from Nick.

"I remember thinking while I was watching the games that you were handsome. But in person, you reach a whole different level of gorgeous."

Amused by Rebecca's outspoken admiration, Rowan crossed her arms, waiting to see if Nick's reaction was just as entertaining.

Though suitably flattered, Nick didn't eat up the attention as his due. Instead, he changed the subject, shifting the focus off him.

"Do you work with Rowan?"

"Yes. And speaking of which, I need to hustle along." Rebecca sent Nick a dazzling smile. "If you're going to be in town for a while, I would love to introduce you to my boyfriend. Darren will go mental when I tell him we met."

"I'll be here at least until Wednesday."

Wednesday? As Rebecca drove down the long driveway, Rowan mulled over Nick's news.

"I couldn't get an appointment to see Cartwright until next week," Nick explained, anticipating Rowan's question.

He sounded frustrated. Knowing how Leo operated, Rowan wasn't that surprised. Not that Leo played games—exactly. But sometimes, he wielded his power in odd, inexplicable ways.

"You didn't tell Leo why you wanted to see him?"

"Seems like more of a face-to-face kind of thing."

As she grabbed the handles on the wheelbarrow, Rowan wondered how to tell Nick a few hard truths. Three steps ahead of her, he saved her trouble.

"If Cartwright is half the businessman he's purported to be, he already knows who I am. Who my mother is. And the probable reason I'm in Jasper."

They took the path toward the bed of roses near the back of the property. Nick strolled by her side. He didn't try to do the *manly* thing, muscling her aside. Instead, he let Rowan do her job.

Another major round of brownie points for Mr. Sanders.

"Leo has a crack team of investigators on retainer. You're right. By now, they've checked you out pretty thoroughly."

"Yet, no phone call moving up our meeting. I guess Lenny isn't terribly anxious to meet his long-lost son."

For the first time in her life, Rowan wished she was somebody else. A person not connected to Leonard Cartwright. Her loyalty to him was more about gratitude than affection, but the reason didn't change the facts.

Leo was her stepfather. Married to her mother. Her brother worked for him as his right-hand man and heir apparent. Rowan's refusal to conform to her stepfather's idea of how a young woman should behave had made her a bit of an outsider. But the fact remained. They were the only family she had.

"You can't take my side, Rowan."

Funny, hearing Nick give voice to her thoughts suddenly brought them into complete clarity.

"I'm not taking sides."

Not yet. Rowan would cross that bridge if and when she came to it. Reaching the end of the path, she set down the wheelbarrow.

"I'm helping a friend find the answers he deserves."

"Some friend." Without asking, Nick handed Rowan one of the nearby shovels, taking another for himself. He followed her lead, distributing the compost around the roses. "More like a pain in the ass."

"Not mine. Yet," Rowan laughed.

"Rowan. Lunch is here."

"We'll be right there, Minnie. Come on." Rowan took Nick's hand. Even through her thick work gloves, she liked the feel of his fingers closing over hers. "There's a place in the greenhouse where we can wash up."

"Word is going to get around that we're spending time together."

"Some of the biggest gossips in Jasper saw us together this morning," Rowan said as she opened the door to the large, domed building. To the right, she stopped by a ceramic sink. Turning on the taps, she shrugged. "I can't control what people say—or who hears what they say."

"That's a nice way of looking at things, Rowan." Nick squirted a dollop of soap into his palm. "But you don't strike me as the head-in-the-sand type. I have nothing to lose in all of this. You, on the other hand..."

"Why are you here, Nick?"

"In Jasper?" Nick frowned. "I told you."

"I mean here." Tossing him a towel, Rowan looked him straight in the eyes. "With me. If you're so worried about unsettling my life, why not stay away?"

"Because at heart, I'm a selfish bastard."

Rowan wouldn't argue Nick's assessment of himself. The man was a professional athlete. She imagined selfish had to be part of the package. But he had given her a pretty sizable peek inside himself. Self-centered? Sure. To some degree, who wasn't? Self-obsessed to the exclusion of anybody else's feelings? No. Rowan wasn't buying that as an explanation.

"Try again," she said.

When Nick hesitated, Rowan simply crossed her arms and waited.

"What other reason could there be?" he hedged.

"Maybe that you like my company? You think I'm funny and easy to talk to?"

"True."

Copying a model's stance, Rowan posed as if in front of a camera. The incongruity of her old jeans, worn work boots, and dirt-smudged face added to the image she deliberately created for Nick's amusement.

"Beautiful." Rowan batted her naturally long eyelashes. "And sexy as hell."

Lips twitching, eyes twinkling, Nick nodded. "Don't forget humble."

"Why state the obvious?"

Deliberately, Nick stepped toward Rowan, his arms closing around her waist until his body pressed fully against hers.

"There is nothing obvious about you, Rowan. Subtle curves." He ran his hand down her side, grazing her breast, coming to rest on her denim-covered hip. Leaning close, his lips brushed the side of her neck. "Subtle scent. Yet so intoxicating."

"Compost and sweat. Every man's dream smell."

A moan of pleasure as Nick bit lightly into the soft flesh right below her ear quickly followed Rowan's self-deprecating laugh.

"I have a friend who sells pots of potions, lotions, and tempting fragrances. If she could bottle your scent, she would make a fortune."

The sound of Nick's voice—the low, raspy rumble—sent shivers through Rowan's overheated body. She wasn't listening to the nonsense of his words as much as the tone. Bone melting. Hormone inducing.

At that very moment, Rowan would have agreed to anything Nick asked. Though one thing quickly sprung to her mind.

Sex on the floor of her employer's greenhouse? Sure. Absolutely. Yes. Please.

"Gorgeous."

Opening her eyes, Rowan found Nick staring. She didn't consider herself a vain person. But she knew when she made a little effort, turning heads wasn't out of the question.

At the moment, though, Rowan wasn't at her best. Her hair was in a simple braid held in place by the usual rubber band, shoved under her knit hat. Not a lick of makeup adorned her face. Her coat hung open, leaving little doubt that she was a woman. But most of the time, an onlooker would be hard pressed if asked to describe her shape hidden beneath.

However, the open admiration—the unfettered desire—in Nick's eyes left little doubt in her mind that he spoke the truth. To him—dirt smudges and all—she was indeed gorgeous.

"We could skip lunch." Nick cupped Rowan's cheek, his thumb running over her skin with a gentle caress. "But your crew would probably guess what we were doing in here."

"They're a sharp bunch," Rowan agreed, her sigh laced with regret. "Not that they would need much of an imagination."

"Just as well. What I have in mind is much better accomplished on a bed. King sized, if possible."

"I own a queen."

"Please tell me that's an invitation," Nick said as he matter-of-factly buttoned Rowan's jacket.

"More of a let's see how things go. With a big *probably* added on for good measure."

"Fair enough." Nick took Rowan's words with good humor. A major twinkle in his dark eyes. "I plan on doing my best to change that probably into a definite yes."

"I'm sure I'll enjoy your efforts," Rowan chuckled.

Her laugh turned into a gasp when Nick pulled her close for a quick but breathtaking, intense kiss.

"You'll enjoy every second. Guaranteed," Nick assured her, holding open the greenhouse door.

Rowan searched for a clever quip—one designed to let a little air out of the man's inflated ego. But she had nothing. Her brain was thoroughly scrambled. If she tried to speak, she would only embarrass herself as she fumbled to string words into a simple, cohesive sentence.

Instead, Rowan gave him what she considered her best cool, withering look. The one that had sent more than one lounge lizard slinking away, his balls shriveled to the size of dried prunes. Nick simply smiled, his gaze seeming to say he wasn't intimidated.

If anything, Rowan had the impression Nick's interest in her had intensified. Great. A professional athlete, he undoubtedly possessed a finely honed competitive side.

How was she supposed to make a rational decision when the sexiest man she had ever met focused all his considerable talent on getting her into bed?

They had until Wednesday. Much longer than Rowan had anticipated. Her insides jumped at the idea of having Nick around for the better part of a week. The calm, logical side of her brain wasn't as sure, throwing out warning signals like crazy.

Dangerous flashed in big, bold neon letters.

Not physically. Rowan knew with the certainty of the sun coming up in the east that Nick would never raise a hand to cause her harm.

Her body would be fine.

Her heart was another matter.

After only a day, Rowan knew more about him than most of the men she had dated for months. Her fiancé—the man she planned to spend the rest of her life? She had never cracked the surface of what made him tick. Though to be fair, the blame fell on her as much as Wilton. She hadn't tried to make him open up simply because she hadn't cared.

Almost from the moment they met, Rowan wanted to know everything about Nick. And there lay her problem. For perhaps the first time in her life she had met a man who made her want…

Everything.

"Don't look so worried," Nick teased, blissfully unaware of the direction of Rowan's thoughts. "I'm not going to jump you during lunch. A little seduction here. A little there."

To illustrate his point, Nick brushed his hand against hers as they made their way to where her crew already tucked into the delivered sandwiches and hot soup. One light touch, yet enough to make Rowan's heart race with anticipation for more.

Oh, yes. Nick was a danger to Rowan. In so many ways. And the crazy part? He had absolutely no idea. And for the sake of her peace of mind—and the rest of her—Rowan knew the best thing would be to keep him in the dark.

CHAPTER SIX

● ≈ ● ≈ ●

OUT OF HABIT, Rowan stopped to check her reflection in the oval mirror hanging in the hall. As far as she knew, the antique silver-framed glass had been there as long as the house.

Built just after the Civil War by Leonard Cartwright's direct ancestor, Langford Cartwright used the money he made off government contracts. His company supplied the North with anything and everything he could get his hands on. From bullets to tents. Anticipating the conflict to come, the wily up-and-coming businessman bought cheap. Stockpiling warehouse after warehouse. Then, when demand peaked, he sold at a premium.

Langford Cartwright began the 1860s with a decent fortune. By the end of the decade, he was one of the wealthiest men on the eastern seaboard.

The mansion of sizable proportions sat on the outskirts of Jasper with a sweeping view of the ocean. Generation after generation lived there. Some happy. Some, not so much. But year after year. Decade after decade. As one century flowed into the next. Two things continued to grow.

The Cartwright money. And the power that a family with great wealth and burning ambition, inevitably wielded.

Smoothing her already neat-as-a-pin hair, Rowan wondered, as she often did when visiting the house she lived in until she was eighteen, how she had lasted that long.

Just after Leo and her mother married, Rowan's natural exuberance was temporarily subdued by the dark halls and somber-faced portraits that seemed to watch with disapproval every time she walked the grand, curving staircase.

In those days, Leo's mother was alive. Sternly unsmiling, she had little patience for children. Though Agnes Cartwright warmed a little toward Rowan's brother. Possessing the right combination of chromosomes, Geoff—as a boy—held more value. He wasn't a Cartwright by blood, but until their mother did her duty and produced an heir, Geoff was the next best thing.

Blessed with the kind of personality that didn't dwell on what was wrong with her life, Rowan quickly—happily—discovered that in the Cartwright household, her sex—that of a lowly girl— paid major dividends.

Once beyond the claustrophobic confines of their precious mansion, the Cartwrights couldn't have cared less where she went or what she did. Her friends—like Rowan—didn't matter. As long as she didn't attract attention, she was free to do as she pleased.

The year Rowan turned fourteen, the sum of her worth—at least in the eyes of her step-grandmother—took a dramatic tick upward.

Suddenly, as Rowan matured. Shooting upward. And outward—in all the proper places. As her somewhat pretty face lost the girlish softness becoming interesting. Some might even say beautiful. Which meant she could attract the right kind of husband. One from the right kind of family.

Rowan spent the next four years under Agnes Cartwright's eagle eye. Her activities were closely scrutinized. As were her friends. To keep the peace, she went along with the old woman's archaic notions of how a young woman should behave.

Or rather, Rowan *pretended* to conform.

With a little ingenuity, and a lot of false smiles, she lived a double life. Demure when in the range of what she tagged the *propriety police*, a bit of the wild child the rest of the time. Compared to some, Rowan's teenage escapades were pretty tame. But she did her share of crazy. Things that would have turned Agnes Cartwright's fashionable silver hair stark white.

From the kegger parties out at *Starlight Pond,* to losing her virginity in the back of Moss Goldberg's beat-up *Civic,* a big part of the thrill was knowing she wasn't supposed to be having so much fun.

As the excitement of sneaking around wore off, Rowan cut back on the fun and games, concentrating on school and her future. College. Starting her own business.

Agnes Cartwright didn't live to show her disapproval over Rowan's choice of professions. On that subject, Leo—in his unique, cool, unemotional manner—would have made his mother proud.

Quite simply, Leo hated that Rowan insisted on getting her hands dirty for a living.

Landscaping wouldn't have been his first choice for her. However, since she insisted, he generously offered to give her all the money she needed and more to give her a generous start.

One problem. As with anything Cartwright-related, there was a *big* proviso attached. Rowan was expected to supervise the work from a plush, expertly and expensively decorated office located in the downtown building owned by Leo. The one where his very, very, very successful consulting firm occupied the entire top floor.

For so many reasons, Rowan would never have considered taking Leo's offer. An offer her mother and brother pointed out—again and again—was beyond the realm of generous.

And they were right. If Rowan wasn't bothered by the long, thick, and ever-changing strings that came attached any time Leo opened his bank account.

Rowan was lucky. She received a small inheritance from her maternal grandmother. The house she now lived in and enough money to put her through four years of school at the college two towns over.

Though Rowan's independence hadn't set well with her family, she knew on some level Leo respected her need to be successful—or fall flat on her face—without the crutch of his money and influence.

"That's a nice outfit." Tess touched the collar of Rowan's dark-blue jacket, slowly perusing the lighter-colored silk blouse and matching, long, flared skirt. The knee-high black leather boots were several years old but looked like new. "Did you get it in New York?"

"No. Here in Jasper." Rowan smiled at her mother. "There's a new boutique just off Main Street. *Lilac and Lace*. They have some great things. And all the accessories. You should stop in."

"Perhaps."

Perhaps. Maybe. We'll see. All Tess Cartwright speak for *not in this lifetime or any other*. At heart, Rowan's mother was a snob. Twice a year, she traveled to New York. Or London. Or Paris. On occasion, Rome and Milan. She only wore designer originals— purchased from the design house.

Beautiful. Stylish. Well-spoken. And vain to her very core. If Tess Cartwright couldn't travel to the best, she brought the best to her. The perks of marrying a very rich man who liked his wife to look the part.

Tess flew in a top stylist once a month to cut and color her hair the perfect shade of honey blonde. Tess watched every morsel that went into her mouth. Exercised regularly. Though smart, she knew Leonard Cartwright hadn't married her for her brains.

Catching a rich husband was work. Holding onto one was a career.

Other than the shape of their face and slender build, Rowan had little in common with the woman who gave her life. She topped her mother's five-foot-three-inch frame by almost six inches. Preferred denim to silk. Tess had a manicure every week. Rowan barely had time to keep her nails trimmed.

However, for all their differences, Tess was her mother. And she loved her. Sometimes liking her wasn't easy. But the love was bone deep.

"Is Leo in his office?"

"Yes. He's been here most of the afternoon. Did you have an appointment?"

The fact that Rowan needed to schedule time to see her stepfather spoke volumes about their family dynamic. Warm and fuzzy they weren't.

"He asked me to stop by."

Actually, Leo's assistant did the asking. But why split hairs?

"I see."

"That's it? Aren't you curious why I was summoned by the great man?"

Tess raised an eyebrow—a well-practiced gesture perfected over the years.

"Sarcasm rarely appeals to the opposite sex, Rowan."

For as long as she could remember, her mother recited things the *opposite sex* didn't like. Rowan stopped paying attention long ago. But she was fairly certain that sarcasm fell somewhere between a smart mouth and not wearing lipstick.

"You look lovely."

As she was known to do, Tess switched gears for no discernable reason. Smiling, she reached up, adjusting the length of Rowan's long hair, leaving the ends of the simple ponytail cascaded over her shoulder instead of down her back.

Rowan didn't protest. What would be the point? No matter how perfect, her mother liked to tweak things. The flowers in a vase. The settings of silverware. Her daughter's perfectly fine hair.

"Thank you," Rowan smiled, as her mother finished fussing. "So do you. I like your hair that way."

Tess preened, plumping the ends of her new chin-length bob. Though her mother would have preferred to live in a more cosmopolitan city, she embraced her role as Jasper's Queen Bee. Part of her job—as she saw it—was to mix up her look from time to time. To be a trendsetter amongst her peers.

"Not too short?"

Knowing her part, Rowan stood back as if contemplating her answer.

"Perfect," she said.

"If you like, I can have my stylist fix you up the next time he's in town. Your hair is so thick, a little thinning wouldn't hurt. Bangs would look good on you. Maybe one of those modified shags?"

"We'll see." Which in Rowan speak meant, *not now, not ever.* "I don't want to keep Leo waiting," she checked her watch. "He said five o'clock."

"Why didn't you say so?" Tess gasped. Punctuality wasn't taken lightly in the Cartwright household. "Go. Can you stay for dinner?"

"Not tonight." Nick was taking her out for the meal they skipped the night before. "I'll stop to say goodbye before I leave."

The office was located at the end of a narrow hallway painted a pale lime color. The long walk gave a visitor plenty of time to consider the fate awaiting them.

Once, and only once, Rowan jokingly dubbed it *The Green Mile.* Her stepfather wasn't amused. Then again, in her experience, he rarely was.

Defused lighting cast shadows on the pictures lining the walls. Black and white photos of family through the years, they always struck Rowan as something out of an old movie. The horror variety.

Pausing outside the carved oak door, Rowan took a deep breath, sorry that every meeting with Leo felt like a chore instead of a pleasure.

Growing up, Rowan rarely tried to hide her rebellious side. And Leo hated not getting his way. Not the best combination. They didn't exactly butt heads. Leo didn't argue. With anybody. When displeased, he became a glacier. Solid ice. More than once he had frozen her out, the thaw—whether or not she could be persuaded by her mother to apologize—was slow.

Eventually, Rowan learned to keep her opinions to herself. Which meant biting her tongue whenever she and Leo were in the same room.

Their relationship at best was strained. Now and then, Rowan asked herself if she could have done something to bring them closer. To her sorrow, the answer was always no. She and Leo were too different. Oil and water.

Rowan's engagement to Wilton Jacobs was the only time she could remember receiving Leo's full approval. He still blamed her for breaking things off.

When Rowan explained why, Leo shrugged, imparting a bit of wisdom. Two words. Spoken in a calm, matter-of-fact manner.

"Men cheat."

To this day, Rowan's head almost exploded when she thought of the way Leo shrugged, his sympathy firmly with her ex-fiancé.

However, time moved on. Rowan had gained perspective. If she hadn't exactly forgiven Leo for his callous take, she had shrugged off most of the hurt. Mostly because she hadn't been in love with Wilton. Infatuated. But her heart had never been in danger.

As for the engagement. Their families weren't entirely convinced the problem that ended things so abruptly couldn't be fixed. *How crazy was that?*

Shaking off her thoughts, Rowan raised a hand, giving the door a brisk knock.

"Come in."

Squaring her shoulders, Rowan turned the doorknob, flicking the hair her mother had so neatly arranged back over her shoulder.

"Hello, Leo."

"Rowan. Please, take a seat." Not looking up, Leo continued reading the paper he held in his hand. "Would you like a drink? Tea? Coffee?"

"Nothing. Thank you."

Patiently, Rowan sat in the chair opposite Leo's desk. She didn't need to look around, easily conjuring a picture of the office.

Meticulously organized. Not a speck of dust to be seen. The features never changed. One wall was covered with floor-to-ceiling bookshelves, leather-bound first editions that she learned the hard way were there to be seen, not read. Heavy wooden furniture that included an antique desk passed on to the oldest son from generation to generation.

Leo, as the latest Cartwright to lord over his holdings, sat relaxed as if the world were his and no one would dare challenge his supremacy. Which, for the most part, was true.

But that didn't mean Leo's world couldn't be rattled. Why else would Rowan be sitting in his office as Friday afternoon slid into evening?

"I understand your job for Marsha Frederick is progressing nicely."

Surprised, Rowan nodded. Leo never discussed business. His or hers.

"We're ahead of schedule."

"Good thing. Forecast is calling for the first hard freeze end of next week."

"I heard this afternoon. My crew is working through the weekend to finish up by Monday. Tuesday at the latest."

"Smart."

Leo rose, moving to the bar trolley that the staff kept fully loaded, replacing the ice several times a day. He poured himself a whiskey—neat—repeating his offer to Rowan.

"Nothing for me."

Pushing sixty, Leo could easily pass for twenty years younger. Still handsome and slender, with a full head of dark hair lightly salted with gray. He was an active man with the same youthful vigor as when he and Rowan's mother first married.

He drank a bit too much. And his office smelled of fresh smoke from one of those imported cigars he liked so much. However, he was a stickler for watching his diet.

As for exercise, Leo finalized many a business deal on the golf course. He had a personal trainer who came to the house every other day.

Leo's love was tennis. He even had an indoor court in the basement. Though finding a worthy opponent wasn't easy. Her stepfather—as with every aspect of his life—expected to win. To say he wasn't a gracious loser would be like saying the Pacific

Ocean was a vast body of water. Both gross understatements of the obvious.

"Morton Simpson has added a four-season conservatory to the back of his home."

"Always a good look."

"Mm." Instead of sitting, Leo walked to the window, staring out at the backyard. "He wants to fill the thing with all kinds of tropical crap. Fountains. Lights. Hell if I know," he said with a dismissive shrug. "Told him you could help."

Rowan didn't know what to say. Never—not once—had Leo pushed business her way. Considering his attitude toward her chosen profession, she wasn't surprised.

So why the sudden change in attitude?

Rallying her thoughts, Rowan gave Leo a speculative smile.

"With holidays coming, we're not taking any new jobs before the first of the year. But tell him to call the office."

Leo turned, sporting the stern frown she recognized all too well.

"He's a friend, Rowan."

Rowan knew about Leo's crony network. Rich, powerful men scratching each other's backs. Not literally. Though the image made Rowan's smile widen.

"Did I say something amusing?"

Leo? Make a joke? Rowan liked to think he was capable of genuine humor. But she had never been witness to him sharing so much as a bad pun. Wisely, she kept her thoughts to herself.

"The best I can promise is a consultation."

"Morton is a busy man."

"And I'm a busy woman."

Leo raised an eyebrow. Never mastering that particular power move, Rowan simply tilted her head, her eyes never wavering. Wondering if her imagination was playing tricks on her, she thought she saw a flash of admiration in his dark gaze. But the moment passed before she could be sure.

"He may decide to go with someone else."

"If you like, I'll give you the names of several excellent people Mr. Simpson can call."

Leo's eyes narrowed. He expected capitulation. Always. No exception. Those who dared challenge him quickly felt the sting of his wrath. Sometimes socially. Sometimes professionally. But he never let a perceived slight go unpunished.

Family wasn't immune. However, on occasion, Leo would let an annoyance slide with only a withering glare. Once upon a time, Rowan dreaded him turning that look on her. Back when she still harbored a sliver of hope he would be the father figure she longed for.

Those days were long gone. As were the effects of Leo's perpetual displeasure.

"Are you doing so well you can afford to turn away a paying customer?" Leo asked, sipping his whiskey.

Rowan shrugged. "Business will never be that good. However, making promises I can't keep is the best way to lose those paying customers. Don't you agree?"

"Are you staying for dinner?"

End of conversation. Rowan sighed. What had she expected? Agreeing with her would be tantamount to Leo admitting he was wrong.

"I wish I could, but I have other plans."

Leo's gaze sharpened. Rowan had given her stepfather an opening to finally bring up the subject of Nick. She waited to see if he would step through.

"A date?"

"Yes."

"Anyone I know?"

A loaded question if ever there was one.

"You've never met."

Even from across the room, Leo's frustration was palpable. Without asking directly, he expected Rowan to give him the

71

information he wanted. He should have known better. But Leo never understood her. Sadly, she doubted he ever would.

"Was there anything else you wanted to say?"

"No." Leo set his glass on the trolley. "And you? Is there something you'd like to tell me?"

"Not right now." Rowan stood. "Perhaps we'll have something to say to each other at another time."

"Perhaps." Leo watched as she crossed to the door. "Do you know what I prize about all things, Rowan?"

Instead of giving Leo the obvious answer—*Money? Power? More money?*—she simply shook her head.

"Loyalty. You might want to keep that in mind." Having made his point, Leo turned his back on her. "Have a good evening."

Rowan silently closed the door behind her. *Damn the man*, she thought as her stomach clenched. Leo was the guilty party here, not her. If he had agreed to see Nick right away, all his questions would have been answered.

Taking a straightforward approach—something Leo rarely did—would mean giving as much information as he received. He preferred holding his cards close while those around them spilled their guts.

How dare Leo play his games with her? Rowan felt her stomach settle, a wave of anger replacing the guilt.

Nick's story wasn't for her to tell. Knowing what he had to say, keeping the information to herself, wasn't disloyal. If she thought for a moment that Nick meant Leo harm, she would have come to him immediately.

Leo already knew who Nick was. And why he had come to Jasper. Nothing Rowan told him would have mattered.

Loyalty. Maybe Rowan's had shifted. She waited for her stomach to protest the thought. Nothing. Not a single twinge.

Foolish? Reckless? Rowan wouldn't argue. But sometimes she had to follow her instincts.

Maybe Nick didn't deserve so much blind faith. Maybe he would prove her wrong. Until then, it seemed she had planted herself firmly in his corner. Though she had only known Nick a short while, she knew Leo very well. And what he was capable of doing.

Leaving the house after a quick goodbye to her mother, Rowan buttoned her coat against the brisk breeze that blew off the ocean. Thoughtfully, she slid into her truck, starting the engine and turning the heat on full blast.

More than ever, Rowan believed Leo was Nick's biological father. And if she was right, her stepfather was the one who had to do the explaining.

CHAPTER SEVEN

● ≈ ● ≈ ●

"DO THEY SERVE pie?"

"Naturally." Rowan smiled at Nick's teasing question as he drove around the last winding corner into the close-to-overflowing parking lot. Luck was on their side, a car pulled out as if anticipating their arrival. "But not the every day, made by Mom kind. The chef thinks outside the pie box. There's a different kind every day with some very unusual combinations."

The building that housed Jasper's most popular restaurant sat on a bluff overlooking the town. Originally, the location contained little more than a rundown shack used as a lookout station to watch for summer fires. When the forest service moved to newer, more state-of-the-art digs, the owners of *Pie in the Sky* jumped at the chance to buy the land and build their dream restaurant.

Elegant yet understated, the cuisine was eclectic, changing with the seasons. The chef filled her menu with as much locally supplied items as possible. Unique. Fresh. And most of all, delicious. *Pie in the Sky* was a huge success.

Getting a table on a Friday night meant making reservations weeks in advance. Or, in Rowan's case, the fact that last summer she turned the yard behind the restaurant into a gardener's paradise—including a state of the art greenhouse—at a price nobody else was willing to match.

Rowan made a reasonable profit. Even better, having chef/owner Lanny Raye as a friend meant she could get an in-demand table anytime she wanted.

"Wait," Nick said when Rowan tried to leave the SUV.

Jumping to the ground, Nick's long legs carried him around the vehicle while Rowan did as he asked, feeling a bit bemused. She could never remember a date opening the car door for her. The gesture was a little old-fashioned. Something Cary Grant would do for Grace Kelly in an old movie.

The perfectly tailored suit in the color of a moonless midnight sky didn't hurt. However, that certain undefinable something radiated from Nick twenty-four hours a day.

While how he dressed accentuated the moment, Rowen knew Nick could pull off the move with a smooth confidence wearing jeans and a faded t-shirt.

Nick came across as a completely modern man. Yet, he managed to help her from her seat with the suave aplomb of another era.

"Careful," Rowan warned, tucking her hand into the crook of his proffered arm. "Behavior like this might spoil me for other men."

Rowan used a light tone, an accompanying smile on her lips. The way Nick looked at her made her heart skip a beat.

"I was thinking the same about you and other women."

All Rowan could think was, *I don't know if that's a line he uses all the time. And if it is, right now, I couldn't care less.*

Then, to top things off, Nick raised her hand for a warm kiss.

Dangerous, Rowan sighed to herself. That's what he was.

Like the parking lot, the restaurant was full. Designed with such a contingency in mind, the building's acoustics muffled most of the noise. Dimly lit, the main room provided a warm, intimate dining experience with a panoramic view of Jasper and the ocean just beyond.

"Hello, Rowan." A tall, thin man with a mop of bright red hair and a brighter smile greeted her, ignoring the other people waiting to be seated. "I saw your name in the book."

"Hi, Dwayne." Rowan returned his friendly hug. "Lanny was kind enough to fit us in."

"She made me promise to tell her when you arrived. Something about a new man in your life." Dwayne gave Nick a long, speculative look. "You dating is news enough. Lanny didn't mention he was such a tall, yummy drink of water."

Rowan was used to Dwayne hitting on every man he met, but she wasn't certain how Nick would take her friend's mostly teasing perusal.

Adding to his ever-growing list of sigh-worthy qualities, Nick sent Dwayne an easy smile, holding out his hand.

"Nick Sanders."

"Dwayne Plank. Welcome to Jasper." Dwayne sighed. "Why are all the good ones either married or straight?"

"You do all right."

Better than all right. Dwayne was notorious for his coterie of boyfriends. With his job running the business side of a very successful restaurant, Rowan didn't know where he found the time.

"Yes, I do," Dwayne said with a self-satisfied smirk. "However, that doesn't stop me from coveting what I can't have."

"*We* covet a table," Rowan reminded Dwayne why they were there.

"Come on then," Dwayne chuckled, his laughter directed at himself.

The restaurant was designed so patrons could circle around the main floor without disturbing other diners. However, that didn't stop them from turning heads as Dwayne led Rowan and Nick to a table by the window.

"The stars are out. Perfect for enjoying the view." Dwayne commented, seating them with his usual flair. "We have a set menu on Friday nights. However, if you would like something a little less adventurous, I'm sure Lanny could accommodate you."

Rowan was an adventurous eater, open to almost any culinary concoction. She turned to Nick. "Any allergies or dietary restrictions?"

"Snails." Nick's face mirrored the distaste in his tone. "I'm not thrilled about eating anything that leaves a trail of slime. And please. No internal organs. Or testicles."

"Free-range chicken," Dwayne assured him. "You can push its feet to the side if they don't appeal."

"Chicken feet? Is he joking?" Nick asked after they were alone.

"You never know." Rowan laughed when Nick grimaced. "Relax. Lanny believes in using every part of the animal. But rarely during the same meal."

"Once I would have eaten the sole from a dirty shoe and been grateful. Thankfully, those days are long gone."

Rowan understood that Nick wasn't seeking her sympathy. The fact that he could speak of going hungry in such an off-hand manner amazed her. The combination of money and, most of all, the passing of time helped, she supposed.

The raw pain in Nick's eyes when he spoke of his childhood was burned into Rowan's memory. The wounds had healed. But the scars would never completely fade.

"I saw Leo this afternoon."

Rowan wanted to be as upfront with Nick as possible. If for some reason he found out about the meeting, she didn't want him to get the wrong idea.

"He's your stepfather," Nick's expressive eyes shuttered—just a bit. "I imagine you see quite a bit of him."

"Not really. And I wouldn't have today if he hadn't asked me to stop by."

"A little fact-finding mission?"

Rowan couldn't tell what Nick was thinking. However, in his place, she… Honestly, she had no idea. She couldn't imagine what she would be feeling.

"Yes."

"And? What did you tell him?"

"About you? Nothing."

Nick stared at her. Hard. Disconcerting. Knowing the knowledge wouldn't be welcome, Rowan didn't tell him that only a few hours earlier, Leo had looked at her the same way. Waiting.

Unlike Leo, Nick didn't wait for her to crack, expecting his will to crush her own.

"Okay," he said.

"That's all? Okay?"

"Unless you lied? Did you tell what you know about me?"

Rowan shook her head.

"Then, yes. That's all." Nick picked up the wine menu. "Would you like something to drink?"

"Nick—"

"Not tonight, Rowan." Laying his hand over hers, Nick's eyes pleaded. "Tomorrow, I'll have a dozen questions. Followed by at least a dozen more. But right now, let's enjoy each other's company, a spectacular view, and what I hope will be a great meal. Can we do that?"

Turning her hand, Rowan squeezed Nick's fingers.

"Yes. We can do that. And yes, I would love a glass of wine."

The waitress was across the room, delivering an order of drinks. Nick would have called the way the woman miraculously looked his way the second he smiled a coincidence. Rowan would have agreed. Until she noticed the way the young woman hustled, weaving her way around tables. When she arrived, her eager-to-please smile was all for Nick.

"What can I get for you?" she asked in a breathless voice.

Though the question was directed at him, Nick sent an inquiring glance Rowan's way. When he winked, she had to smile.

"I'll have the house Chardonnay."

"And a beer for me."

"Any particular kind?"

Nick mentioned a brand new to Rowan, but the waitress simply nodded.

"I'll be right back with your drink."

"Drinks," Nick reminded her.

"Oh," the young woman frowned as if noticing Rowan for the first time. "Right. Chablis?"

"Chardonnay."

Alone again, Rowan laughed, shaking her head. She wondered how Nick felt knowing he could turn a woman's brain to mush with little more than a casual smile?

"What would I get if I googled you?"

Nick seemed surprised by her question.

"I assumed you already had."

"Until this moment, the idea never occurred to me." Rowan frowned. "Not smart, but there you go. Want to give me the highlights? Or maybe the lowlights?"

"I'm not a saint," Nick told her. "But my sins haven't been bad enough to shake the world."

"Models? Actresses?"

Rowan wasn't a big believer in fairy tales. And she certainly wasn't in the market for a prince. But the way Nick hesitated, a frown marring his forehead, she had to wonder if this was where he morphed from a charming man into a wart-riddled frog.

"In my earlier days, I was involved in a bar fight—once. My face gets in the gossip columns from time to time because of me or who I took out to dinner. I had a stalker—not a pleasant experience. So, yes," Nick said with a glint of what will be, will be in his eyes. "You can google me. You'll see my follies and a few of my triumphs."

"Have you killed anyone? Kicked a dog?"

"No and no."

Rowan smiled. She hadn't been holding her breath—exactly. But hearing Nick confirm what she already believed in her heart didn't hurt.

"Then, I would rather form my own opinions about the man in front of me. I don't care about the famous baseball player. Or what you did as a hotheaded kid. Tell me about Nick Sanders."

"I can do that."

Waiting patiently as their server delivered their drinks, her eyelashes batting with such force Nick had to feel a breeze, a thought crossed Rowan's mind.

"Did you google me?" she asked.

"Once. Indirectly. I had to find out if you were Leonard Cartwright's biological daughter."

"Very important information," Rowan agreed.

"Vital."

"I think we should have sex. Tonight."

Nick, in the middle of taking a drink of beer, sputtered, sending a spray of foam across the table. Luckily, the force only carried the liquid to the edge of the tablecloth, missing Rowan altogether.

"Tonight?" Nick wiped his mouth. And chin.

"What's the matter?" Rowan teased, enjoying the oddly endearing look of surprised panic on Nick's face. "Do you have other plans?"

Nick made a fast recovery, his sexy smile causing Rowan's breath to catch in her throat.

"Nothing I can't cancel."

Enjoying their banter—and unwilling to let his initial reaction pass without one more little jab at his ego—Rowan leaned forward, lowering her voice.

"There's no shame in admitting to a bit of performance anxiety. Happens to every man now and then. Or so I understand."

"Rest assured. My *performance* never fails me." Nick's dark eyes seemed to spark with gold fire. "If we were alone, I would be happy to demonstrate."

Catching Nick's meaning, Rowan's gaze dropped. She couldn't see what was going on under the table, but she could imagine.

"Right now?" she asked.

"What do you expect? You say we should have sex. My hormones spring to attention—so to speak. Thank God for a long tablecloth."

"I'm sorry," Rowan apologized, not sounding a bit contrite. "That must be... hard."

"Funny," Nick shook his head as Rowan snickered. "I'll be fine. As long as I don't have to stand in the next five to ten minutes."

Rowan knew how the human body worked. Involuntary blood flow, and all that. But nature aside, she couldn't help the thrill that raced through her knowing the effect she had on Nick.

Dinner turned out to be delicious. Nothing too odd for Nick's taste, with plenty of spice for Rowan's

As the meal progressed, Rowan discovered Nick to be a gifted storyteller. He regaled her with his early days in the minor leagues. And she learned more about the game of baseball. He started with a single A club. The Tallahassee Tornadoes were an off-shoot of the Cyclones, pretty much as low on the ladder as a young second baseman could start.

"I was full of piss and vinegar in those days. We all were. Knowing we had the talent to get to the big club was one thing. Proving we weren't just a flash in the pan was another."

"The odds must be astronomically against getting to the top."

"There are thirty major-league teams. Twenty-five players on each. Take away the pitchers, which leaves somewhere between seventeen to eighteen spots for the guys who go out on the field every day."

Rowan didn't need to do the math. In many ways, Nick was a miracle. Fulfilling a dream that so few ever achieved took more than talent. He needed dedication and determination. And yes, a bit of good old-fashioned luck.

"I know men who were happy just to have a cup of coffee in the majors."

"A cup of coffee?" Rowan had never heard the term.

"A week or so with the big club. Usually when an everyday player has a minor injury or a brief illness, the team brings up a temporary filler. Sometimes, if he's lucky, he'll dazzle management. Usually, he's sent back down, never to make the jump again."

"That sounds brutal."

"That's baseball."

Nick seemed philosophical. And Rowan supposed he was right. But to make it—ever so briefly—and know that one moment was probably all you would get? She couldn't imagine.

"Did you have a contingency plan? Just in case?"

Nick's gaze didn't waver. "Failure was never an option."

"Do you always get what you want?"

"Yes." His smile was slow to form, giving Rowan's heart rate time to accelerate accordingly. "Every time."

"I see you enjoyed the chicken."

The heat between Rowan and Nick had risen to a dangerous level. Dwayne's arrival tempered things down to an acceptable level for a public venue.

"Give the chef my compliments." Nick placed his fork on his empty plate. "I can't remember the last time I enjoyed a meal as much."

"Lanny wanted to stop by to say hello, but she's swamped tonight. Her sous chef called in sick at the last minute. But she took a peek."

"And," Nick asked. "Did I pass muster?"

"Lanny's response—and this is a direct quote. *Holy crap.*" Dwayne let out a delighted chortle. "Short and highly accurate."

Nick looked amused.

"I'll take that as a compliment. Dessert?" he asked Rowan.

"Cheesecake," Dwayne answered for her. "The day Rowan orders anything else I'll eat my Italian leather loafers."

"A feat I would love to witness. But not tonight."

Lanny made the best cheesecake Rowan had ever tasted. Considering she ordered the dessert whenever she found it on a menu, the praise was well-earned.

"Not to put a damper on your evening," Dwayne's smile disappeared. "I had hoped you would be gone before his party arrived. But…"

For an instant, Rowan thought Dwayne was talking about Leo. Seeing the flash in Nick's eyes, he must have jumped to the same conclusion. But she quickly realized her mistake. She left her stepfather and mother about to sit down for a quiet dinner at home.

"Who do you mean?" Rowan asked, giving Nick a look that told him to relax.

"Wilton Jacobs IV." Dwayne raised his nose several inches, looking at Rowan down the newly formed slope. "He just arrived. I won't say his date has her plastic surgeon on speed dial. But that girl is a walking Barbie doll. God never made boobs that big and perky."

Rowan sighed. She thought she had moved past trying to convince people that she didn't care what—or who—her ex-fiancé did.

"What is a Wilton Jacobs IV?" Nick asked.

"Scum. Pretty in a capped-teeth kind of way. But that boy oozes fake charm like a leaky septic tank."

Nick glanced at Rowan, a question in his eyes.

"Consider the nail hit firmly on the head," she laughed. "Wilton and I were engaged in what I call my delusional period."

"You wised up?"

"She caught him slipping his secretary his Vienna sausage." Dwayne raised his hand, showing about an inch of space between his thumb and forefinger. "And that's generous."

"Dwayne." Rowan rolled her eyes.

"Honestly. We go to the same gym."

"Well?" Nick asked.

"No comment." Rowan couldn't believe they were discussing the size of her ex's penis.

"Mr. Gherkin is headed this way," Dwayne sang out. "I'll send over your cheesecake."

"You're over this jerk?"

Nick could have been asking Rowan the time of day. Except for the glint in his eyes as he looked over her shoulder.

"Dumping Wilton was the best move I ever made. And no, he didn't break my heart. More of a dent to my pride."

The smart thing for Wilton to do would consist of taking a wide berth around Rowan's table. Smart. Gentlemanly. Considerate. However, Wilton had political aspirations. With his eye firmly on the state Senate and beyond, he treated every situation with the mentality of a natural vote whore.

Wilton had the process down to a science. From his not too firm, dry-as-a-bone handshake to the smarmy, hold onto your wallet smile.

For the gazillionth time, Rowan asked herself. *What did I ever see in this man?*

"Rowan." Wisely, Wilton neither held out his hand, not tried to brush a friendly kiss across her cheek. "What a pleasant surprise."

Pleasant wasn't the word Rowan would have chosen. But what the heck.

"Friday night in Jasper," she shrugged.

"Exactly." Wilton's ever-alert gaze shifted to Nick. He held out his hand. "Wilton Jacobs."

"Nick Sanders."

"Right. The baseball player. I heard you were in town."

Wilton was blessed with what Rowan's mother called Ivy League good looks. Average height. Slender build. Blond. Blue eyes. On his own, Wilton was just fine. Compared to Nick? Well, what was the point?

Like plain, lukewarm oatmeal, Wilton represented—in theory—what her family thought would be good for her. But he turned out to be a cheating bowl of unbelievable blandness. Rowan needed spice in her life. Heat. Variety. Someone who would make each day different and exciting.

Rowan needed...

"Nick."

Realizing she spoke his name, Rowan tried to cover. "Nick is only in town for a few days."

"Not a resident of our fair state?"

"No."

"Ah." Wilton's interest quickly dimmed. "Have a good evening, Rowan. Nick."

"You don't have a vote, so you aren't worth his time," Rowan explained as Wilton glad-handed his way across the room to the table where his date waited patiently.

Nick rubbed the back of his neck, giving Rowan a crooked smile.

"Your taste in men..."

"Has improved. Greatly."

"At the risk of sounding egotistical, I have to agree."

Subject closed. Rowan didn't want to spend another second thinking or talking about Wilton Jacobs. Nick, thank goodness, was happy to follow her lead. They enjoyed their dessert accompanied by light, easy conversation.

However, as they waited while their waitress brought them the bill, the mood shifted as Rowan remembered her earlier declaration. From the look in his eyes as he placed his credit card in his billfold, Nick's thoughts traveled along the same line.

"Sex?" he whispered in Rowan's ear, helping her on with her coat?

Rowan simply took Nick's hand, retracing the steps they took earlier that evening. She waved to Dwayne as they left the restaurant. Crisp and clean, she took a deep breath, her arm brushing Nick's. She stopped when they reached the SUV.

"Sex?" she asked, winding her arms around Nick's waist. She smiled, tipping her head as his lips grazed the side of her neck. "Yes. Please."

CHAPTER EIGHT

● ≈ ● ≈ ●

EXCITEMENT BUZZED THROUGH Rowan's blood.

As Nick drove down the mountain, one hand gripping the steering wheel, the other lightly brushing her arm, her hand, her thigh, she waited for her nerves to kick in.

And waited. And waited.

Nothing. Not even a twinge trying to warn Rowan she had made the wrong decision by going so far outside her normal behavior.

Rowan Cartwright didn't invite men back to her home with the sole purpose of having sex. Not their first time together.

Her date would walk her to the door. Kiss Rowan goodnight. If something sparked, she would initiate another kiss. She might invite him in for a drink. The process would be a slow build. A progression of steps with the looming question of maybe they would, or maybe they wouldn't.

Almost from the moment she met Nick, she knew the answer. Yes, they would. The only question was how soon.

Rowan hadn't expected tonight to turn into *the* night. In fact, she had talked herself into waiting. Anticipation was a potent form of foreplay. Knowing Nick would be leaving town on Wednesday provided her with a time limit. Tuesday night they could sleep together. If the experience were great, Rowan would be left with a nice memory.

If Nick turned out to be an unexpected dud, Rowan wouldn't have to worry about a repeat performance. Or an awkward phone call explaining why she didn't want to see him again. *Been there, done that.*

Rowan should have known better. Nick wasn't like any man she had ever met. And the chemistry between them? Off the charts. The more time she spent with him, the logical reasons for not

86

sleeping with him as soon as possible—and as often as possible—dissolved like tissue paper in a tsunami.

"You're awfully quiet." Keeping his eyes on the road, Nick lifted Rowan's hand to his lips. "Second thoughts."

"A lot of thoughts. None of them second ones."

"Talk to me, Rowan. What's going through that wonderfully complicated mind of yours?"

Rowan wondered if this was the time to keep her thoughts to herself. She wasn't prone to spilling every word and idea that popped into her head. But with Nick, she felt the need to share... everything. From the smallest observations to the biggest emotions.

Off the top of her head, Rowan could think of a dozen reasons she couldn't say any of those things to Nick. Beginning with the one that had been at the top of the list from the moment they met.

Too soon. And since Nick was leaving in a few days? Rowan added a big, fat never. Why embarrass herself—and send him running for the hills? Better she edit her words. For both their sakes.

"On average, how many times do you have sex in one night?"

"With the same woman? Or are we talking multiple partners?"

"Wow. Not the answer I expected."

Fascinated, Rowan shifted, turning her body toward Nick as much as her seatbelt would allow.

"New question. How often do you have multiple partners in one night? Do you go from woman to woman? All at once? And how does it work? When you're servicing one, do the others play with each other? Do they watch? Or—"

"Slow down before you blow a gasket," Nick laughed. Hard. "Do you really want to know?"

"Definitely." Rowan decided she needed to clarify so Nick wouldn't get the wrong idea. "As long as you understand I'm merely curious. Whatever you and I do is strictly one on one. No extra participants. No rubberneckers."

Nick slowed the SUV, stopping outside Rowan's house.

"Hold that thought."

Bemused, Rowan waited as Nick jogged around the vehicle, opening her door and taking her hand which he kept in his after helping her alight.

"For me, sex is fun. Always has been," Nick said in a conversational tone as they strolled toward the front door. "Pretty much anything goes as long as everybody involved can legally buy a beer and is fully on board."

"Whips? Chains? Nipple clamps? Other men?"

Chuckling, Nick leaned against the doorjamb as Rowan turned the lock.

"Yes—soft. No. Once. No."

Rowan quickly matched Nick's answers to her questions.

"Were your nipples on the receiving or giving end?"

Nick followed Rowan into the house. He shut the door, turning the locks.

"Giving. Are you asking these questions out of a general curiosity? Or…?"

Rowan unbuttoned her coat, shaking her head.

"I'm not the tie me up, tie me down kind of woman. However, I do wonder about the appeal."

"My partner at the time enjoyed the lifestyle. So, I dipped my toe in the water. Turned out the whole bondage, flagellation, pain equals pleasure, isn't my thing. "

"But you enjoy more than one woman at a time?"

Handing Rowan his coat, Nick sighed. But his indulgent smile didn't waver.

"A baseball season is a long, sometimes exciting, occasionally tedious, campaign. Sex takes the edge off. Multiple partner sex perks up an otherwise routine Wednesday night. But only if the Cyclones don't play on Thursday."

Rowan had never met a man who was so naturally open about… anything. But especially concerning his sex life. To be fair, the idea of asking never occurred to her before.

"Have I scared you off?"

"Are you going to invite another woman to join us?"

"No." Kissing her lightly, Nick slid his hands up Rowan's arms. One stopped at her neck, cupping the back. The other took the clip from her hair, wrapping the length around his fingers. "Besides, who would I call? All the interested women I know live three thousand miles away."

"Good," Rowan made an encouraging sound of pleasure when Nick kissed the side of her neck. "Tonight, I need your undivided attention."

"You have it. Tonight. Tomorrow. As long as I'm in Jasper."

Nothing Nick had told her about his sexual history bothered her. Not a twinge of concern. Rowan didn't care how many women—alone or in bunches—he'd been with.

As long as I'm in Jasper.

Rowan appreciated Nick's honesty. He didn't make any promises. He told her right up front. Sex was fun. And their time together had a definitive beginning, middle, and end. A fact she would deal with when the time came.

But tonight was their beginning. And Rowan would enjoy every second.

"I like this suit."

Rowan could feel Nick's lips curve as he continued to explore her neck.

"What do you like? The color? The fit?"

"Yes, and yes. I enjoyed looking at you while we ate. But right now, I like how easily I can remove your jacket."

To prove her point, Rowan undid the single button, pushing the butter-soft material from his shoulders and down his arms until the jacket lay in a pool at his feet.

"The pants come off almost as quickly—in the right hands."

"Good to know."

Rowan's laugh had a low, husky quality she didn't recognize. She liked the sound. And from Nick's low growl, so did he. Or perhaps his reaction had something to do with how her hands kept brushing the bulge between his legs as she carefully lowered his zipper. She was fine either way.

"You were right. Off in a heartbeat."

How Nick managed, Rowan would never know. Before giving her more than a glimpse of his long, muscular legs, he removed his shoes, lost the socks, and gently nudged her onto the couch.

"Smooth," Rowan laughed.

"Just wait," Nick knelt, his hand disappearing under Rowan's skirt. "You ain't seen nothing yet."

"I thought you might want me to keep my boots on."

Nick simply raised an eyebrow, baring Rowan's right foot, then her left, her boots joining his shoes in a nearby pile. He kissed the inside of Rowan's thigh.

"So damn soft and warm."

Closing her eyes, Rowan breathed deeply as her blood heated and her heart began to pound as if planning to burst from her chest at any moment. Nick's kisses were like gasoline near an open flame. Her body felt ready to explode.

"White lace?"

After a busy week, the panties were the only clean pair Rowan had left. Along with the matching bra, they were a gift from her best friend that were too impractical for everyday wear.

"Don't let the color fool you. There is nothing virginal about me."

Nick met her gaze. Talk about heat. His dark eyes almost scorched her skin with their intensity.

"You aren't innocent and sweet?"

As Rowan slowly shook her head, Nick let out an exaggerated sigh of relief.

"Thank God. If you told me you were a virgin, I wouldn't turn you away. Hell, I'm not crazy. My head is filled with a million fantasies involving you naked, and tempering them—even a little bit—would be disappointing."

"A million fantasies?" Rowan was on board. "How many can we get through?"

"Don't worry. We'll make a sizable dent. But you know the old saying." Nick removed the slip of white lace. "Every journey begins with the first step."

As first steps went, he outdid himself.

Nick pushed Rowan's skirt higher, higher, until the material was bunched just above her thighs, kissing each exposed inch of skin as he went.

"You said you weren't sweet," he lightly admonished with a swipe of his tongue. "Believe me, I've never tasted anyone sweeter."

Rowan gasped. Her head falling back, she let every thought fly from her head so she could concentrate on what was important. Nick. His magic tongue. And the otherworldly pleasure coursing through her body.

Nick made her feel as though she was all that mattered. The house could tumble down around them, he wouldn't notice. At this moment, nothing—nobody—else existed.

Clutching at the cushions, she never wanted it to end. Yet at the same time, she reached for that final burst, the crashing crescendo. Up. Up. Holy—

"Nick!"

Rowan reached the top alone, but Nick was with her for the fall. Holding her as her body shook. Encouraging. Soothing. And yes, from the look on his face as she finally had the strength to open her eyes, gloating. Just a little.

"Don't look so smug," Rowan said with all the rancor she could muster. In this case, very little.

"Do I?" Nick sounded pleased. "I wonder why?"

"Maybe you have the right."

"Maybe I do." Chuckling, Nick pulled her close, smoothing back her hair. "You called out my name."

Did she? Rowan tried to remember. The pleasure she experienced was front and center. Whatever words might have come out of her mouth were blurred by a warm, fuzzy haze. Nick seemed pleased. So, what the heck. Why argue?

Since the energy involved was minimal, Rowan used one hand to unbutton Nick's shirt. Her reward was his chest, bared to her very appreciative gaze.

"Do you shave?" she asked, starting her explorations with his rock-hard abs. "Wax?"

"Are you kidding?" Nick sounded as if her question was a major insult.

Rowan really wanted to laugh, but she bit the inside of her lip instead. She had found a tender spot in Nick's seemingly impenetrable ego. Who would have guessed?

"Manscaping? Isn't that what you cosmopolitan types call it?"

"You got the term right. But I don't. I remove the hair from my face. The rest of me is all natural."

To make up for her unintended gaffe, Rowan intensified her caresses, adding her mouth to the mix, soon losing herself in the task that was much more a treat than a chore.

"Mm," Nick hummed his approval, his fingers lacing through her long hair.

Rowan made her own humming sound as she lifted the waistband of Nick's shorts. "Oh, my."

"Are you laughing? Cause FYI. No man alive wants a woman to chuckle at his dick."

Nick grinned as he spoke, showing Rowan he wasn't worried about her reaction to what he carried between his legs. Nor should he be?

"Nothing to be ashamed of from this angle." Rowan turned her head. "Or this one. Just to be certain, why don't I get a closer look?"

"Sounds like a plan. But first." Nick groaned when Rowan kissed the region of his bellybutton before he could stop her.

"You made me miss my target."

"Try again as soon as we're in your bed. I won't move a muscle." Nick took Rowan by the hand, pulling her to her feet. "Lead on."

"Drop the shirt, and you have a deal."

"Negotiating? After what I did for you?"

"Yes."

"You're wearing more than I am."

Without a second thought, Rowan removed her jacket. Her blouse was next. As she shimmied out of her skirt, she paused, waiting for Nick to catch up.

"Sorry," he said, unbuttoning first one cuff, followed by the other. "You distracted me with that fast, but entertaining striptease. Nice bra."

"Matches the panties. Angie will be glad to know they finally saw the light of day. Or rather night."

"Your best friend?"

Rowan nodded. "She likes to give me lingerie as a gift."

"Tell her I said thank you." With an expert touch, Nick unfastened the closure. "I love bras that open in the front. But not as much as what's underneath."

Laughing, Rowan took a step back, avoiding Nick's reach.

"Hands to yourself, fella. Shorts next. Then you can feel me up to your heart's content."

Nick didn't hesitate. Nor was he shy about his body. Why would he be? Top to bottom—and everything between—was the highest form of eye candy. He waited, content to let Rowan look her fill.

"Nice."

"Nice?" Nick raised an eyebrow. "Surely you can do better than that."

"Very nice. And don't call me surely."

"I didn't think I could want you more. But a woman who quotes *Airplane*? Irresistible."

"Then come and get me."

Rowan took off, knowing that Nick would be close behind. He could have easily caught her as she zipped through the living room and up the stairs. But glancing over her shoulder, she could see he enjoyed the chase. The game. Playing.

Laughing, slightly out of breath, Rowan collapsed onto her bed. Rather than pounce, Nick paused in the doorway. To use his word, she realized they were having fun. A new experience for her.

Rowan had always enjoyed sex, but the idea of combining lighthearted play with wild passion would never have occurred to her. The two had always seemed like polar opposites. Now, she wondered how she could ever go back to anything else.

Holding out her arms, Rowan beckoned Nick to join her.

"Hello, gorgeous," she whispered as his hard body covered hers.

"That should be my line." Nick's kiss left her gasping, wanting more. "I wish I had the words. Rowan—"

Rowan laid a finger over Nick's lips. She found herself torn between wanting to know what was going on in his head and worrying that if she knew, saying goodbye would be hard. Harder than that moment was already bound to be.

"Not now. Let's enjoy each other." She pushed at his shoulder. Nick wrapped his arm around her waist, reversing positions. "Let me make you feel good."

"Having you near makes me feel good." Nick touched her face. Slowly, he grinned. "But I'm happy to take whatever you have in mind."

"Damn right. I don't do this every day. So, consider yourself one of the lucky few."

"You don't have to."

Nick's words said one thing. The look—the need—in his eyes said another. Even if she wanted to, how could she disappoint him? Luckily, stopping was the last thing on her mind.

"Relax." Rowan gave him a lingering kiss. Then winked. "Lie back and think of England."

With a bark of laughter, Nick fluffed the pillow, his hands cradled behind his head.

"I'll be too busy thinking of you."

"If after thirty seconds you can think at all, I should brush up on my technique."

As a prelude—and because she couldn't resist—Rowan started with Nick's spectacular chest. Smooth, hard, her lips feasted. She breathed deeply, taking in his scent. Clean and spicy.

As a test, Rowan licked his rippling abs. Just as she suspected. Nick tasted even better than he smelled. And the way he sucked in his stomach followed by a deep moan, told her she wasn't the only one enjoying her ministrations.

"You doing okay?" Rowan asked, peeking at Nick through the curtain of her hair.

"One thing. I want to watch. But..."

Nick tried to push her hair behind her ear. The tresses were too thick and silky to stay in place for long.

In the drawer of her nightstand, Rowan found a barrette—the kind she kept in almost every room in the house. Twisting her hair into a topknot, she clipped the messy mass into place.

"Problem solved. I've thought about going for a shorter cut. Something practical."

"Are you crazy?" Nick protested.

"One day. Maybe," she reassured him, surprised yet pleased by his reaction. "But not anytime soon."

"Good."

"Now, where was I?"

Nick took Rowan's hand. "Right here."

Chuckling, Rowan shook her head, grasping the long, hot length of him.

"I'm pretty sure you jumped ahead a bit. But this is your party."

Oral sex wasn't Rowan's favorite activity. After all, there was a reason somebody named it a blow*job*. However, after a hesitant start, she quickly realized that with the right person—namely, Nick—she didn't mind. Just the opposite. She felt a burst of power.

Rowan literally held the key to Nick's pleasure. And as his excitement rose, so did hers.

"Time out," Nick said, air rushing from his lungs.

"I haven't finished."

"Another time." This time when he took her hand, he settled her next to him, on her side, face to face. "I want to be inside you. But my condoms are in my coat pocket."

"FYI? Modern women are always prepared."

Straddling Nick, Rowan plucked a foil packet from the nightstand.

"You can put this back." Nick unclipped the barrette, running his fingers through her hair. "Feel like running the show?"

Nodding, Rowan watched as Nick quickly and efficiently donned the condom.

"Ride 'em, cowgirl."

"Don't make me laugh," Rowan's cautioned, resting her forehead on Nick's chest. "If I slip, you might end up in a hole I'm not interested in letting you explore."

Rowan heard Nick snort, his entire body shaking.

"Jesus, woman. The way you think. I want to crawl inside that head of yours and watch the wheels turning."

"My head is fine. Just stay out of my a—"

Nick covered her mouth with his, stopping her words. As for her thoughts? Gone. If he were to make any observations at the moment, all he would see would be the pleasure center of her brain shooting skyrockets like the Fourth of July.

Every color of the rainbow and some Rowan was fairly certain were new to the spectrum.

Resting her hands on Nick's chest, her eyes locked with his, Rowan slowly, inch by excruciatingly wonderful inch, lowered her body onto his. They had no more room for banter. Or smiles. Or laughter.

Rowan spiraled higher, Nick with her all the way. He sat up, fingers tangling in the wild fall of her hair, his arm around her waist, anchoring her to him. His breathing matching hers. Their rhythm in perfect sync.

When they fell—after reaching so high Rowan swore she almost touched the sky—they fell... together.

CHAPTER NINE

● ≈ ● ≈ ●

TAKING ONE LAST glance at Rowan, sleeping peacefully, Nick reluctantly slipped from the warm bed. The soles of his feet protested when they hit the cold hardwood. Cursing his lack of foresight, he left the room, naked, hurrying down the stairs.

Nick used his memory, and the shaft of light from the street that filtered through the closed curtains, to find his clothes. He dressed quickly. Pants, socks, shirt. In his jacket pocket, he found his phone.

Using the light from the screen, Nick entered the kitchen. With a quick search, he discovered where Rowan kept the coffee and filters. A few minutes later, he had a pot brewing.

While Nick waited for his first shot of morning caffeine, he made a call. Yes, the hour was early, but he knew for a fact that Travis liked to work out at an ungodly hour. By now, his friend was either in the middle of his run or ready to hit the showers.

"Unless you're in prison or near death, fuck off."

Nick frowned. The voice sounded like Travis, but his hostile words and surly tone didn't fit. If he didn't know better, Nick would think he was speaking to himself.

"Hello to you too, sunshine."

"What the hell are you doing up so early?"

"A better question would be, are you still in bed at quarter to six?" Nick grinned. "Unless you aren't alone. If so, I apologize for the interruption."

"Wrong on both counts, asshole. I haven't been to bed yet."

"There's your problem. Get some sleep. And get yourself laid. I can highly recommend both."

"You've been there less than two days, and you've already talked some tootsie out of her clothes?" Travis growled, his voice laced with exasperation. "Unbelievable."

Normally, Nick would have laughed. Maybe bragged a little. But Rowan wasn't his usual conquest. She wasn't a conquest at all. And she certainly wasn't a tootsie.

"No comment."

"Since when?"

"Since..." Nick never hesitated to confide in Travis. But something stopped him. "You know what? Never mind. Tell me what crawled up your ass? Problems? Do you need backup?"

One word from Travis would have seen Nick on the next plane south. Rowan would understand. Or—he smiled when an idea popped into his head—she could come with him. A mini-vacation. The more Nick mulled over the possibility, the more his enthusiasm grew.

"I appreciate the offer." Most of the piss and vinegar had drained away. Mostly, Travis sounded tired. "Small towns. I'd forgotten what a pain in the ass they can be. How are you doing? Outside of the sex department? You always do well there."

"Daddy dearest is a bigger asshole than I imagined."

"Considering your attitude toward him going in, that's saying something. Did he try to excuse his behavior toward your mom?"

"I haven't met Leonard Cartwright."

Nick gave Travis a quick rundown of the situation—deliberately leaving Rowan out of the mix.

"He put off seeing you until Wednesday? I'm surprised you didn't say fuck Cartwright and headed out of town."

Nick chuckled. His friend knew him well.

"I figured now or never. The answers are here in Jasper. A few more days won't matter."

"Looks like we ended up in the same proverbial boat," Travis said, his voice tinged with frustration. "My situation turned out to be more complicated than anticipated."

"So much for sandy beaches and lazy afternoons."

"Mm."

Nick noticed neither of them mentioned bikini-clad babes. A lot had changed in a short period of time. When he thought of Bermuda. Warm nights. Tropical drinks. The only woman he could picture by his side was Rowan. She filled his senses, leaving little room for erstwhile thoughts of random hookups.

"We'll get away before the first of the year," Travis assured him. "Maybe we can convince Spencer to come along. If you don't mind him bringing Blue."

"I like Blue," Nick said. "If Spencer had to go and fall in love, he couldn't have made a better choice."

"Too good for him, I say."

"Ditto, brother."

Hearing Travis chuckle, Nick grinned. When he and his best buddies took off for some R&R, girlfriends were strictly verboten. However, Spencer's reckless bachelor days were over. Nick and Travis were more than capable of raising hell on their own.

"Good morning, gorgeous."

Rowan brushed past Nick, her hand briefly touching his. Dressed in a bathrobe, her long hair bundled into a messy topknot, and her face glowing, healthy and freshly scrubbed.

Without the slightest attempt to glam herself up, Rowan had more allure than any woman Nick had ever known.

"Call if you need anything," Nick told Travis as he watched Rowan take two mugs from the cupboard.

"Same goes."

"Standing in the dark isn't necessary," Rowan said, handing Nick his coffee. "I can afford the electricity."

"Habit." Nick's entire body sighed as he took a sip of the steaming brew.

"From when you were a kid. Or now?"

"Both."

With a shrug, Nick wrapped an arm around Rowan's waist, kissing the concerned frown marring the area between her brows. He was tired of rehashing his childhood. He had grown up with a loving, supportive mother. She was the one who suffered. She sacrificed so much for him. Every day. In so many ways.

With the blithe ignorance of youth, Nick had assumed he would have years, decades, to shower his mother with luxury. Now, he would have settled for hearing her voice, seeing her smile—untainted by pain—one more time.

"I ran out of time."

Rowan didn't ask what he meant. Somehow, she knew.

"I'm sorry."

His mother would have liked Rowan. A strong, independent woman, Annie Sanders recognized the qualities when she saw them. Nick hated regrets. But every life was littered with a few. He would add the fact that Rowan and his mother would never meet to his short, but unavoidable, list.

"When do you have to leave for work?"

"Twenty minutes. Why?"

Nick took Rowan's cup, setting it next to his in the sink. Lifting her, he gave her a long, heated kiss before heading up the stairs.

"Oh," she said, smiling.

Some regrets Nick couldn't avoid. Not taking every chance he had to enjoy warm, naked Rowan wouldn't be one of them.

ROWAN ADDED ANOTHER bag of yard waste to the growing pile near the back fence. The morning had been a non-stop race against the clouds moving in from the east. As each minute ticked from the clock, the temperature dropped a corresponding degree.

One more week and *RTC Landscaping* would have come up short on the promise Rowan made to Marsha Frederick. And the bonus her crew counted on to make the upcoming holidays a little merrier would have blown away with the nasty wind currently nipping at their heels.

Two more bags hit the pile. Rowan shot Nick a sideways glance as he stood beside her.

"I appreciate the help. But—"

"You didn't ask. I volunteered."

"And I'm grateful. But there's fresh snow on Mt. Blaire. I hear the skiing is fantastic."

"Are you trying to get rid of me?"

Hardly. Rowan only had a few days with Nick. If she had her way, she would spend as much time with him as possible.

"Just pointing out your options," she said, keeping the rest of her thoughts to herself.

"I'm where I want to be." Nick stretched his back, grimacing. "I thought I was in good shape. Now, I'm not so sure."

"Different set of muscles." Rowan admired the view as Nick bent over, picking up a stray piece of cardboard. "Nothing wrong with your gluteus maximus. Or any other part of you."

"You should know." Nick's gaze dropped to Rowan's mouth. "You kissed every inch of me. From top to bottom."

Yes, she had, Rowan thought with satisfaction. And if Nick voiced no objection, she planned to do so again. Next time from bottom to top—for the sake of variety.

"You want to trek out to the dump, or should I?" Rebecca asked. She usually spent weekends with her children. But today, all hands were on deck.

"You get rid of this load. I'll run the other pile to the center."

Not only was making their own compost a win for the environment, every successful DIY project they initiated meant a hefty chunk of money saved.

"I shouldn't be more than an hour."

Rowan shook her head. "By the time you drive there and back, we'll be done. Go home. Hug your kids. And that man of yours."

"Darren doesn't want for attention." But Rebecca didn't argue. "We made a masterpiece."

Returning Rebecca's hug, Rowan nodded.

"Janna is taking pictures as we speak. Check your inbox tomorrow afternoon. She should have everything downloaded, edited, and sent out to everyone by then."

Normally, Rowan played photographer. She enjoyed walking every inch of a project. Double checking that everything was as close to perfect as possible. Mostly, she liked to take the time to savor a job well done.

However, Mother Nature had graciously given Rowan a window which wouldn't stay open much longer. Leisurely strolls through the garden weren't on her agenda.

Janna Stapleton had expertly documented the job before and during. Rowan trusted her to take care of the after.

"What's next?" Nick swung a friendly arm around Rowan's shoulders.

"Don't laugh. I have a little ritual I always do at the end of every job. Sort of a superstition."

"I'm a baseball player. We love superstitions. When I was still in the minors, I had a teammate who wore the same underwear for three weeks straight."

Rowan grimaced. There were times—often, in fact—when the habits of men left her utterly confused. Apparently, male athletes rose to a whole different level of odd.

"Why?" she asked. "And how did you find out?"

"He bragged. Damn proud of those stiff, crusty suckers. Randy was on a hot streak. During those twenty-one days, his batting average rose over a hundred points. He became an RBI machine. Doubles. Triples. Twelve home runs."

In spite of herself, Rowan found the story fascinating.

"And then?"

"One day he went 0-for-5. Ritualistically—in the locker room shower—he burned the underwear right after the game."

"You didn't find the whole thing a bit odd?"

Nick shook his head, grinning. "Randy's antics were mild. I could tell you tales that would curl that pretty blond hair."

Rowan could tell that Nick was kidding. Not about the stories, but about sharing them. But she wasn't letting him off that easily. He had opened the door to her curiosity.

Besides, learning more about the oddities of baseball meant she learned a little more about Nick. Or at least the world he inhabited. Knowledge was almost always a good thing.

If nothing else, Rowan simply enjoyed the sound of Nick's voice.

They stopped near a pile of yard waste. She handed a bag to Nick, taking one for herself.

"Tell me more."

"Really?" Nick seemed surprised—and a little pleased—by Rowan's interest. "I didn't think baseball was your thing."

"Baseball isn't. But— I can always use a laugh."

"Okay. Just remember, you asked for it."

Rowan let out a silent sigh of relief. Thank goodness she caught herself before saying, *but you are*. Somehow—maybe last night, maybe today—when she wasn't paying attention, Nick had become her thing.

As she filled the bag, Rowan waited for the warning bells telling her she was a fool to jump when Nick wouldn't be there to catch her. He would be thousands of miles away, probably forgetting her as quickly as he moved on to one of his glamorous models.

Rowan waited. And waited. The bells, pealing their warning, never came. Great. Fine. No, even better. Terrific. How often did a man like Nick come into a woman's life? Into *her* life? The answer was simple.

Once in a lifetime.

Instead of worrying about how she would feel after he left, shouldn't she embrace every second she had with him?

Again, Rowan found her answer without much digging. Yes. To everything.

Wednesday. Until then, Rowan would fill her head with as much information—as many memories—as possible. Thursday would be soon enough to deal with the consequences.

"By then, stopping him wasn't an option," Nick finished another tale covering the antics of a minor-league teammate, blissfully unaware of Rowan's thoughts. "The manager's office was filled with fifteen goats. Trust me, they weren't housetrained."

"Who cleaned up the mess?" Rowan asked, laughing.

"Tuffy, and the two guys who helped him pull the prank. But the entire team paid the price. No amount of showering could completely eliminate the smell of goat shit. Naturally, we started a road trip the next day. Tuffy and his cohorts were relegated to the back of the bus for the next week."

"What about you?"

"Me?" Nick tied off his bag, reaching for another without missing a beat.

"All your stories are about teammates. Tell me one of your misadventures."

"I kept my nose choirboy clean." The twinkle in Nick's eyes told a different tale. "Maybe I slipped. Once. Twice at the most."

"Go on," Rowan urged.

"Have you ever been to Wilbur, Missouri?"

"Can't say that I have."

"Don't bother. Blink, and you'll miss the one highlight. *Miss Sally's*."

Chuckling, Rowan shook her head at the improbable name. "Sounds like a brothel."

"Close enough."

"You're joking."

"Scout's honor." Nick placed a hand over his heart.

"Were you a Scout?"

"No," he admitted, the edge of his lips twitching upward. "But the principle's the same."

Rowan had known a few Scouts. Some were trustworthy. Some? Not so much. As for Nick? In this case, she would give him the benefit of the doubt because... he was Nick. But mostly, she really, really wanted his story to be true.

"Though Wilbur is a small town, *Miss Sally's* catered to a wide-reaching clientele. Including visiting baseball teams. With nothing else to do for hundreds of miles, we naturally gravitated there after the game."

"Boys will be boys."

Rowan said the words tongue in cheek. Nick's nodding agreement was devoid of the irony she intended.

"I'd always avoided paying for sex—still do. But if a young man played minor league ball. And his team landed in Wilbur." Nick shrugged. "Miss Sally's was a rite of passage."

"What kind of passage? Years later, you can all brag that you caught the same STD?"

"Miss Sally's ladies were clean." When Rowan sent Nick a skeptical look, he backed down—a bit. "The only time I visited, I came away clean."

"A ringing endorsement if I ever heard one." Rowan finished filling the last bag. With a sense of accomplishment, she placed her hands on her hips. "Is Miss Sally's still standing?"

"Hell if I know. Probably."

Prostitution wasn't something Rowan could comfortably expound upon. However, she knew the practice wasn't all laughter and good times—despite what Dolly Parton and *The Best Little Whore House in Texas* wanted everybody to believe.

As far as Nick and his youthful indiscretion? She asked. He willingly volunteered. Subject closed.

"I'll get my truck. Once we've loaded these bags, we're done. Except for telling the lady of the house that her showpiece garden is finished. On time and, yay, under budget."

NICK WATCHED AS Rowan walked away, her long legs eating up the distance between her and her waiting truck. She was a sight to see. Strong. Confident. Carrying a heavy load of responsibility and more than capable of doing the job.

Outside of his mother, Nick couldn't think of a woman he admired more.

"You're the first person with a dick to work on Rowan's crew. How does that distinction make you feel?"

Glancing at Marsha Fredericks, Nick smiled. He met her briefly when he joined Rowan for lunch. A dynamic personality, she struck him as someone who spoke her mind and to hell with what the world thought. He liked her immediately.

"Rowan isn't sexist."

"No. She hired women because she had to. Then stuck with them because they could do the job and didn't grouse about working for a woman." Marsha scoffed. "Men."

Nick didn't know how to respond without sounding... male. So, he flipped the subject to a different angle.

"Why start a project like this?" Nick motioned toward the newly renovated backyard. "Why now? You could have waited until next year. What was the hurry?"

"Not just a pretty face, are you?" Marsha said with a considering glance.

"I appreciate the compliment. However, I'm certain the same thought crossed Rowan's mind a time or two."

"Undoubtedly. But she didn't ask."

"Because she's a good businesswoman. You wanted the job done, paid her well. Why question the goose and her golden egg?"

"Interesting imagery." Putting her hands in the pockets of her unapologetically, un-politically correct sable coat, Marsha pondered the view—and Nick's question. "Rowan has talent. However, her success has come through bullheaded determination. There are people in this town—some very close to her—who tried to keep her down. More than she even realizes."

Nick did a bit of pondering of his own. Someone close to Rowan. Someone who would be just as happy if she didn't succeed. Marsha didn't name names. She didn't have to. The only person who fit the bill was Leonard Cartwright.

"Were you testing Rowan?"

"Rowan tested herself. Otherwise, she wouldn't have taken the job. If the byproduct is the turning of a few previously skeptical heads in her direction, all the better."

"Men don't like a woman in charge. I'll guarantee the hardline, good old boys won't change their attitude no matter what Rowan does."

Marsha's eyes widened as if surprised by Nick's prescient observation.

"Enough people have Rowan's back."

"Including you."

"Mm." The sound could have been interpreted several ways. Nick figured the hum was Marsha's way of agreeing with him, saving herself from saying the actual words.

"What brought you to our town? And if you say the road, I'll smack your pretty face."

Figuring a response of *my SUV* would end with the same result, Nick kept the quip to himself.

"I'm on vacation."

"In Jasper, Maine?" Marsha managed an expert eye roll. "Do you know somebody? Friends? Family?"

"Do my reasons matter?"

"To me? No. But you latched onto Rowan awfully fast. *She* matters."

Nick wouldn't explain himself to Marsha Fredericks. However, the woman obviously cared about Rowan. He didn't mind eliminating a few of her concerns.

"Rowan isn't in the dark about me or my business."

"Fair enough." Marsha shivered, the pelts on her coat unable to block the frigid wind. "I've had enough nature for one day. Come with me."

"Rowan will be back in a second. I don't want to leave her to do all the work."

"You won't be gone that long." Marsha opened the sliding glass door. "Well?"

Nick hesitated before following, curiosity getting the better of him. Besides, he would know the second Rowan returned.

"I did some checking on you."

Eyes narrowed, Nick crossed his arms, waiting.

"Don't get pissy. I investigate everyone I meet. Sort of a hobby of mine. Another life, another time, I would have enjoyed working as a private investigator." Marsha poured herself a drink before offering one to Nick. "No? I heard you weren't much of a drinker."

"Did you?"

"I couldn't find much about you pre-baseball. Not that I care. I'm more interested in the man you are today. Ross Burton sang your praises to the rafters, by the way. Then wanted to know what the hell you had done and how much your escapades would cost him."

"You know the owner of the Cyclones?"

"I met Sherry Burton through our charity affiliations. Through her, I met Ross. Don't worry, I assured him you haven't been up to anything untoward."

"I'm not worried."

However, like any smart employee, Nick preferred to stay on his boss' good side.

"After a nice, long conversation—not all of which concerned you—I've decided to trust you with something very precious."

Opening a drawer in an antique armoire, Marsha picked something up, tossing it to Nick. He snagged the item midair, his second baseman's reflexes working without a second thought.

"Keys?" Nick asked, frowning at two pieces of metal bound by a simple silver chain. "Unless these are made of platinum, I would hardly call them precious."

109

"The keys are to a cabin in the mountains. You are welcome to use it for as long as you like. The person you're taking with you? She's more precious than any silly chunk of ore."

"No arguments here," Nick muttered. "A cabin. For Rowan and me? I don't know..."

"Ask her or don't. She could use a few days away." Marsha's expertly arched eyebrow rose a little higher. "Unless your interest in Rowan is different than I presumed?"

Nick gently tossed the keys in his hand. He wanted to get away with Rowan. He'd imagined a four-star resort with twenty-four-hour room service and a huge tub they could use for sexy water games.

However, Marsha's cabin might be a better solution. Complete privacy with no chance of anybody recognizing him. Nothing but Rowan. No interruptions. No distractions.

"She might not be interested."

"Smooth talking Rowan is up to you. Though something tells me you won't have much problem convincing her." Finishing her drink, Marsha set down the empty glass. "The directions for getting there are on the table by the door. I instructed my caretaker to fully stock the cupboards and refrigerator. If you need anything, give me a call. But I suggest turning off your phone. At least for the first day. You'll be amazed how freeing leaving technology behind can be."

Without another word, Marsha exited, leaving Nick behind, grateful if a bit bemused. Sticking the keys in his pocket, he paused by the glass door just as Rowan arrived. Picking up the paper on the nearby table, he perused the contents.

Handwritten on heavy, embossed paper, Marsha's directions were thorough, detailed, and left Nick little doubt he could find the cabin in full daylight or the dark of night.

"I took a little longer than expected. The rest of the crew was ready to go. Before they went, I gave my word all bonus checks would be ready to pick up by the end of next week." Rowan grinned as she opened the truck's end gate. "I've never seen so many happy faces in my life. Now I know how Santa Claus must feel."

"Any plans for the next few days?"

Nick tried to keep his tone casual. Holding his breath, he waited for Rowan's answer.

"Nope. Wonderfully free as a bird until after Thanksgiving." Picking up a bag, she paused. "I can't remember the last time my schedule was completely clear."

"What do you say we get away? Just the two of us."

Rowan threw the bag onto the truck. Turning, she met Nick's gaze.

"Sounds great. Just tell me what to pack."

CHAPTER TEN

● ≈ ● ≈ ●

"YOU'VE ONLY KNOWN him two days."

"Two days, seven hours."

Rowan took two sweaters from her closet, adding a third just to be safe. On her bed, next to her open suitcase, sat her best friend. Full of questions.

Angie Fiorina sported short, dark hair, a round, pretty face, and dark espresso-colored eyes. Smart, driven, full of fun, and fiercely loyal, she knew Rowan better than anybody.

"You've already had sex. Now you're going away to some unknown location for who knows how long?"

"Marsha Fredericks' cabin. But yes to the rest."

"Who are you and what have you done with Rowan?"

"I'll admit, Nick brings out a different side of me." Socks. Underwear. Toiletries. Condoms. Check. Check. Check. And double check. "You always said I should loosen up."

"Did I sound like I disapproved? Just the opposite. I was about to ask if your Nick has a tall drink of water teammate I can borrow for a few days."

Barely five foot two, Angie had a thing for men who topped her by a foot or more.

"Sorry. Nick hit town flying solo."

"My misfortune," Angie sighed. Spying what Rowan planned to pack next, she jumped from the bed. "No. Absolutely not."

"But the cabin will probably be cold."

Angie snatched the thick, granny nightgown from Rowan. Shaking her head, she returned it to the dresser, handing Rowan a flimsy piece of silk instead. Another gift, best friend to best friend.

Holding up the nightie, Rowan frowned.

"What is the difference between this and naked?"

"Watch Nick's eyes. You'll see the difference."

Laughing, Rowan packed the pink silk. When Angie looked away, she snuck in the flannel nightgown more out of stubbornness than the idea she would actually wear the thing.

"One piece of advice." Angie took the smaller of the two bags, following Rowan into the hall and down the stairs. "Don't fall in love with him."

"We're having fun. Enjoying each other's company." Rowan hadn't told Angie why Nick was in Jasper. For one simple reason. Though she trusted her friend implicitly, the secrets weren't hers to share. "To quote Tina Turner, *What's Love Got to Do with It?*"

"Just saying. You don't fall easily," Angie admitted. "But I've never known you to sleep with a man this quickly. Mistaking lust for love? Take a warning from somebody who's been there, done that."

"Terry Reardon," Rowan nodded. "He was a jerk."

"True." Picking up her coat, Angie donned the black, knee-length Anorak. "But jerks can charm part of the time. I was so bowled over by the instant chemistry, I convinced myself he was the one. Getting over my bruised heart was a lot easier than getting rid of Terry."

"Nick's life is on the other side of the country. He will leave. Comparing him to clingy Terry isn't fair or accurate."

"Knowing the relationship has a firm sell-by date is a good thing."

"I agree."

In all the years they had been friends, Rowan had never told Angie a deliberate lie. Until now. If she had a vote, Nick would stay in Jasper. She wanted the chance to build on their instant connection. To find out if there could be more.

Rowan wouldn't say the L-word. Not even to herself. But she was honest enough to admit what she wanted. More time. More days and nights.

More Nick. Period.

The doorbell rang, ending the conversation.

"Nick comes to the door?" Angie looked impressed. "The last guy I dated stayed in his car and honked. I was lucky if he actually remembered to unlock the passenger side. Most of the time, I had to pound on the window to get in."

"Stop exaggerating," Rowan said as she opened the door.

"Only a little."

Grinning, Angie turned her full attention to Nick. What she saw had her letting out a low whistle of approval.

Casually dressed in jeans, a navy-blue coat, and sturdy hiking boots, the ends of his dark hair peeked out from under a knit cap. But his face was on full display. Rowan knew what to expect, and Nick's good looks still sent her heart racing. She knew exactly the impact he had on Angie. Especially when he turned his smile on her for the first time.

Gobsmacked covered the expression on Angie's face pretty well.

Amused, Rowan took her heavy coat from the closet, checking to make certain her gloves and hat were in the pocket.

"Ready?" Nick asked, holding the coat as she slipped it on.

"All set. Nick, this is my best friend. Angie Fiorina. Angie. Nick Sanders."

"Pleasure to meet you," Nick sent Angie a warm nod.

"Believe me, the pleasure is all mine." Angie took Nick's hand. Looking up, she sighed. "Have any single brothers?"

"I'm an only child." Nick's lips twitched, his eyes flicking Rowan's way. "Sorry."

"I'll survive." Turning serious, Angie's grip tightened. "I love this woman. She's the sister of my soul. Bring her back in the same condition you found her, or you'll have me to deal with. Along with my five, big, burly, fight-loving brothers. Are we clear?"

"Crystal."

"Good." After patting his hand like she hadn't just threatened him with a beating, Angie hugged Rowan. "Have a good time. Call me if you need anything." She gave Nick one more, long, telling look. "I mean anything."

114

"Down, Killer," Rowan chuckled. "I'll be fine."

Nick picked up Rowan's luggage.

"Can we give you a lift?"

"Thanks, but no. I have my car."

Rowan locked the house. The walk to Nick's SUV was made in a companionable silence, Angie content to have checked him out and issued her warning.

"I like your friend," Nick said when the luggage was stored, and they were in the vehicle, buckling their seatbelts.

Rowan didn't apologize for Angie's behavior since Nick wasn't offended and, if the situation were reversed, she would have done the same. Using different words. And her brother couldn't be counted on to swat at an annoying fly. However, the sentiment would be on point.

"Angie's one of a kind. The good kind."

"My mom used to say, *you get your pick of friends, choose wisely*." Nick slowed for a stop sign before pulling onto the street heading north out of town. "She was worried I would fall in with a bunch of deadbeats who only cared about riding my coattails."

"Do you have somebody? A person to call when you're in trouble or just need to talk?"

"Travis Forsythe and Spencer Kraig."

"Teammates?" Rowan asked, trying her best to suppress a yawn, failing miserably.

"Why don't you close your eyes? I'll tell you about two of the best men I've ever known."

Rowan did as Nick suggested, trusting Nick to get them where they were going. The sound of his voice as he spoke of his friends, filled with affection, humor, even a trace of exasperation. They had his back. He had theirs. No matter what happened. A trade. Retirement. Even—God forbid—if one of them signed with a different team. He knew nothing could weaken the bond.

"Sound like keepers."

Rowan was nowhere near sleep, simply pleasantly relaxed.

"Making friends with teammates is easy. We play toward a common goal. Warriors in arms—so to speak. But Spencer and Travis? We clicked on a different level."

"I know what you mean. Sometimes—" Rowan groaned when her phone rang. She glanced at the screen. "My brother. Sorry. I really should take this."

"Go ahead."

"Hello, Geoff."

"Where the hell are you?"

Typical, Rowan thought, fighting the urge to hang up. Geoff couldn't begin with *how are you*? Or a common hello. He threw his words at her using an accusatory tone, as if the fact that she wasn't where he expected was a deliberate slap at him.

"I'm on my way out of town."

"At this time of night? Why? Are you alone?"

Rowan and Nick decided to leave tonight while the roads were in good shape. If they waited until morning, the chance of snow might have turned into a certainty, making their trip a little iffy.

If Rowan thought for a second Geoff's questions had to do with concern for her, she might have been more inclined to answer. However, since he rarely worried about anybody else, his curiosity was most likely self-serving.

Besides, where Rowan was going, why, and most of all, with whom, weren't any of Geoff's business.

"Why do you need to know?"

Geoff heaved an exasperated sigh.

"Rowan."

"Geoff."

"Get off your bitch horse and answer my question."

"Tell him to fuck off," Nick said, his anger palpable. However, unlike Geoff, he pitched his voice low so only Rowan could hear.

Shaking her head, Rowan laid her hand on Nick's thigh, her touch gentle.

"Goodbye, Geoff."

116

"Wait! At least tell me how long you'll be gone."

"A couple of days. Three, maybe four at the most."

Without another word, Geoff hung up. Rowan set her phone in her purse, rubbing her free hand over her face.

"Your brother sounds like a jerk."

"Geoff is… difficult. For the most part, we get along."

"What happens when he pushes too far?"

"A lot of yelling."

Rowan tried to avoid arguments. They never ended well, even when she won. Her superior vocabulary could reduce her brother to a muttering fool. Satisfying in the short run. Unfortunately, Geoff's way of getting even usually involved running to Mommy. Not very dignified for a married, thirty-year-old father of two.

But a dent to his pride never stopped Geoff. Always quick to jump to her boy's defense, Tess would chastise Rowan. In person. For a good hour. Reminding Rowan where she picked up her extensive knowledge of words.

"Why put up with his crap?"

"I suppose the easiest explanation is Geoff's my brother. We grew up together."

"If you say so," Nick placed his hand over hers. Warm. Strong. "I'll say he needs a lesson on manners and leave the rest of my opinion unsaid."

"Your restraint is greatly appreciated. Concerning Geoff's lack of manners? I won't disagree."

"Leaving Jasper," Nick read the bright red sign. "What do you say we leave everything and everyone behind at the city limits?"

Rowan loved the sound of Nick's suggestion.

"Do you think we can?"

"Marsha said we should cut off the world for twenty-four hours." Nick took out his phone. "Power off. Care to join the revolution?"

Immediately, Rowan followed Nick's lead, knowing if she thought too hard, she might come up with at least a dozen reasons not to.

"We have officially traveled back in time. What's your guess? Twenty years?"

"Close. Hand it over." Rowan opened the glove compartment, depositing their phones before snapping shut the door. "Cold turkey. Think we'll have withdrawal symptoms?"

"Phones turned off. No internet." When Rowan let out an over-the-top gasp, Nick smiled. "No television. We're dumping a lot of technology all at once."

"I can make the sacrifice if you can." Rowan let her hand drift toward the inside of Nick's thigh, her touch morphing from friendly to enticing. "Of course, finding some way to occupy ourselves will be a challenge."

"If we put our heads together, we'll think of something."

"I had in mind putting together something other than our heads," Rowan said, her fingers brushing his zipper. "Do you think you can *rise* to the occasion?"

"If you want to find out, move your hand a little further. Ever had sex on the side of a well-lit highway?"

"Threat?" Rowan asked. "Or promise?"

Somehow, Nick managed to keep his eyes on the road while simultaneously sending her a smoldering look. Talent, indeed.

"Threats are for wimps."

Rowan looked out the window. There were a surprising number of lights. Why hadn't she noticed before? Her reputation would survive getting caught having sex on a public thoroughfare. But why risk the embarrassment? They weren't horny teenagers unable to control their hormones.

Glancing at Nick, Rowan felt a rush of electricity. Not a teenager, but her hormones weren't acting as if they were aware of that fact.

"How soon until we turn onto a dark side road?"

On cue, the built-in GPS system told Nick to turn right in two miles.

"I can wait that long. Can you?"

Nick hissed—pleasure, not pain—as Rowan cupped him through the material of his jeans.

"You're playing a dangerous game," he warned, gripping the steering wheel hard enough to turn his knuckles white.

Unconcerned, Rowan squeezed, her breath hitching when she felt Nick's hard length grow until she wondered how he could stand the tight constraints imposed by the unforgiving denim.

"I thought you liked to play."

"I do. When I get a turn."

Nick swerved off the highway onto an unpaved side road. Rowan bounced in her seat, but not enough to displace the hand. Perhaps her grip tightened—just a bit—causing him to suck in his breath.

"Are you okay?" Rowan asked, trying to sound contrite. She failed miserably.

"I will be. Soon."

The side road had a side road. How Nick found what was really little more than a path hidden by a group of trees—in the dark— Rowan would never know. He rolled to a stop, turning the engine off.

"We'll get cold without the heater."

Rowan grinned at her own foolishness. The fire in Nick's eyes alone could heat a small town.

Unsnapping Rowan's pants. In one motion, he had them and her underwear down her hips.

"Raise your legs.

The position should have been awkward. Because Rowan still wore her boots, her jeans were firmly ensconced around her ankles. Nick slipped between her thighs, spreading them wide enough to snugly accommodate his lean, hard body.

Gasping, Rowan closed her eyes as Nick entered her in one powerful thrust.

"Mm." The man was good. Very good. "You've done this before."

"Sex?" Nick breathed in her ear, making Rowan shiver. "Sure. Once or twice."

Since turnabout was fair play, Rowan found Nick's ear with her teeth.

"You know what I meant."

"Never like this. Cars are too small—as a rule. But with you, I've changed my mind." He sank deeper. "Best. Place. Ever."

Five minutes later, adjusting her clothes, Rowan had to agree. Still winded and thoroughly satisfied, she couldn't stop smiling.

"So beautiful." Nick gave her a lingering kiss. Sweet and tender. "Ready to continue our journey?"

"Think we can get there without another unplanned stop?"

Chuckling, Nick started the engine.

"Probably. If you keep your hands to yourself."

"I'll try," Rowan said, laughing with him. "But I can't make any promises."

CHAPTER ELEVEN

● ≈ ● ≈ ●

"MARSHA CALLS THIS a cabin? I don't think so."

Rowan stared at the building wondering if they had the wrong place.

"A little shack in the woods doesn't need a caretaker," Nick told her as he unloaded their things. "But I agree. Marsha undersold this place just a little."

Rustic chic? Was that even a thing? Rowan figured the term fit. The logs—hewn by hand, no doubt—were huge. Which made sense. So was the house. The porch alone could hold a hundred people comfortably. She could almost see the beautiful people dressed in white, sipping some ridiculous cocktail invented especially for the occasion.

"Too many Dynasty reruns."

"Whatever you're daydreaming about, save it for tomorrow. The temperature is dropping as we speak. Let's get inside."

"How many rooms do you think this place has?"

"While I light a fire, you can count." Nick opened the door, standing aside for Rowan to enter.

"Somebody beat you to the punch."

On the far side of a huge living room, a stone fireplace dominated the wall. The wood inside was ablaze.

"A cheery welcome."

"And a dangerous one."

"Don't worry. I would never leave a fire untended."

Startled, Rowan spun around. A small, wiry-looking man of indeterminate age set their suitcases by the stairs. A big, welcoming smile on his face, he held out his hand.

"Name's Jimmy Sears. No relation to the store."

Shaking his hand, Rowan had to smile back. Jimmy had that kind of face. One that drew a person in.

"You must be Marsha's caretaker," Nick said.

"Right the first time. I live about three miles up the mountain. Take care of several homes 'round these parts. Lots of city folks build vacation places. I'm one of a handful of year-round residents."

"We appreciate the fire."

"All part of the job. There's plenty of split wood in a pile just outside the back door." Jimmy tipped his head in the direction of the kitchen. "I'll bring in the last of your bags then get out of your way. If you need anything, don't hesitate to call. If I'm not around, my wife will take a message."

"Thank you, Jimmy." Rowan looked at Nick. "Want some tea?"

"Sounds good. And something to eat. Marsha mentioned that Jimmy stocked the fridge."

"Angie already took care of dinner."

Rowan picked up the wicker basket sitting next to their suitcases, sitting it on the granite countertop.

"You unpack that while I heat up the water."

The cupboards were well organized—another thank you to Jimmy. With little trouble, Rowan found a canister of loose-leaf tea and two heavy ceramic mugs. She filled the electric kettle which sported more buttons and settings than she had ever seen on a small appliance.

"There's enough food here for a small army." Nick lifted the lid on one of the containers, breathing in the aroma. "I don't know what this is, but I think I'm in love."

"When food is involved, Angie believes the more, the better." Rowan opened another container. "Ravioli. My favorite. Green salad with her special dressing. Black olives. Spaghetti. Manicotti. Chicken Parmesan. Antipasto."

"Tiramisu?" Nick showed her the luscious dessert.

"Angie developed most of her own dishes. But the tiramisu is her Grandma Fiorina's secret recipe. I don't know what's in it, but I've never tasted better."

"Remind me to send Angie a dozen thank-you roses." Nick swiped his finger through the sauce covering the spaghetti, his eyes closing with pleasure. "Roses aren't good enough."

"Angie's favorite flower is a gardenia," Rowan said, amused by Nick's reaction.

"Mm. The woman could open a restaurant in any city in the world. Including Rome. The lines would be around the corner."

"You hit Angie's dream right on the head. World-famous restaurateur. She has the drive and ambition."

"I know some investors who are always on the lookout for a new, surefire project. If you don't think Angie would mind, I could give them a call."

Rowan stared at Nick. Was he for real? All Angie needed was that first hand up. But finding somebody to believe in her—as Rowan knew from bitter experience—wasn't easy.

A phone call might not seem like much. But for Angie, Nick's one gesture could change her world forever.

Rowan wrapped her arms around Nick. He wasn't playing games. He didn't expect a favor in return. She had always hoped men like him existed. Finding proof lightened her outlook on his sex considerably.

On tiptoe, she kissed his cheek.

"You're a good man."

"Is that a yes?" Nick asked, smoothing back her hair.

"Yes, please. With a cherry on top."

"I can't make any guarantees. But I'll call as soon as we get back to Jasper."

They ate in front of the fire, spreading their feast out on the mahogany coffee table. A little of this, a lot of that. In no hurry, they sampled everything ending with a shared helping of dessert.

"Is Grandma Fiorina still around?"

"Happy, healthy, and living with her third husband in Arizona."

"Any chance she might leave him for a younger man?"

Rowan chuckled. "I've met husband number three. He's a babe. Seventy-six. Has a thick head of hair. Works out daily. And absolutely adores his wife. They share the same interests. Go dancing every week. And he makes her laugh."

"Sounds nice."

"Yes. It does."

Nick rolled to his feet. Across the room, he perused a stack of CDs, picking one. A slow, romantic tune filled the air.

"I'm a little rusty, but if you're willing, so am I."

Surprised, Rowan took Nick's hand.

"You dance?"

"I shuffle." He moved them off the rug, onto the hardwood floor. "Sorry I can't promise any fancy moves."

"Fancy is way overrated." Rowan rested her head on Nick's shoulder. "I can't remember the last time I danced. With a man."

"You dance with women?"

"Sure. Angie and I will get out on the dance floor anytime the music moves us. And we've been nicely lubricated by a margarita or two."

"I hope I live up to Angie's standards."

"Better." Snuggling closer, Rowan hoped the song never ended. "So much better."

Rowan lost track of time as one song led to another and another. The fire crackled, the lights were low. The night was... perfect. No other word fit. She wouldn't have changed a thing.

"Why don't you head up to bed? I'll bank the fire and put away the food."

"I can help."

Nick's kiss held the promise of more.

"Tomorrow, you can handle clean up duty." He turned her toward the stairs. "Go. I'll be up in a few minutes."

Before Jimmy left, he carried their bags up to the master bedroom. Though they tried to insist the gesture wasn't necessary. *All part of my job.* Jimmy took pride in what he did. And wouldn't hear of taking Nick's offered tip.

Rowan easily found the room at the end of the hall. She hadn't gotten around to counting, but on this side of the house, there were six doors before she reached the master. She wondered how often they were all filled. Or perhaps Marsha simply liked variety. A different bed every night?

Huge was Rowan's first impression. Truly a room fit for the master of the house. Or in this case, the mistress. In a pinch, Marsha could have rented out the walk-in closet. And the bathroom. Combined, their square footage surpassed Rowan's entire house.

Maybe Rowan exaggerated. But not by much.

Her nightly rituals were complicated. With a clean, moisturized face and freshly brushed teeth, she was ready for bed. Opening her suitcase, she had the choice of silk or flannel. One was practical. The other a wispy male fantasy.

All day, Nick had put her first. Even now, he tidied up so she could relax. He deserved a treat.

Quickly shedding her clothes, Rowan slipped the whisper of silk over her head. Feet bare, she walked to the fireplace. Ready to light, she had the blaze going in no time.

All she had left to do was turn down the covers, crawl into bed, and arrange herself in what she hoped was an alluring, provocative pose.

Nick didn't keep her waiting long. And Rowan quickly discovered Angie was right. *Look in his eyes.* The flair of pleasure told her she'd made the right choice of nightwear.

"All for me?" he asked, unbuttoning his shirt.

"Like what you see?"

Silly question. But Rowan, her skin tingling as Nick's dark gaze devoured every inch of her, couldn't wait to hear the answer.

"Oh, yes," he nodded slowly. His shirt hit the floor. Followed by his boots and socks. "I'm a very, very, lucky man. Give me five minutes. And don't move."

Where would she go? Everything Rowan wanted was right here. She kept her eyes on the thin line of light under the bathroom door. When it went dark, she took a deep breath of anticipation.

The door opened, Nick stepped out. Naked. Exactly how Rowan liked him. The firelight highlighted every rippling muscle as he walked across the room, stopping at the foot of the bed.

The mattress dipped. Nick crawled toward her on his hands and knees.

"We aren't going to get much sleep," he warned, his hand sliding up Rowan's leg.

Rowan sat up with a welcoming smile.

"I can sleep anytime. Tonight, all I want is you."

SNOW BLANKETED THE ground, the skies having deposited several inches the night before. But the white stuff didn't stop Nick from taking his morning run. He knew the dangers of slacking off on a regimented off-season routine.

More times than Nick could count, he'd been witness to teammates reporting to Spring Training overweight and out of shape. Months were spent trying to catch up, time they should have spent simply playing the game.

The fresh snow cushioned the sound of Nick's feet hitting the road. His shoes—the ones he packed when he traveled—were designed for all-season running. Another time, he would have veered off into the woods to enjoy a little tougher terrain.

However, sometimes the snow literally was a blanket, hiding obstacles from his ever-vigilant eyes. The last thing he needed was a twisted ankle, or worse, a broken one. Not to mention the possible collateral damage to his hands or arms as he tried to cushion his fall.

Better safe than sorry. Nick's body was his livelihood. Some injuries were unavoidable, but he couldn't take a chance on his own stupidity knocking him out of the game.

Knowing his body, Nick estimated he'd run close to his seven miles a day target. Once the regular season started, he would cut back on the roadwork. A treadmill and time in the weight room were enough during the long six-month campaign.

The cabin came into view as Nick rounded the corner. Sprinting the last hundred yards, he jogged up the steps, tapping the snow from his shoes before removing them. The laces were soaked through, so instead of untying them, he toed off the sneakers.

Taking the key from his pocket, he opened the front door. He could have left the door unlocked. Who would try to break in way out here in the middle of nowhere? Nick wasn't worried about thieves. His concern had to do with leaving Rowan alone.

Weirdos, creeps, and villains didn't just lurk in cities.

A burst of heat greeted Nick, reminding him that though the exercise had provided his body with the illusion of warmth, in truth, the temperature outside barely skimmed the upper teens. His skin felt clammy *and* icy cold.

The thought of a long, steamy shower put an extra spring in his step.

"Coffee." Breathing deeply, Nick dropped his shoes, detouring toward the kitchen. "I smell coffee."

"And bacon." Rowan rushed to pour Nick a cup of liquid caffeine. "The waffle batter is ready for the iron as soon as you're ready for a waffle."

"I hoped you'd still be in bed."

"You're lousy at sneaking out of bed. After you left for your run, I explored the house, taking advantage of the workout area in the basement. You should check the place out. I've been to high-end gyms with less equipment."

Conscious of his sweaty state, Nick tried to spare Rowan, planning on a quick kiss. She wasn't buying.

"I'm a mess," he protested when she hugged him close.

"You're like ice." Rowan's warm hands snuck under his hoodie and t-shirt, rubbing his bare back vigorously. "Why don't I draw you a bath? From the size of the tub, you can have a good soak all the way up to your neck."

"I'll start the bath. You grab the coffee."

Nick nipped at Rowan's neck, eliciting a low, husky moan. The sound had zoomed to the top of his favorites, beating out the roar of a crowd after he lofted a long, high home run over the centerfield fence.

"Me? I've already had a shower."

"We're going in the water to get dirty, not clean."

"Where do you get the stamina?" Rowan asked. But her disbelief didn't stop her from turning off the waffle iron. "After last night, I thought you would need at least half a day to recover."

"You inspire me. Five minutes. And don't forget the coffee. You know what?" Nick grabbed a mug, filling the dark liquid to the rim. "I'll take mine with me."

Brushing another kiss across her lips, his gaze locked with Rowan's. Her blue eyes brimmed with laughter—and desire. A potent combination.

"Make that four minutes." Nick took a sip of coffee before hurrying up the stairs. At the top, he leaned over, catching Rowan's attention. "Three and a half."

"If you don't hurry, I'll be there before you start."

"Start without you?" Nick slowly shook his head. "Never."

IN A BLINK, Saturday became Sunday. Then Monday. And Tuesday. Nick didn't have much difficulty talking Rowan into staying until Wednesday morning. His appointment with Cartwright wasn't until the afternoon. Why not enjoy each other and their surroundings until the last minute?

They went for long walks. Talked for hours about nothing and everything. Nick told Rowan about his mother's last days and her wish to have her ashes strewn over a flower-covered hillside.

Rowan told him about her engagement. To this day, she wasn't certain why she agreed to marry Wilton Jacobs. A lapse in good judgment? Temporary insanity. Though according to her family, she was crazy for not taking him back.

When Rowan spoke of her early childhood—before Leo—her voice took on a wistful quality.

"I don't know if I remember my father. Maybe my memories are wishful thinking. But in my mind, he was wonderful. He loved us. We had a good life, never wanting for anything. I know my mother was happy. A thirty-six-year-old man isn't supposed to die of a massive heart attack."

Nick squeezed Rowan's glove-covered hand, tucking it into the crook of his arm. "Why did your mother marry Cartwright? Money problems?"

"Dad had a generous life insurance policy. The house was paid for. We would have been fine. Mom has always been open with me. She preferred the life of a wife to that of a widow. Several of the men who showed interest were nice enough. But she had already married for love. When Leo asked, she said yes without hesitation. She married for money."

"Your mother must have liked him at least."

"She did. Still does, I think."

Rowan hesitated.

"Don't hold back because of me." Nick didn't have daddy issues. What he felt for Cartwright had to do with his mother.

"Leo wanted a son."

Nick snorted.

"Believe me," Rowan said. "I see the irony. Mom wanted my brother to fill the role. And Leo was willing. When she gave him a son of his own, things would change. Years went by, and Mom never got pregnant. I sometimes wonder…"

"If she made certain there was no *blood son* to take your brother's place?"

"She may have used birth control. Mom would never volunteer information that sensitive. And I would never ask."

"So, brother Geoff was raised with a silver spoon up his ass."

Rowan's snicker turned into a full-bellied laugh.

"Mom has always indulged Geoff. Leo expected perfection. Neither method of parenting did Geoff any favors."

"You grew up in the same household," Nick reminded her. "Why aren't you a self-important jerkoff?"

"A lot was expected of Geoff. Until I grew breasts, I didn't answer to anybody."

"Bullshit." Nick supposed defending one's sibling was natural. He wouldn't know. But no matter what she said, Rowan knew better. "The way Geoff treats you? That's his choice. And a damned poor one."

Rowan changed the subject, but Nick was right, and deep down, he was certain she agreed. However, as she said, Geoff was her brother. Good or bad, the family tie was strong. Frayed, but holding fast.

A companionable silence fell between them as they took their time going back to the cabin. Nick's mind wandered to the text he received yesterday after they gave in and retrieved their phones from the glove compartment.

The text he deliberately failed to mention to Rowan.

Nick understood the need for secrets. His mother kept hers close, he suspected for her sake as well as his.

Cartwright kept the same secrets. Though chances were, he didn't think that way. His affair with Nick's mother, the child she carried when she left town, might have been embarrassing at the time. However, as time went by, he probably stopped caring or forgot altogether.

Now, the secret was back—and all grown up. Cartwright could no longer ignore his decades-old indiscretion. Unlike his fifteen-year-old mother, Nick wasn't young, inexperienced, or easily intimidated.

Leonard Cartwright could make the rules. But there was no law that said Nick had to play by them.

Which brought Nick back to the text.

Apparently, Cartwright wanted to move up their meeting. He seemed to know everything that went on in Jasper. So, he knew Nick was out of town—and no doubt who was with him. That couldn't be sitting well.

Like a little child who only wanted something when he couldn't have it, Cartwright decided he needed to see Nick. Immediately. Conveniently, his schedule had cleared.

"Be here at two o'clock. Sharp. Or don't come at all."

The text was sent Monday morning. Nick didn't bother to answer. And he didn't tell Rowan. When he said he wanted to leave all the drama back in Jasper, he meant every word. He wasn't going to mar their time together.

Leonard Cartwright's threat was a bluff. He'd see Nick on Wednesday. Or he could go to hell. Nick was good either way.

"Anything sound good for lunch?" Rowan asked as Nick opened the cabin door. She removed her boots, setting them just inside.

Nick watched as she stretched her arms over her head, the berry-colored sweater molding nicely to her breasts. Rowan glanced his way, her eyes widening when she recognized the look in his.

"Really? Again? You were blessed with some industrial strength testosterone."

"I was." Nick grabbed a giggling Rowan before she could evade his grasp. Easily, he tossed her over his shoulder. In three long strides, he lowered her onto the sofa, following close behind. "Any complaints?"

Rowan seemed to consider his question. However, the twinkle in her clear-blue eyes told Nick all he needed to know. He kissed her, the coolness of her lips warming quickly.

The next time they thought about food, the sun was about to set. And lunch had become dinner.

CHAPTER TWELVE

● ≈ ● ≈ ●

NICK LOVED TAKING a vacation.

He loved his job and worked hard. Time away was important for both his mental and physical health. After a long, grueling—sometimes heartbreaking—season, he looked forward to getting away.

Someplace. Anyplace. Where nothing mattered but relaxing and having fun.

However, there always came a moment when his thoughts inevitably turned back to his first and overriding passion.

Baseball.

When Nick was with his buddies, he could go a week—maybe two—without thinking about the game and the season to come. Either he, Spencer, or Travis were always thinking up some adventure. The crazier, the better. But like him, they were athletes. Hardwired for the kind of competition they could only find on a field, between the crisp white lines.

Nick's patience—or rather impatience—surfaced much faster when his leisure-time companion was a woman. Whoever said variety is the spice of life must have had Nick in mind.

Tall. Short. Rounded. Lean. Smart. Slightly dim, but sweet and funny. Nick enjoyed all types. For short, intense bursts.

The blame lay firmly on Nick's shoulders. He had no interest in anything long term. And he made certain the women he dated knew the score. A good time was had by all. Never had he walked away with an ounce of regret.

Never—not once—had Nick looked back. Or felt the slightest urge to do so.

After four days with Rowan where they spent almost every minute together. After marathon sessions of mind-blowing sex—followed by equally long hours just sitting and talking and never running out of things to say—Nick should have been done. Over. Out the door.

Yet, after dropping Rowan at her house, Nick found himself looking at his watch, counting the minutes until he would see her again.

Nick had come to Jasper with one objective. To close the door on his past, once and for all. His meeting with Leonard Cartwright was only two hours away. Where were the pre-game nerves? The anticipation he always felt before meeting an opponent?

Make no mistake, Cartwright was his adversary. Neither of them expected a sentimental, moist-eyed, father and son reunion. Nick didn't give a shit what Cartwright wanted. Most of the time— in his mind—the meeting ended in one way. With the bastard on the floor, lip bleeding, Nick's hand singing with the satisfying pain of knocking Daddy Dearest on his ass.

Nick smiled as the image played out behind his closed eyes. Then the image flickered and disappeared, replaced—surprise, surprise—by Rowan. Light snuffing out dark. Good triumphing over evil.

With a groan, Nick flopped onto the bed. Light and dark? Good and evil. Where the hell was that crap coming from? Not from him. What had Rowan done to him?

And why, Nick asked himself, scrubbing a hand over his face, wasn't he freaking out? Running for the hills? Jumping the first plane west to Seattle—or anyplace that wasn't here? He should deal with Leonard Cartwright, then head straight out of Jasper, pedal to the metal.

What Nick should do, and what would happen were two different animals. Without trying, Rowan had burrowed under his skin, into his blood, and damn close to his heart.

"Trouble, son," Nick said to the empty room. "You're running straight toward a big, flashing danger sign. The window may be closing, but you still have time. Change direction. Now!"

As he stared at the ceiling, Nick wondered what was wrong with him. Where was the overwhelming sense of panic? The flop sweat? Just a tinge of unease?

Nick waited. And waited. Nothing. The emotions he expected—even craved—were nowhere to be found. Considering the thoughts running through his head, he felt relaxed. Calm. Almost—dare he say—happy?

Sitting up, he started to laugh. At himself.

"Well, shit."

Who could have seen this coming? It seemed Nick Sanders was well and truly hooked.

THE RECEPTION AREA of Leonard Cartwright's wasn't any different than thousands of offices all over the world. Change the color scheme, the art on the walls. Powerful men seemed to like the same things. Plush carpets. Soft, dark leather chairs. Attractive women sitting behind wooden desks, the finish complementing the rest of the décor.

Nick hadn't expected anything else. What surprised him was the greeting he received. A big change of attitude from Ms. Havisham. Expecting a stern—even harsh—reception, the woman's smile seemed out of place. As did the way she rose to her feet, meeting him as soon as he stepped off the elevator.

"Mr. Sanders. Welcome."

"Ms. Havisham."

A little older than he imagined—a youngish forty— Cartwright's assistant ticked all the boxes. The posh accent was a nice touch. For whatever reason, when a person sounded British, they automatically seemed smarter.

Nick knew for a fact the truth was somewhere between, but first impressions were always important, and Ms. Havisham presented an elegant, attractive, well-heeled front for her boss.

"May I get you something? Coffee? Tea? A soft drink?" She laughed, flirting a little. "One of those energy drinks I hear athletes are so fond of?"

Nick wasn't the least interested in a refreshment. Or flirting back.

"Nothing. Thank you."

"If you change your mind, let me know." Her meaning was clear. A drink? Me? Both were still on the table. "I'm afraid Mr. Cartwright is running a bit late."

Shocking. Mentally, Nick scoffed. Adding an eye roll for good measure. He would have laid down good money—no matter the odds—that Cartwright would throw come kind of delay at him.

"Ms. Havisham—"

"Please. Call me Megan."

If she expected Nick to return the favor, *Megan* was sorely mistaken.

"Ms. Havisham." Nick couldn't think of her any other way. "We both know your boss isn't running late. He wants me to wait. How long?"

"I…" Ms. Havisham swallowed.

Nick wondered how many people dared call Cartwright on his bullshit. From his assistant's uncomfortable expression, he might be the first.

"How long were you supposed to keep me twiddling my thumbs? And then what? Was he planning on showing up at all?"

To her credit, Ms. Havisham recovered quickly. Cool and professional replaced warm and welcoming.

"Excuse me for just a minute."

"A minute is about all you have. Any more, and I'm out of here. For good."

Ms. Havisham inclined her head. Rather than return to her desk, she slipped into Cartwright's office. Nick half-expected the man himself to emerge. He prepared himself, just in case.

He needn't have bothered. Ten seconds shy of her deadline, Ms. Havisham closed the office door behind her. With a neutral expression, she met Nick's gaze.

"Mr. Cartwright is at home for the day. He would like you to meet him there."

Nick would like to kick the lot of them firmly in the ass. He didn't move, but some of his thoughts must have transferred themselves to Ms. Havisham. Wisely, she took a step to the side, using the desk as protection. If he'd wanted to do her harm, a piece furniture wouldn't have stopped him. Luckily for her, he didn't hit women.

Nick had a rule. He rarely hit—period. Violence wasn't part of his nature. Unless he count using a wooden bat to annihilate ninety-eight-mile-an-hour fastballs.

However, concerning Leonard Cartwright, he would be happy to break his rule. Just this once.

Walking to the elevator, Nick didn't have long to wait for the car. As he stepped in, Ms. Havisham called after him.

"What should I tell Mr. Cartwright?"

Nick's lips curved into a humorless smile.

"Don't worry. I'll deliver this message personally."

ROWAN SPENT TWO hours in her office catching up on paperwork. A necessary evil that she would have gladly delegated to someone else. Except for one thing. Before she launched her business, she was given a ton of advice. Some she filed away for another day. Some she forgot altogether.

However, a few pearls of wisdom were burned forever in her brain. In her opinion, the biggest—and arguably the most important? Personally sign every check, no matter how small.

From day one, Rowan knew where every penny went. She trusted Rebecca. But the fastest way to bankruptcy was losing sight of the bottom line. And that bottom line was money. Yes, she hired an accountant who double checked Rowan's figures and handled the taxes.

However, nobody had the authority to make a purchase using her company's accounts without checking with Rowan first.

Satisfied, Rowan returned the books to the small wall safe that she'd had installed about a year ago. Fireproof, she kept everything there of any value. From her passport to her grandmother's pearl earrings and everything between.

Rowan's stomach growled, a sure sign she needed food. *Now.*

Because her office was on the second floor, Rowan had to pass her bedroom. And the bags she dumped by the door. Packing was fun. Unpacking? Not so much. However, the job had to be done.

Rather than spoil her lunch with visions of dirty clothes dancing in her head, Rowan picked up her suitcases and shouldered her way into the bedroom.

Frowning, Rowan took a deep breath. Something was off. Slowly setting down her bags, she breathed again. The smell was familiar. Pine? Not the natural, real tree kind. But from an aerosol can. And something else. Perfume.

Out of the corner of her eye, Rowan spied a scrap of red peeking out from under her pillow. Approaching the bed, she tentatively tugged, leery about what she would find.

A bra? Rowan held up the lace and spandex. The cups were huge. Double. Maybe triple D? Definitely not one of hers.

Reading the tag, Rowan dropped the bra like a hot potato. One by one, pieces fell into place.

Pine air freshener—something she never used. Musk perfume—not her scent, if she had one. And a bra big enough to hold a regulation-sized bowling ball.

All the not-so-subtle clues added up to one nasty, unsettling conclusion. Patrice Dandridge had polluted her home with her god-awful scent. And—if the bra were any indication—ruined Rowan's bed beyond saving. Fumigation might help the room.

The bed had to be burned. Immediately.

Sadly, Rowan didn't have to tax her brain to figure out how and why Patrice had been here. Her brother. Geoff.

Another mystery solved. Rowan now knew why he called her on the night she left town with Nick. He wanted to screw around with his girlfriend. What better place than his sister's house?

Getting the extra key from their mother would have been easy. Make a copy. Return it. Mom would never be the wiser.

Rowan's neighbors wouldn't question Geoff's arrival. Why would they? He didn't visit often, but they knew who he was. As for Patrice? The alley behind the house was fairly private. After dark, she could enter through the back gate.

Easy-peasy.

Rowan opened both windows. A frigid gust of air beat lingering Patrice any day.

Damn, Geoff. Rowan thought he'd gotten the urge to cheat out of his system years ago. During the first few years of his marriage, he refused to change from a carefree bachelor to a responsible husband. Why his wife put up with his wandering, Rowan could never understand. Allison was sweet and kind. And she loved Geoff with a devotion he hadn't deserved.

However, after their twin girls came along, Geoff settled down. Or so Rowan thought. She didn't know if Patrice was a sudden slip, or if he learned how to hide his indiscretions. Either way, Allison and his daughters deserved better.

Using her house meant Rowan had been pulled into Geoff's ugliness. She liked Allison. More than she liked her brother. She deserved to know what her husband was up to. If she—and the rest of Rowan's family—chose to shoot the messenger, so be it.

Rowan had weathered worse. And probably would again.

Suddenly tired, Rowan went to the kitchen, intent on making herself a cup of tea. Food was out. She wasn't one of those people who found solace in eating. Just the opposite. The more upset she became, the less she could face the idea of anything in her stomach.

After Rowan had broken off her engagement, she ate an entire pumpkin pie. She didn't need a psychologist to analyze that.

When her phone rang, Rowan checked the screen, hoping Nick was calling with news about his meeting with Leo. Between the paperwork and her brother drama, she'd successfully kept herself from worrying. He'd promised to come by as soon as he was finished. She hoped he hadn't been held up.

Rowan glanced at the screen. Geoff. Fine. Great. She was in the mood to tear him a new one. Though she would have preferred a face-to-face confrontation, the phone would do.

"Where are you?"

Nick was right. Her brother was an asshole.

"Where are you?"

"Outside your front door. Open up."

Rowan squared her shoulders as she stomped toward the door. She'd give her brother credit. He had a lot of nerve.

"Only idiots return to the scene of the crime."

Geoff barreled past her, stopping, ironically, by a picture of their father. They had the same coloring. The same fine features. And the same tall, slender build.

Too bad the son couldn't have inherited a bit of his father's character.

"I don't know what the hell you're talking about. And I couldn't care less."

"No." Rowan crossed her arms, planting her feet. The battle was on. "But your wife will care."

"Allison? What does she have to do with any of this?"

"You used my house to screw around. Patrice's husband may turn a blind eye to what she gets up to. Allison—for whatever reason—cares about you."

"Stay out of my business, little sister."

Rowan hated when Geoff called her that. Emphasis on the little. When they were kids, he could knock her down. And did whenever nobody was looking. She hoped he tried again. Because little sister was no longer a pushover.

"My home. My business. Give me back my key. And by the way, you owe me a new bed. The old one smells like a whore," Rowan paused for effect, "house."

"Fuck you. Fuck your bed. And fuck your motherfucking boyfriend."

"Watch your mouth."

"That's all you have to say?" When angry, Geoff's face turned red. At the moment, he resembled a mottled, overripe tomato. "You expect me to believe you spent the last four days with Nick Sanders innocently frolicking in the woods?"

"I couldn't care less what you believe."

"Do you know who he is? Of course, you do." Geoff threw his hands up in the air. "Unbelievable. You're screwing Leo's son. Where's your loyalty?"

"Stop right there." Of all the people she knew, Geoff was the last person to throw a lack of loyalty in her face. "Whatever you know—or think you know—none of it has anything to do with you."

"I know plenty. Probably more than you. The file I found in Leo's home office was very thorough."

"Leo would pop a gasket if he knew you went through his personal papers."

"He shouldn't have left the thing laying around," Geoff said with a careless shrug.

Rowan knew better. Leo terrified her brother. Not physically. For all his faults, their stepfather never raised a hand to them. But Geoff's future as heir apparent could flip on a whim.

Or—Rowan suddenly saw the light—Geoff could lose everything if Leo finally had the biological son he always craved.

"Nick isn't a threat to you." A little of Rowan's anger waned as she felt a flash of sympathy for her brother. "He has a very good life in Seattle. And he certainly doesn't need Leo's money. Nick has plenty of his own."

"Jesus." Geoff slapped a hand to his forehead. "Are you really that naïve? Hear my words. Nobody. Ever. Has. Enough. Money."

Rowan knew she couldn't reason with Geoff. Like their mother and stepfather, he believed in the all mighty dollar. First, last, and always. Certainly, Nick didn't need her to defend him.

However, as Geoff's face veered from red toward eggplant, she racked her brain for something to say to bring him down from his upward-spiraling anger high.

"All Nick wants from Leo are answers. Tomorrow, he'll be gone. End of story."

Rowan kept her voice at one level. Calm. Soothing. But as she tried to ease her brother's fears, she felt a shaft of pain, picturing her life without Nick. Reasonable or not, he had become important. Maybe even vital.

When Nick left Jasper, he'd take part of Rowan with him. Whether he wanted to or not.

Geoff—as usual—didn't want to listen to logic. He stalked to the kitchen, opening the cupboard where Rowan kept her alcohol. Her supply wasn't extensive. But the few bottles she had were top shelf.

Wincing, Rowan watched as Geoff downed a shot of twenty-year-old scotch, taking another hit before she could protest.

"The kind of money Sanders makes as a baseball player is a drop in the bucket compared to the Cartwright fortune," Geoff said, sipping his third drink a little more judiciously. "Who in his right mind would be satisfied with millions when billions are just a heartbeat away?"

Rowan reached for the bottle, but Geoff spun away, waving his finger at her.

"Mine."

As she took a deep breath, Rowan slowly counted to ten. She felt as if she were dealing with a disturbingly booze-drenched toddler instead of her older brother.

"Let me drive you home."

"So, you can tattle to Allison about my minor indiscretion? I don't think so."

Rowan realized she had no business interfering. If her sister-in-law were to ask, point blank, she wouldn't lie. However, Allison was a smart woman. Chances were she suspected what Geoff was up to. Perhaps she already knew. Either way, they were on their own.

"I won't say a word."

"I don't believe you."

"Honestly, I—"

"Honesty?" Derision dripped from the word. "Nobody tells the truth. For years, Leo lied to me. He promised me everything. I kissed his ass, played his yes man to perfection. And for what? To have some… some *baseball player* swoop in and take my place."

Taking a seat, Rowan's head dropped back on the cushion. Geoff had wound himself up, all she could do was wait until he ran out of steam.

"I suppose on some level I should be grateful. Leo's known about his precious son for years. What if he'd decided to orchestrate a touching family reunion? I'd have been out on my ass long before now."

Rowan's eyes popped open, her body tensing.

"What did you say?"

Geoff could always hold his liquor. Now was no exception. On steady legs, he crossed to Rowan, leaning down until their faces were inches apart.

"Out. On. My. Ass." His expression grew angry. "I blame you."

What else was new? When in doubt, blame Rowan. She wasn't interested in rehashing a familiar them.

"Did you say Leo already knew about Nick?"

"For years." Straightening, Leo took another swig. "Years, and years, and years."

"And he did nothing to help." Rowan felt her stomach clench. "How do you know?"

"In the file. Everything is in that goddamned file. Thick. Little league. High school. The minor leagues. All the way to the World Series." Geoff sneered as he recited Nick's accomplishments.

Tuning out her brother, Rowan grabbed her phone. Impatient, she waited as Nick's phone rang. When she was sent to voicemail, she grabbed her purse. She didn't know what she would do, but she couldn't sit here and do nothing.

"I could have been an athlete, you know. I could have been a contender. I could have been somebody." Geoff frowned. "Is that from a movie? Wrong sport, I think. But you get the idea."

"Come on, Brando," Rowan took Geoff's arm. "We're leaving."

"I'm not going anywhere with you. Judas. Fucking the enemy. What kind of sister are you?"

"The exceedingly patient kind."

"Piss off."

Geoff shoved Rowan. Hard. She didn't budge. He shoved again. She knew his moves. When he tried to kick her legs out from under her, she easily sidestepped him.

"Knock it off, Geoff."

"Knock it off? Good idea."

In all the years Rowan had known her brother. All the crap she'd dealt with. The verbal tirades. The pouting silences when he didn't get his way. In all that time, he had never hit her in the face. So, when the backhanded slap came, she wasn't prepared.

"Take that, bitch."

Rowan cupped her cheek, ears ringing. Geoff had crossed the line. And she didn't think they could ever go back.

Taking him by the shoulders, Rowan looked at her brother's smirking face, and without the least bit of regret, calmly kneed him in the balls.

"Back at you, bitch."

As Geoff writhed on the floor, crying in pain, Rowan took the keys from his jacket. Walking out the door, she lifted her phone.

"Hello?"

"Allison? This is Rowan. I don't have time to explain. Geoff is at my house. He's been drinking."

"What? In the middle of the day?"

Rowan could hear the concern in Allison's voice. *Good for Geoff,* she thought, slamming her car door. For the time being at least, he had somebody who cared.

"You should come and get him."

"I will. Of course. But, Rowan—"

"Bye, Allison."

And good luck.

Starting the car, Rowan headed toward downtown. But as she came to the stop sign at the end of her street, she turned left instead of right. The proof she needed was in Leo's home office.

Nick deserved the truth—every ugly bit. Leo would only divulge the information that suited him. Whatever put him in the best light.

The file was the key. Rowan would find it if she had to tear the place apart.

Though her sympathies had always been with Nick, Rowan hoped to get through this mess without having to publicly take sides. However, if what Geoff said was true, Leo didn't deserve an ounce of her consideration.

Damn the consequences. Rowan had picked her side. Team Nick. All the way.

CHAPTER THIRTEEN

● ≈ ● ≈ ●

FINDING LEONARD CARTWRIGHT'S residence was easy. Nick already had the address from his mother's letter. He imagined if his GPS had failed, anybody he saw on the street could have given him directions.

The Cartwright mansion was a Jasper landmark. Sprawling over several acres—not counting the grounds—a blind man couldn't miss the monstrosity. Basically, head west and boom.

The building screamed wealth. Loudly, with a side of the obnoxious.

After parking his car on the circular driveway, Nick jogged up the brick steps. How would he have turned out if he had grown up here, the pampered son of a billionaire instead of having to scrape, scrounge, and lie simply to survive?

Nick knew the chances were excellent baseball wouldn't be his chosen profession. But what about the rest? His outlook. His personality? Would he, like Geoff Cartwright, feel a sense of entitlement? That the world owed him deference simply because of his last name. Would he believe a man's worth should be measured by the power his father wielded?

Or, would Nick have been more like Rowan? Independent. Self-sufficient. Fiercely determined that, fail or succeed, she would do so on her own terms. On her own two feet.

As much as Nick liked to believe he would have taken Rowan's path, he couldn't say for certain. Thank all that was holy he never had to find out.

Nick barely pressed the bell when the door swung open.

"Mr. Sanders."

Not a question, a statement. The middle-aged man wearing a neat-as-a-pin dark suit had been expecting Nick. Hardly surprising.

But why assume he was actually Nick Sanders? Unless Cartwright provided his staff with a picture.

Nick would give Cartwright props. He had his staff prepared. Smart on one level. Unsettling on another.

"I have an appointment with Leonard Cartwright."

"This way."

In Nick's younger days, before he had a taste of what money could buy, he might have been intimidated by the gleaming marble floors, grand staircase, and the sparkling chandelier that dripped with hundreds of hand-faceted crystals.

Not that he would have let the butler see him sweat. He would have bluffed his way through with the finesse of the proverbial bull in a china shop.

If Cartwright had invited him here as a show of intimidation, he hadn't done his homework properly. Nick felt at home anywhere. From a sunflower seed-strewn dugout, to an audience with the Queen of England.

The polish Nick wore like a second skin was no illusion. But that didn't mean he had forgotten where he came from. At his core, he was a street rat. A tough survivor.

Whatever Cartwright had planned, Nick was ready. Bring it on.

Down a narrow hall with green walls, Nick followed the butler. He didn't have the time—or interest—to study the photos as he passed. They were Cartwrights. He was one hundred percent Sanders.

"This is Mr. Cartwright's office. As you can see, the elevator door is open. Please enter and push the blue button."

The door clicked quietly, leaving Nick alone to contemplate his next move.

First thought? Who knew he was here? Answer. Not a damn soul.

Paranoia didn't follow Nick around, plaguing his thoughts every time the lights went out, or he answered the phone to find nobody there. He considered himself to be a fairly level-headed guy.

But come on. Only a fool would get into a private elevator armed with only—*push the blue button.*

Better safe than sorry. There was a credo he could get behind.

Nick sent three quick texts. The ones to Travis and Spencer were identical. The address telling them where he was, Rowan's phone number, and instructions to raise holy hell if they didn't hear from him in an hour.

To Rowan—since she was close by and could act fast—he sent a question and statement.

What does Cartwright keep in his basement? And: *You know where to find me.*

Short of hightailing his ass out of here, Nick was satisfied with his chosen safety nets. Most people were lucky if they had one person they could trust implicitly. He had three.

Nick stepped into the elevator, hit the blue button, and waited.

The trip was a short one. Brightly lit, the room into which Nick exited didn't feel like a dungeon. Then again, until now, he had spent his life blissfully ignorant of such things. And would just as soon stay that way.

Frowning, Nick looked around. What the hell? The area looked like a locker room? Was he in the right place?

"I see you found your way without any trouble."

Leonard Cartwright. Nick easily recognized him from his pictures. Except for what he wore. Stern faced, in photographs Cartwright's outfit of choice was a suit. Dark. Mostly black. Expensively tailored. Clothing that told the world this was someone to be reckoned with.

The man standing in front of Nick was in casual garb. A polo shirt. Shorts. Tennis shoes. Very different. Though his expression never changed, his face frozen in a perpetual half frown.

Nick didn't get the memo. Dressed in a light gray suit and red tie, he felt overdressed.

"You'll stay for dinner. After. Right now, everything you need is in the changing room."

"You can keep your dinner, and everything else. All I need is for you to answer a few questions."

"Change your clothes. There should be something that fits you behind the black door. When you're done, meet me on the court."

Cartwright turned to leave, expecting Nick to do as he said. Nick stayed where he was.

"What the hell are you talking about?"

"Tennis. While we play, you can ask me anything you want."

Nick stared at the empty room, alone once more. At any second, he expected to hear the strains of familiar, creepy music followed by a disembodied voice.

You have just crossed over into... the Twilight Zone.

Curious in spite of himself, Nick walked across the room. Black door. Blue button. Was the entire house color coded? One thing was for damn sure. If Cartwright offered to show off his red room, Nick wasn't going anywhere near it.

Whatever Nick expected, a room filled with row after row of white wasn't even close. White shirts. White shorts. Socks. Shoes. All men's. Either Cartwright had a different room for the ladies, or his private club wasn't open to the fairer sex.

Stacked neatly on a long counter were rows of towels—white, naturally. And in a drawer, individually sealed in plastic, were dozens of athletic supporters in varying sizes.

How much tennis did this guy play? Did he conduct all his potentially awkward meetings below ground? Was the act of hitting balls at each other some kind of twisted metaphor?

Or—as Nick began to suspect—Cartwright was twisted. Period.

Go or stay? Nick didn't take long to decide. With a resigned sigh, he loosened his tie. Selecting a pair of shoes, Nick let out a whistle when he saw the brand. Cartwright didn't skimp, he'd give him that.

Nick had come this far, why not see the farce to the end. He wanted answers to his questions. Besides, if he left now, he would spend the rest of his life wondering what kind of weirdness Cartwright had waiting for him out on that tennis court.

ROWAN QUIETLY LET herself into the house. She wasn't worried about getting caught. The staff was well trained. They didn't ask questions of family members. However, they knew who paid their salaries. When Leo was home, nothing went on without him finding out. She didn't want him to know she was there. Not yet.

Years of sneaking in and out as a teenager made her path from the foyer, across the living room, and down the hall to Leo's office an easy one. She knew from experience which floorboards squeaked and how to avoid them.

Knowing Leo never locked his door—more ego than blind trust—Rowan slipped in, nobody the wiser.

Breathing deeply, she took a moment to calm her racing heart. Nick was here. And though Rowan didn't believe he was in any physical danger, she hated that she couldn't get a message to him. Part of Leo's remodeling project had included blocking cell phone reception. When ensconced in his lair, he didn't want any interruptions.

She'd tried reaching Nick as soon as she received his text, but she was too late.

What does Cartwright keep in his basement?

Rowan had groaned when she read the words. Why hadn't she thought to warn Nick about Leo and his tennis? Annihilating business associates on the court was one of his greatest pleasures. Why not do the same to his son?

Not that Rowan didn't think Nick could hold his own. He was a trained athlete. In perfect physical condition. However, tennis and baseball required very different skill sets.

Unlike Leo who couldn't stand to lose, Rowan was certain Nick and his ego could handle a defeat. She was the one with the problem. She hated the thought of Nick flailing around the clay court for Leo's warped amusement.

First things first. While Rowan had the office to herself, she was determined to find Nick's file.

Starting in the most obvious place, she looked through Leo's desk. Bless his megalomaniac's heart. Rowan found what she wanted in the first drawer she opened. Guessing his thinking wasn't difficult. His property. His domain.

Which meant every paperclip, every staple, every item was safe because who would dare pry into his private things?

Geoff, for one, that's who. Rowan, for another.

Sorry, Leo. You need to rethink your security.

After today, Leo could electrify the door, surround his desk with barbed wire, and post vicious guard dogs around every corner. Rowan wouldn't care. Today, she had what she needed.

Crossing to the elevator, Rowan caught sight of the portrait that dominated the far wall. Agnes Cartwright had been dead for almost a decade. But her image, the way the artist had managed to capture the perpetual glint of disapproval in her eyes, sent a shiver down Rowan's spine.

With the memory of Agnes' boney fingers biting into her arm, Rowan gave the picture a wide berth.

"I know you can't grab me from beyond the grave." Rowan glanced over her shoulder as she waited for the elevator. "And I know if you were here, you wouldn't care less. But dead or alive, Granny Agnes. You give me the creeps."

"I CONSIDER TENNIS to be a true test of a man's mettle. The rules are simple, yet there is a certain strategy involved. Challenging physically. However, you can't simply power your way through. Without a bit of finesse, the game is lost." Leo took two rackets from a leather case. He held them out. "Take your pick."

"Are we playing, or dueling?" Nick asked dryly, choosing his racket without looking.

"Clever." The corner of Leo's mouth twitched. "I appreciate a nimble mind."

Nick slapped the racket against his palm, contemplating how much force would be required to break the strings over Cartwright's head.

"Are you my father?"

"Yes." Leo took a coin from the bag. "Shall we toss for the serve?"

"How can you be so certain?"

"I'll take heads." Leo flipped the coin. "Heads it is." He took his place on the court. "For every point played and won, you get a question."

"If I refuse to play?"

"You know the way out."

Maybe I'm the crazy one, Nick thought, walking onto the court. *Maybe none of this is happening. Any second I'll wake up from the weirdest dream ever.*

A yellow ball whizzed past, landing just inside the court.

"Fifteen-love," Cartwright said with satisfaction. "You need to play on the balls of your feet. Even distribution of weight is the key."

Or, Nick could try paying attention. But he wasn't worried about losing a point. He wanted an answer.

"How do you know you're my father?"

"I've done my homework. The facts add up. Your mother and I had a brief relationship roughly nine months before your birth. The resemblance between us when I was your age is quite striking."

Nick didn't agree. As he told Rowan, he had his mother's eyes, which he trained on Cartwright.

"She was fifteen."

With a shrug, Cartwright took a ball from his pocket. "The sex was consensual."

Briefly, Nick saw red. He couldn't let his emotions get the better of him. Not yet.

"So you say." Nick gritted his teeth. "The law doesn't agree."

"Ready?"

151

Leo sliced his racket through the air, sending the serve toward Nick's backhand. Better prepared, Nick used his natural speed to track down the ball. He used his strength and skill to rifle the ball over the net, well out of Leo's stumbling reach.

"Not bad." Leo's gaze narrowed as if retaking stock in his opponent's level of talent. "You've played before."

"Once or twice. Did you know my mother was pregnant?"

"No. Fifteen all."

Nick had little trouble returning the serve. Though Cartwright was in good shape for a man his age, besides the age difference, there was no comparing their fitness levels.

Plus, as he said, Nick knew his way around a tennis court. Nick's first year in the majors, he dated the top-ranked woman in the world.

Nick helped Celia improve her technique in bed, she helped him develop a killer ground game. His serve wasn't bad either. He hadn't played in years. But, the muscle memory was still there. Like riding a bike. Once he learned, he never forgot.

Back and forth, Nick ran Cartwright around the court without an ounce of guilt. He enjoyed making the bastard huff and puff.

"My point," Nick said after a sizzling put-away shot. "Next question."

Red faced, Cartwright gave Nick a terse nod.

"She was an easy mark, wasn't she? No family. No money. You were married. Older. Why not pick somebody who knew the score?"

Cartwright gave Nick a pitying look.

"You formed this idealized picture of your mother. Sweet. Innocent. The big, bad wolf took advantage, enjoying her, then tossing her away without a backward glance. Am I right?"

"Close enough."

"Well, let me tell you. Annie Sanders was fifteen going on thirty. She worked in a diner down on Main, wiggling her hips like a pro. I wasn't the first to take what she offered."

Like so many men, Cartwright didn't get the point. He never would. But Nick had to say something, or he would never forgive himself.

"I don't care if she served food in her birthday suit. I don't care if she propositioned you and every man who walked through the door. My mother was fifteen. *Fifteen*. Little more than a girl. And, no matter how she behaved, not close enough to a woman to justify your actions."

"You should thank me. Without my sperm donation, you wouldn't be here."

"Shame on you," Rowan shouted as she stormed onto the court.

"Go away, Rowan." Leo made a flicking motion as he would if confronted with a gnat. "You know nobody is allowed down here without an invitation. And street shoes are expressly forbidden on the court."

"Too bad. I'm here, shoes and all. I'm not leaving without Nick." She raised her chin. "I'm the cavalry."

"I appreciate the thought." Rowan looked a bit disheveled and altogether gorgeous. A true sight for his sore eyes—and heart. "Cartwright still has a few questions to answer before I go."

"I can speed things along." Rowan handed Nick a file. "Everything you need to know is in here."

"Where the hell did you get that?" Leo demanded.

Ignoring him, Nick thumbed through the thick stack of papers. He could see the information had to do with him. Reading every word would take more than a quick glance.

"Want to give me an overview?"

"I only read the first two pages while in the elevator. They told me enough." Rowan's clear-blue eyes clouded. "Leo's known about you for years. I don't know how he found out. But—"

"A fluke." Casually, Leo picked up a towel, wiping his face. "I was in Los Angeles on business. I rarely watch television, but an associate had on the local news. Imagine my surprise when I recognized your mother beaming with pride over her baseball player son. You were about twelve years old, I believe. As soon as you came onscreen, I knew I was your father."

Nick remembered the story. His mother was so proud. She called it his first brush with fame.

"If you were so sure Nick was your son, why run a DNA test?"

"What?"

Rowan nodded. "The results are on page two of the file. The technical stuff is a mystery to me, but under results is the word positive."

When Nick asked how he knew they were father and son, Cartwright lied without hesitation. He wasn't surprised. But he wondered why he bothered. Everything out of the man's mouth was some form of bullshit—unless the truth suited his agenda.

"How did you get my DNA?" Nick figured as long as he was here, he might as well ask.

"Don't be naïve," Leo said. "Every day you leave samples of your DNA laying around. We all do. Chewing gum. A drinking glass. Hair in the shower drain. Even a condom carelessly left in a wastebasket."

"Jesus." Nick's skin crawled as Cartwright ticked off the possibilities as if running down a grocery list.

"You were still quite young. I don't believe my people had access to your semen."

Head spinning, Nick couldn't settle on one emotion. Anger mixed with incredulity and a massive dose of old-fashioned disgust. He knew there were questions to ask, but for the life of him, he couldn't form a single one. Thankfully, he had Rowan.

"You knew Nick was your son, but you did nothing? At the very least, why not provide financial support?"

Leo opened a bottle of water, taking a sip.

"I still had hope that your mother would provide me with a son."

"What does one thing have to do with other?"

"My blood wasn't pure enough."

Cartwright met Nick's gaze. Steady. Unapologetic. "Your mother was part of the problem. However, if you had been raised properly, I could have overlooked her contribution."

"Leo!" Shock washed over Rowan's face.

"Why bother to keep tabs on me?" Nick settled on one emotion. Cool, razor-sharp, anger. "I wasn't worthy of the Cartwright name? What was the point? Unless...? Was I your backup plan just in case your new wife didn't produce?"

"Clever and quick." Cartwright smiled. "I was curious to see if you could make something of yourself without my help. A test, if you will."

Rowan grasped Nick's hand. He realized for the first time that he wasn't the only one affected by Leo's revelations. No matter how complicated their relationship had been, she grew up under Cartwright's roof. He was married to her mother.

Nick gave her hand a squeeze.

"I'm sorry, Rowan."

Rowan's eyes were filled with sadness, more for him than herself.

"Don't worry about me."

"Cut the melodrama," Leo scoffed. "Neither of you has a reason for a long face. You," he pointed at Rowan. "You'll inherit a nice sum when I'm gone. As for Nick? You've risen from nothing to become somebody of merit. Sports isn't a top-notch profession. But as a stepping stone, you chose well."

"Everything, since I arrived in Jasper, has been a test." Nick wasn't asking. He'd already figured out how Cartwright operated. "The runaround when I first tried to set up a meeting. The asinine now or never text I received when Rowan and I were out of town."

"What text was that?" asked a puzzled Rowan.

"I'll explain later. And this." Nick made a sweeping gesture. "Which would get me further into your good graces? If I won, or lost?"

"Either."

"Since when?" Rowan demanded. "Everybody you play knows they aren't supposed to win. Give you a decent game? Sure. But they better lose, or else."

Cartwright's expression hardened.

"I always win because I'm always the better player."

Rowan snorted but kept the rest of her thoughts to herself.

"We're done."

"Wait." Cartwright couldn't believe Nick would leave. "My empire is yours for the asking. You can't mean to walk away."

"Right the first time."

"I don't expect you to give up baseball. Play as long as you want. When you decide to retire, you can move to Jasper." For the first time, an air of desperation entered Cartwright's demeanor as if he suddenly realized Nick and all he represented was about to slip through his fingers.

"Keep your fortune. Keep your empire and all your power. I'm not interested."

"You'll change your mind. But when you do, the offer might be off the table," Cartwright warned.

"Sounds fair." Nick, his fingers laced with Rowan's, headed toward the door.

"I should have known. Annie was trash. Why should I expect anything else from her son?"

Stopping, Nick kissed the back of Rowan's hand before letting go. He walked to the edge of the court, picking up his racket and two balls.

"Call me anything you want, but don't even breathe my mother's name."

"She spread her legs the first night I took her out. Didn't even wait for me to buy her dinner."

Nick's grip tightened around the wrapped handle. In one fluid motion, he tossed a ball in the air. Whoosh. A yellow streak sailed at Cartwright, striking him in the chest.

"Are you out of your mind?" Cartwright tried to rub the sting from his chest. "Put that racket down. Now."

"No problem." The racket hit the red clay with a dull thud. In his bare hand, he lightly tossed another ball. "Tennis isn't really my sport. But baseball? I won my third straight gold glove last year. For defensive excellence. I never miss my target."

"What does that have to do with—?"

Laser straight backed by every bit of his considerable strength, Nick threw the ball. Letting out a screech of pain, Cartwright hit the ground, his hands covering his face.

"I'm bleeding. Goddamn it. I think you broke my nose."

Maybe not quite as satisfying as using his fist, but all things considered, Nick thought a ball—even the tennis variety—to Cartwright's face seemed fitting.

"Impressive," Rowan said, not the least upset by her stepfather's agonized groans.

"I'm damn good at what I do." Nick held out his hand. "Ready?"

"One second."

Rowan pushed a panel on the wall, revealing a phone. She picked up the receiver, pushing a button.

"Mom? Yes, I'm by the court. Call Dr. Brill, Leo's bleeding. His nose. Mom." Rowan glanced at Nick, shrugging. "Mom! I don't have time to explain. Call the doctor. Bye."

As Rowan hung up the phone, she smiled.

"Do you want to change your clothes?"

Shaking his head, Nick paused only long enough grab his clothes with one hand and Rowan with the other before getting into the waiting elevator.

"All I want is to get out of here and never look back. And spend the next few hours holding you. Sound good?"

Rowan's smile widened, her eyes bright as the summer sky.

"Sounds perfect."

CHAPTER FOURTEEN

● ≈ ● ≈ ●

OUTSIDE THE CARTWRIGHT mansion, Rowan waited while Nick stowed his clothes in the back of the SUV. As great as his bare legs looked, shorts weren't snowy, cold weather apparel.

"What do you want to do with this?"

Rowan held up Leo's file.

"Why print the damn thing out? A computer is convenient and snoop-resistant." Nick took the stack of papers, testing the weight in his hand. "Waste of a few good trees."

"True. But you didn't answer my question."

"There's enough paper here to start a roaring fire. Several. We can settle in for the night at your place and enjoy the blaze. You go first," Nick said, pulling on his heavy jacket. "I'll be right behind."

"Do you mind if we go to your hotel instead? No fireplace, but we'll figure something out."

Rowan assumed that Allison had collected Geoff by now. But just in case, she didn't want to deal with her brother right now.

"Does the reason have anything to do with the bruise on your cheek?" Nick held Rowan's chin, turning her head to get a better look. "A light greenish blue, and slightly swollen. Give me a name so I know who to kill."

A chill raced up Rowan's spine that had nothing to do with the bitter wind swirling around her feet. Nick wouldn't kill Geoff. But he might knock out a tooth or two. Something she didn't want.

In spite of everything that occurred today, Rowan strongly adhered to a policy of non-violence. Geoff paid for what he did, and—she hoped—would suffer longer than she would.

"Don't get me wrong," Rowan said, snapping shut the button at Nick's throat. "I love that you want to defend my honor—such as it is."

Nick chuckled, giving Rowan hope she could talk him down.

"I dealt with the problem. On my own and quite satisfactorily."

"Who'd hit you, Rowan?"

"If I tell you—"

"If?" Nick asked, his dark gaze unwavering.

"If." Rowan didn't blink. Did he think he's cornered the market on stubborn? "I will tell you. You'll take a deep breath. We'll open a bottle of wine—the one Angie will send with the pizza. By then, you'll be so relaxed, killing somebody will be the furthest thing from your mind. End of story."

"Most of that sounds good. As for the rest? No promises." Nick held out his hand, catching one of the sparse snowflakes peppering the air. "We'd better go before a few flurries turn into a blizzard."

Rowan started her truck with more force than necessary. *Men. Were. Impossible.* Plus, irresistible—at least in Nick's case. Such a frustrating combination.

The hotel was on the other side of town. Rowan took her time in deference to the snow falling with increasing urgency. By the time she pulled to a stop, the ground was entirely blanketed in white.

"Looks like we're in for the night," Rowan said, his fingers crossed.

Nick didn't respond, taking her hand as he helped her from the truck. Five minutes later they, were in his room, shedding their coats.

Feeling better already, Rowan turned in a slow circle.

"I've eaten at the restaurant, but I've never been in one of the rooms." She breathed deeply. No weird smells. Always a plus. "Nice. Generic, but clean."

"When you've seen as many hotel rooms as I have, clean hits pretty high on the must-have list." Nick stripped, his borrowed clothes ending up in a heap by the door. "Those can burn along with the file. Come on."

"Where?"

"Shower."

The Nick she'd come to know could never be called a man of few words. He could talk for hours about anything and everything, never running out of steam. Never boring. Considering the afternoon he'd endured, Rowan didn't blame him for needing a hot shower and some blessed quiet.

"Do you need a little alone time?"

"No."

"Okay."

Laughing, Rowan let Nick pull her into the bathroom. While he turned on the taps, his heated eyes watching her every move, she removed her clothes.

"Roomy." Rowan stepped under the water's spray. "Most hotel room showers are pretty generic. This one—"

"Shh."

Nick quieted her with a soft kiss. Then another, deeper, more intense. Sinking in, Rowan ran her hands down his smooth, strong back. With a sigh, she closed her eyes, enjoying the feel of Nick's fingers running through her hair, massaging her scalp.

"You always smell so good." Nick bit Rowan's neck. Not too hard. Just hard enough to make her sigh with pleasure, moan with need. "And taste even better."

"Haven't all the women you've showered with tasted good?" Rowan teased.

"They tasted… different. Not as sweet."

"I shower every day. Sometimes twice. That could be the problem. Dirty women. Holy crap."

Rowan gasped, her head falling back. She hadn't realized her ear was a major erogenous zone. Thanks to Nick and his magic tongue, now she knew.

Cupping her bruised cheek, Nick tenderly kissed the swollen flesh.

"This is criminal," he said, his eyes troubled.

"I'm fine," she assured him, pushing back the wet, dark hair that covered his forehead.

"Thank you for coming to my rescue. My own personal cavalry."

"You would have been fine without me."

Pressing Rowan close, Nick whispered, "Fine, maybe. But I *needed* you, and you were there."

ROWAN COULDN'T SEE the clock—didn't feel like rolling over to check. Wrapped in Nick's arms, knowing two juicy burgers from room service were on the way, she wished time would stop. Right here. Freeze this moment. Not forever. Just long enough. Whatever *enough* meant.

"Nick?"

"Hmm?"

He sounded relaxed. Content. Rowan didn't want to ruin Nick's mellow mood by dredging up an uncomfortable subject.

"I can hear the wheels turning," Nick lightly tapped her temple. "Spill the beans, gorgeous."

"What Leo said about your mother?"

Rowan felt him tense.

"Lies."

"Yes. I agree." Rowan hurried on. "But there must be people in town who remember her. Who knew her. We could find them. Ask—"

"I appreciate the thought, Rowan. But I don't need anybody to tell me about Annie Sanders. Kind. Funny. Strong. To the bone beautiful."

"At fifteen, she may have been careless with her heart. With who she trusted. But she learned from her mistakes. She grew up fast. And she was the best mother. The best woman." Nick's chest rose, his breathing ragged with emotion. "The best. Period."

Nodding, Rowan kissed Nick's shoulder. He was right.

What if Nick found a dozen people who remembered Annie Sanders? Would their opinions—good, bad, or indifferent—change his memories? Or his opinion of the woman who raised him? Of course not.

Through the circumstances beyond the scope of Rowan's imagination, Annie raised her boy alone. Like his mother, her boy became a kind, funny, strong adult.

Beautiful to the bone.

"Now." Nick ran a finger across Rowan's lower lip. She felt a familiar stir in her blood. "Time to tell me who hit you."

"For the love of..." Rowan rolled her eyes. "You're like a dog with a bone."

"You took care of my bone," Nick chuckled at his own joke. But his eyes didn't lose their razor-sharp glint. "Black and blue aren't your colors, Rowan."

Just a few words—spoken with quiet conviction—and Rowan's heart melted. If he asked, she would hand the organ to him on a platter. Always and forever. But Nick hadn't asked for her heart. Perhaps he never would.

When would Nick leave? Tomorrow? The next day? Rowan had a day or two—at the most. She would deal with the pain when she had to. Right now, she had another problem.

How to keep Nick from turning her brother into a pile of broken bones.

"He was drunk. And before you blow your top, I know alcohol is no excuse. He hit me. I crushed his balls with my knee." Crushed was a good word, Rowan decided. Hopefully violent enough to take the edge off Nick's blood lust. "When I left, he was still on the floor. Crying and whimpering."

"Your brother needs a reminder that a man never hits a woman."

"How did you know—" Angry that she would fall for such an old trick, Rowan flopped onto her back, the mattress bouncing with the weight of her frustration. "Smartass."

"I suspected from the start." Nick leaned over her. Anger lingered in his eyes, but mostly, Rowan felt his concern. "Men—with a few exceptions—are bigger and stronger. You can take care of yourself. I get that. But if Geoff decides to retaliate, he could hurt you."

Frowning, Nick's gaze moved to the darkening bruise. "Seriously hurt you."

"For the sake of argument, what good will beating him up do?"

"He'll know his actions have consequences."

"You give Geoff, what? A fat lip? A black eye?"

"Sounds like a good place to start."

"And when you aren't here?" Keeping her expression neutral, Rowan's heart raced. "After you leave town, who's going to remind him then? Theoretically, won't he be angrier than before? What's to stop him from taking that anger out on me?"

"Maybe I should just kill him."

"I know you're joking, but look close." Rowan, her face an inch from Nick's. "Not funny."

With a sigh, Nick rested his forehead against hers. "Poor taste. But the facts haven't changed, Rowan."

"You're right. Fact one. You won't be here to fix things every time my life goes a little sideways. Fact two. Even if you were, I wouldn't run to you with every problem. Like my blond hair or my blue eyes. The need I have to take care of myself is a part of me. That won't change. Ever."

"I don't want you to change, Rowan." Nick kissed her. "I hope you feel the same about me."

"Asking you not to beat up Geoff isn't the same as asking you to change."

"I hate when I can't think of an argument," Nick said, his voice gruff.

"Because you know I'm right."

A sharp rap sounded on the door.

"Saved by a burger." Nick rolled out of bed. Pulling on a pair of sweats, he opened his wallet. "Here's the best I can do. I won't seek your brother out. However, if I see him. Say, walking down the street. I *will* give him a piece of my mind."

"Only a small piece," Rowan called after Nick. "You can't afford to lose very much."

"Funny woman."

Grinning, Rowan snuggled under the covers. Waiting, she played back their conversation, her smile slowly fading.

Nick had addressed her worries concerning Geoff. And acknowledged her need to take care of herself. What he hadn't mentioned—whether by design or not—was the fact that soon, he would leave Jasper—and Rowan.

The reason was obvious. Rowan hated the idea of him going. Nick? The thought didn't bother him.

Nick liked her. Enjoyed her company—and her body. But from day one, he made himself and his plans crystal clear. Nothing had changed.

When they said goodbye, it would be forever.

"I'm starving. How about you?"

Nick set the tray in the middle of the bed. Shucking his sweats, he climbed under the sheets, giving Rowan a long, lingering kiss.

"A cheeseburger and a beautiful woman. Who could ask for anything more?"

"Swap out the woman for a sexy man, and I'm right there with you."

What choice did she have? Rowan would be happy with tonight. A hot meal. A glass of wine. And whatever else Nick had to give.

CHAPTER FIFTEEN

● ≈ ● ≈ ●

"JUST LIKE THAT? Wham bam, thanks for helping me clear up my murky past, ma'am. And then? Nick rides off into the horizon? What is he, a baseball player, or the Lone Ranger?"

"Nice reference." Rowan added a foil-wrapped loaf of garlic bread to the basket.

"I do my best." Angie handed Rowan several takeout containers with her restaurant's logo on the side. "I can't believe you're preparing a going-away meal. Inside, you're dying. But God forbid Nick Sanders goes hungry between Jasper and the airport. You need to find a way to keep him around, not fix him a glad to see you go care package."

"I could cry."

Angie nodded. "A few tears are always a good way to go."

"Or beg."

"Not your style," Angie said with a dismissive wave.

Rowan's lips curved, though smiling was the last thing she felt like doing.

"I know. After a few weeks, I'll drop him a text. *Surprise. You're going to be a daddy.*"

"Any chance a baby could be possible?"

"For the love of Pete, Angie! Of course not."

"Just a thought."

Rowan tossed a handful of napkins in the basket before shutting it tight.

Nick was leaving in less than an hour. Rather than watch him pack, Rowan enlisted Angie to help her take her mind off the awful truth. Time to say goodbye.

She couldn't complain. Well, she could. But Rowan knew she had no right. Nick had stayed an extra two days. Forty-eight hours she hadn't thought she would have.

Most of the time, they spent sequestered in her house. Laughing. Eating. Sitting in front of the fire—after burning Leo's file. Rowan drew the line at Nick tossing in the tennis clothes.

The smell of burned rubber would have polluted the house for days.

In the end, Nick was content to settle for tossing everything in the trash.

As for Rowan's bed, she didn't know how he managed, but a new mattress and box spring arrived within hours of them walking through the front door. She didn't care what happened to the old one as long as it—and the lingering smell of musk—were far, far away.

"Nice of him to wait until the last second to announce his departure." Angie huffed. "Probably didn't want a scene."

Rowan didn't answer. She was glad Nick waited. If she'd known the exact day and time, a heavy shadow would have fallen over their last night. Instead, she enjoyed their last time together.

Intensely sweet. Nick gave her pleasure over and over again, the sun peeking through the bedroom window as he held her while she dozed.

Rowan's phone buzzed. Reluctantly, she let the incoming text pull her back to the present.

"I have to go. Nick has checked out of his hotel. He should be at my place in a few minutes." Rowan gave Angie a quick hug. "Thank you. For the food. For... everything."

"Say the word, and we'll spend the night binging on rom-coms, emptying a bottle of wine or two, and *not* talking about Nick Sanders."

"I'll let you know."

Nick waited for her, closing the door to his SUV as her truck came to a stop. Was his usual smile a bit subdued as the gravity of the moment finally hit him? Or was Rowan seeing something that wasn't there? She wanted him to feel regret, so she looked for some sign—any hint—to prove he might miss her. Just a little.

"All packed?" Rowan asked, her tone cheery

Inwardly, Rowan cringed, chiding herself. *Dial back the fake happy.* Nick wasn't expecting a joke a minute. Taking the basket, she handed it to him.

"What's this?"

"A few goodies courtesy of Angie. I know you can't take them on the plane, but if you get hungry on the way, you won't have to stop at a restaurant with iffy cuisine."

"Thank you." Nick opened the passenger door, stowing the basket. "And thank Angie."

"Want to come in for a few minutes? Or do you have to get going?"

Nick took her hand, walking with her to the front door. Once inside, he took her in his arms. *Don't,* she thought. *Whatever you do, don't cry.* But the tears were close, lurking behind her eyes.

Why couldn't he be a little less sweet? If he called her a name. Or drove off with a careless wave. Anything to make saying goodbye easier.

But no. Not Nick. He had to hold her in his strong, warm arms, reminding her one more time what she was about to lose.

"I wish I could stay a little longer." Nick cupped the back of her neck, looking into her eyes. "Thanksgiving with the team is a tradition. Anybody who lives in Seattle. We make a point of getting together every year."

"That's nice. Where do you meet?"

"One house or the other. Depends. I don't know who's up this time."

"And Christmas? Any fixed plans?"

"Really? Small talk?" Nick paced away. When he spun around, Rowan saw what she'd been hoping for. Raw emotion. "All we can do is talk about my plans for the holidays?"

"We've talked about everything else."

"Not everything."

Rowan didn't pretend to misunderstand.

"What's the point? You have to leave. And I have to stay."

Nick took a step closer. "Yes, I have to leave. I signed a contract with the Cyclones. For the next six years, they agreed to pay me a very nice salary—with some very nice performance-related bonus money. In return, I agreed to put on the uniform and do my ever-loving best to help the team win."

"I know."

Rowan knew Nick had to be heading somewhere. She clutched her hands behind her back and waited.

"I'm stuck. No, I'm not stuck. I could quit. Or demand a trade. But I don't want to. I like Seattle. I love my team. We're good, Rowan. And we should be for a long time. I'd be a fool to walk away."

"I wouldn't ask."

"And I can't ask you to leave your life here in Jasper. Your family is more than a little suspect."

"I wish I could argue," Rowan said.

"Your friends, on the other hand, are top notch. And your business is here. You've made nothing into something pretty damn great."

"Which brings us back to—"

Nick stopped her, placing his finger to her lips.

"I don't want to say goodbye."

Rowan swallowed, biting the inside of her cheek, to stop the tears from flowing.

"Long distance relationships don't work."

"Who says?"

Nick's unexpected question threw her. Needing to think, Rowan headed toward the kitchen.

"Well?" Nick followed on her heels. "What law says two people have to be in the same city—or state—to have a relationship?"

"I'm sure I could find a boatload of statistics." For something to do, Rowan set about preparing a cup of tea she had no desire to drink. "Plus, you're a professional athlete."

"Hardly news."

"Temptation. A different woman in every port."

"I think you have me confused with a sailor," Nick smiled. "Can we sit down? Following you around is making me dizzy."

Rowan abandoned the unwanted tea for a seat on the sofa. She had a point, and Nick would listen.

"We met just over a week ago. Yes, we have a strong connection. But will we feel the same when you're three thousand miles away?"

"Rowan—"

"You're a physical man, Nick. You like sex." Rowan didn't like where her thoughts had taken her. But she refused to put her head in the sand. "Temptation is everywhere. Especially for a man like you. You could be strong. And start to resent me because you made a commitment. Or, you'll cheat. And resent me because you feel guilty."

"Thanks for the vote of confidence."

Rowan braced herself against the hurt she saw in Nick's dark eyes, certain he would thank her—in the not-too-distant future.

"Maybe I'll be tempted. Obviously, my theory works both ways."

"Bull. Shit." Nick glared. Hurt mingled with anger. "You know you wouldn't cheat. But you really believe I would?"

"I believe you are used to a certain lifestyle. If we tried a long-distance relationship, you would feel obligated to change." Flailing, Rowan grasped at the word. "Remember? We said we didn't want to change each other."

"You think I'm a man-whore."

"I think you're wonderful. Exactly as you are."

Nick opened and closed his mouth, for once, at a loss for words. Throwing his hands in the air, he surged to his feet.

"I should go."

"Now?"

"Why stay? We're running in circles."

Speaking of running. Rowan could either hustle her butt after Nick or stand in her living room, her mouth hanging open as he drove away.

"Damn it." Rowan grabbed Nick's arm before he could leave the house. "At least say a proper goodbye."

Taking her face in his hands, Nick kissed Rowan. A bone-melting, knee-collapsing, ruin her for any other man kiss.

"I'm not saying goodbye," he told Rowan, making certain she was steady on her feet before letting go. "We aren't over. If you need time. Fine. I can wait. A month?"

"I…"

"Six? Will six months work for you? Or a year?" Nick frowned. "Personally, I think a year is a stretch."

"Nick—"

"I will call. And Skype. And text. If you like, I'll even write by snail mail. As long as you promise not to send the letter back unopened."

The fact that Nick could joke about something that a few short days ago was no laughing matter, amazed Rowan. And made her admire him even more.

"I—"

"Don't answer. We have time." Nick opened the door. "I'm leaving Jasper, Rowan. But I'm not leaving you."

ROWAN SPENT THE rest of the day in an odd haze. Part sad. Part confused. And part—the best part—hopeful.

As she puttered around the house doing the usual chores that had to be done no matter her state of mind, she cranked up her tunes to work by playlist. Two hours later, the downstairs sparkled from floor to ceiling—windows included.

And, she received a text from Nick.

Meatball sub is my new favorite thing. I'm sure I never mentioned my love for root beer. How did you know? Great minds, Rowan. Great minds.

Rowan clutched her phone to her chest, trying her best not to get carried away. One text didn't a lasting relationship make.

The doorbell saved Rowan from butchering any more famous phrases—or trying to remember who said the original.

Plato? Socrates? Maybe Aristotle. She always mixed them up.

"Mom!"

Grasping the doorknob, Rowan couldn't keep the lack of enthusiasm from her voice. She'd known her mother would show up eventually. But she'd hoped for a longer reprieve.

"Hello, Rowan." Smartly dressed—as always—Tess Cartwright fussed at the collar of her long, gray cashmere coat. "May I come in?"

"Of course."

Her mother looked as if she were headed to afternoon tea with the Queen of England. Rowan, in jeans, an old flannel shirt, and bare feet, wouldn't be allowed to clean Buckingham Palace's floors.

The thought made Rowan smile as she hung Tess's coat in the closet.

"I'm glad to see you're in a good mood. Word is your friend left town today."

"Word is correct. Would you like something to drink before we get down to business?"

Sitting, Tess smoothed a nonexistent wrinkle from her pleated skirt.

"Water. Flat, no ice. And in a glass. I can't abide drinking from a plastic bottle."

Rowan was used to how her mother made every request sound as though she was speaking to the hired help. After all these years, she barely noticed.

"Your house looks nice."

"We both know why you're here, Mom." Sitting, Rowan crossed her legs.

"You can save your breath. I am not going to apologize to Geoff. He's lucky I talked Nick down. I only kicked his balls. Nick would have ripped them off."

Tess winced. "Geoff did contact me. He swore you acted with little provocation. I can see—as usual—he lied."

Rowan's hand went to her face. She kept forgetting about the bruise. The pain was long gone, the color now more green and yellow than black and blue.

"You admit Geoff lies? What brought about that revelation?"

"I've always known." Tess sipped her water. When she looked at Rowan, her eyes were troubled. "I'm sorry."

"For…?"

"Everything. Anything. For making excuses for Geoff's weakness. For making him weaker by ignoring the problem."

Tess spoke the truth. However, Rowan found no satisfaction in hearing the words. Not when they caused her mother so much distress.

"Geoff's a big boy. You aren't responsible for what he does."

Rising, Tess walked toward the fire, the heels of her boots clicking on the hardwood floor. When she ran her hand over the mantel checking for dust—almost without thought—Rowan shook her head. Some things would never change.

"One of the reasons I married Leo was because I hoped he would treat Geoff as the son he always wanted."

"I thought you married Leo for his money."

"I did." Unashamed, Tess didn't flinch from the truth. "But why not shoot for the stars? Don't get me wrong, I tried to give Leo a child. I even became pregnant after five years of trying."

"I had no idea."

"No one did. I wasn't very far along." Tess stared into the fire. "I might have told Leo. I might have kept trying. But one night, not long after your ninth birthday, he made a comment that changed everything."

Tess glided to the sofa, taking her seat. For the first time, she met Rowan's gaze full on.

"We were in bed. Leo had one of those endless reports he's always reading. Without looking up, he said, *too bad Rowan isn't a boy*. One sentence. But I knew what he meant."

"I was a tomboy."

"Geoff was a disappointment, while you had all the qualities Leo admires. Unfortunately, you didn't have the one thing that matters most."

"A penis." Rowan had heard the refrain before. But the part about Geoff was new.

"I hadn't thought about equal rights or women's liberation. What was the point? But when Leo dismissed you because you had the gall to be born a woman? Something in me finally stood and took notice. I promised myself I would never give him the son he craved."

"Your own little revolution."

"I suppose. As I said, your brother is weak. He needed me. You never did." Tess sighed, running the tip of her finger along the rim of her glass. "Perhaps you did, and because I was so preoccupied with Geoff—at some point—you stopped trying to make me notice."

"Mom." Rowan leaned forward. She wanted to sit on the sofa, to feel her mother's arms around her. But habit made her stay where she was. "I wish you'd told me sooner."

"I didn't know how to start."

Tess, hope in her eyes, patted the cushion. Rowan didn't hesitate.

"I love you, Mom."

"Oh, baby. I love you, too." Tess patted her back. "Did you really kick your brother in the balls?"

"I used my knee. But, yes. I did."

"Good."

Rowan laughed.

Keeping one arm around Rowan, Tess picked up her glass, downing the contents. "Eating humble pie is a thirsty business."

"Would you like some more?"

"I'm fine. You know Geoff will never change. Not because he can't."

"Because he doesn't want to," Rowan finished for her.

"As for Leo…"

"Is his nose broken?"

"Very." Tess didn't sound upset. "Dr. Brill had to reset the bone. The jury is out on whether Leo will need plastic surgery. The swelling has to go down before they'll know."

"Nick will be happy to know."

"Nick Sanders. Leo's biological son, according to your brother."

"According to everyone, including a DNA test."

Suddenly, Rowan needed the tea she had passed on earlier. Without asking, she decided to make a pot, removing two cups from the cupboard.

"Leo didn't say a lot. But your young man… He is your young man?"

"To be determined," Rowan said, adding a sugar bowl and a small pitcher of cream to a serving tray.

Tess raised her eyebrows, but let the topic drop.

"Leo was quite impressed. Mad as Hades, but impressed. Something tells me he hasn't given up his dream of bringing his son into the fold."

Something told Rowan that Leo needed his head examined.

"I knew Leo wasn't perfect. Not by a long stretch. But now…" Rowan searched for what to say. "He's not a good man."

"Not compared to some. Shall I pour?" Tess asked after Rowan set the tray on the coffee table.

"Mom—"

"I like my life, Rowan. At this point, Leo and I have very little to do with each other beyond entertaining his business associates." She handed Rowan a filled cup, adding a splash of cream and half a teaspoon of sugar to her own. "I'm content most of the time. Happy when I have my grandchildren around."

"I would want more than content."

"You're young. You should want more." Tess's eyes took on a faraway look. "Your father loved us."

"I remember."

"You do? I'm glad." She sipped her tea. "So many years have gone by. If I had never known him, I wouldn't believe a man like that existed outside of a fairytale."

"He made you laugh."

Tess smiled at the memory. "Your father was steadfast. Not the sexiest word. And a little old-fashioned. But believe me, if you ever find a man who will stand by you, no matter what. No questions asked. Who lights up when you walk in a room. And holds your hand—just because. Never let him go, Rowan. A man like that? He spoils you for anybody else."

Rowan rubbed her chest. The spot right above her heart.

"I think I already found him."

"Nick?"

"It's complicated."

Tess laughed. "Life is complicated. However, when you stop thinking and *know* Nick is the one? All those complications will cease to matter."

"When will I know?"

"You just will."

CHAPTER SIXTEEN

● ≈ ● ≈ ●

ANOTHER SPRING TRAINING in the books. The start of another baseball season was less than forty-eight hours away.

After the flight to Seattle, the bus ride to team headquarters, and the scramble by his teammates to get home to their own beds after a month in Arizona, Nick should have wanted the same thing.

However, the idea of time alone with his increasingly dark thoughts seemed like a punishment, not a reward. Good thing he had friends who could be counted on to chase away the blues—at least for an hour or two.

"You guys want to grab a beer?" Nick asked, slinging his duffel over his shoulder.

"Sorry. Can't. Very important prior plans." Spencer grinned as he watched a bright red Mercedes come to a stop. As the door opened, a pair of long, shapely legs emerged. The woman attached was just as appealing, her eyes all for Spencer.

Blue O'Hara walked into her fiancé's open arms.

"Miss me?"

"Maybe. Just a little."

Nick groaned as he watched the couple kiss. He was happy for them. Honestly. But at the moment, he wasn't in the mood for public displays of affection.

"How about you?" Nick turned his back on Spencer and Blue. He could always rely on Travis to help him kill some time.

"Maybe tomorrow. I plan to sleep for the next twenty-four hours straight. Twenty-six, if I'm lucky."

Nick frowned. He'd been so caught up in his own personal drama, he hadn't noticed that Travis wasn't himself lately. Not frustrated and moody. Nick had the market cornered on those emotions. More pensive, his usual ready smile missing more often than not.

Like Nick's trip to Jasper, Travis' journey to his hometown hadn't ended well. They could form a club.

"Something you want to talk about?"

Travis shook his head. "I've had enough talking to last a lifetime. Either I say too much. Or not enough. Either way, I never seem to say the right thing. You know what I mean?"

"I have absolutely no idea." Nick had never seen Travis so subdued. This version of his friend made him nervous.

"If I leave you alone, you aren't going to do something stupid?"

"Jesus." Travis punched Nick in the arm. Hard. "I'm tired, not suicidal, asshole."

Wasn't that what a suicidal person would say? Nick wasn't taking any chances.

"I plan on calling you every hour or so. If you don't pick up, expect me to show up."

"I need sleep," Travis ground out.

"I don't care."

"He isn't going to kill himself," Spencer, having finally come up for air, watched as Travis slid behind the wheel of his car. "He's having woman problems."

"Why didn't he tell me?"

"Could be he sensed you were in a similar bind." Spencer swung a friendly arm around Nick's shoulders. "Misery may love company, but not when women are involved."

"Travis confided in you?"

"A little. But he was a fount of information compared to you. I know her name is Rowan, and that she's *the one*."

Hearing Rowan's name other than in his head made Nick tense. If he had the time, he would hop a plane for Jasper just to tell her to piss off. Then make love to her for the next week.

Since neither was possible, Nick had to settle for grinding his teeth.

"Right about now, you know as much as I do."

"Things might start looking up."

Ten minutes later, alone in the back of a taxi, Nick closed his eyes. He left Rowan in November, certain he could convince her what they had was worth the risk.

December was good. They were in contact almost every day. Texts. Emails. They even Skyped once a week. From three thousand miles away, Rowan's smile lit up his gray Seattle day.

The old year flowed into the new. Nick asked Rowan to fly with him to Paris. Or London. Rome? Anyplace. Her choice. But she claimed work kept her too busy. Nick wanted to believe her, so he didn't push.

With the rest of the Cyclones, Nick reported to Spring Training in February. By March, when the games began, he was certain they were making progress. Until last week when Rowan all but disappeared from his life.

Rolling his head in a circle, Nick felt his neck pop with tension. He needed a massage. And a good meal. A shower, and his own bed. But most of all, he needed Rowan.

Picking up his phone, he scrolled through her last few texts. Short was the best way to describe them. But not particularly sweet.

Busy. Talk later.

Sorry I missed your call. Mom has a bad cold. On chicken soup patrol.

Nick was glad Rowan and her mother had come to a better understanding of each other. But using her mother's illness as an excuse? The woman needed soup. How bad could it be?

He felt Rowan was giving him the runaround. Something had changed, and for some reason, she wasn't telling him why.

Then, as a big plop of crap on top of an already steaming pile, Nick heard from Leonard Cartwright. Not personally. Cartwright's lawyers contacted Nick's with an offer.

"Mr. Cartwright is offering to make you his heir. Everything would be yours. All you have to do is—"

Nick stopped his lawyer right there.

"No."

"But the offer is quite fair. If you—"

"No. Tell Cartwright's lawyer no deal. I'm not interested. Not now. Not ever."

"But—"

"No buts. Do what I want, or you're fired. Understand?"

"Yes, Mr. Sanders. But I think you're making a big mistake."

Cartwright could go to hell. In fact, Nick wished him there, then put the man out of his mind. Permanently.

However, Nick's lawyer was right. He'd made one big mistake. He thought his heart would be safe in Rowan's care. Now, he wasn't so sure.

Nick let himself into his house, dropping his bags at the front door.

The refrigerator was fully stocked, thanks to his housekeeper, but Nick wasn't interested. After staring at the wide selection of food for several minutes, he shut the door, grabbing a beer.

The house on Lake Washington was more of a stopping-off point than a home. Spencer lived within walking distance. Travis was in the process of building a place several lots over. They often drove to the ballpark together.

Nick had never thought too much about decorating. A comfortable chair sat in the living room. When he wanted to relax, he had a big deck and a view of the lake on one side. A big screen TV on the other.

Beer in hand, Nick opened the French doors, breathing in the crisp, yet surprisingly mild April air. Though the sky was cloudy, a few streaks of sunlight tried their best to break through the gloom. He strolled onto the deck, leaning against the rail.

Nick gazed at the water. Peaceful, he thought, watching the moored boats bobbing up and down. Raising his beer, before Nick could take a drink, he caught a streak of unexpected color out of the corner of his eye.

"What the…?"

The yard wrapped around the house. Not large, but Nick liked the bit of green it provided. A small hill sloped up to a tall row of shrubs, providing the yard with privacy from his neighbors.

Instead of the plain grass he expected, the hill was covered in flowers.

"A hill where spring flowers bloom. Just as your mother asked."

Rowan. Her blond hair swirled into its usual messy bun. Her eyes, so damn blue. And that smile. All for him. Nick didn't know if she were a figment of his imagination. He didn't care.

In two strides, Nick had Rowan in his arms. He kissed her, all his pent-up need and frustration spilling over. The best part? She kissed him back.

"You feel real."

"I am." Beaming, Rowan touched his face. "I'm here. For good, if you want me."

"For good? But how? I— You know what? Explain later." Nick lifted Rowan over his shoulder, making a beeline for the house.

"I can walk," Rowan laughed, grabbing his hips for balance.

"I'm faster."

Slamming the door shut, Nick took the stairs two at a time, cursing the architect who thought putting the bedrooms on the second floor was a good idea.

"Clothes. Off," Nick said the second he set Rowan down.

He took care of his clothing, throwing back the covers. Rowan still had on her bra when he tossed her onto the bed. The sex was wild, out of control. And fast.

"I've missed you," Nick said in the way of an explanation.

"I could tell." Rowan snuggled close. "You won't hear me complain."

"I didn't cheat."

"I know."

After all Rowan's worries, suddenly he had her absolute trust?

"Why?" Nick had to ask.

"You're steadfast."

"Sounds boring."

"Never. I know you'll stand by me, no matter what. No questions asked. Your face lights up when I walk in a room. And you hold my hand." Rowan linked her fingers with his. "Just because."

"You forgot something."

"Did I?" Rowan took a deep breath, her eyes locked with his. "Tell me."

"I love you, Rowan. My heart is yours. My body. My soul. Forever."

"I love you, Nick. Though I didn't know at the time, my heart has been yours from the moment we met. My body. My soul. Forever."

For the first time in forever, Nick felt tears clog his throat. He couldn't cry. Not yet. But something told him, with Rowan—their wedding, the birth of their children—the tears would come.

"Thank you for planting my mother's flowers."

"You think she would approve?"

"I *know* she does."

Content in a way he never guessed possible, Nick held Rowan close, her love—their love—filling the room.

EPILOGUE

● ≈ ● ≈ ●

THE CROWD ROARED. Somehow, they grew louder with every pitch. Rowan wondered how such a thing was possible. Then again, she was new to baseball.

Opening day, Nick had explained on the way to the game, was always filled with a certain amount of pomp and circumstance. But this year, everything was bigger. Better. More intense.

"We're world champs. There's a banner to raise. Rings to hand out. The fans have waited a long time for their team to win the World Series. You can expect a lot of celebrating."

Forget the crowd, Rowan thought. Nick was wound up like a little kid on Christmas morning. She might not understand the intricacies of baseball, but she knew winning the championship was huge. Rowan was thrilled she was here to share the moment with him.

Rowan's decision to leave Jasper hadn't been made lightly. But once she let go of her fear and doubt, she knew she had no other choice. Not if she wanted to be happy. Not if she wanted Nick. And she did. More than anything.

As she told him over scrambled eggs and toast—when he finally let her out of bed—Rowan hadn't meant to cut Nick off.

The actual move had been easier than she expected. But time consuming. She spent every waking second making preparations. Between a massive case of nerves and all the last-minute details, she barely had time to sleep. The weeks flew by, then the last one dragged interminably.

"I wanted to surprise you. Not drive you crazy."

"Yet you managed both," Nick said, too relaxed and happy to do more than gently pinch her on the butt.

RTC Landscaping was about to become a bicoastal operation. Once Rowan made up her mind to jump, she used both feet.

Rebecca would run the end in Jasper. Setting up in Seattle would take time.

"I hope you don't mind. I may have to mooch off you for a while."

"I think I can support both of us," Nick teased. "For the time being."

Rowan adjusted her new Cyclones' baseball cap. Nick was in the...

"What do you call the place Nick's standing?"

"The on-deck circle," Blue O'Hara shouted. "Don't worry. You'll pick up the lingo fast."

Rowan's self-appointed guide—and, besides Nick, her first friend in Seattle—Blue had secured their seats just off the first base side. Hot properties for any game, on opening night, getting tickets was next to impossible. Unless you worked as head of public relations for the team.

Blue informed Rowan that her fiancé's name moved mountains. But just because she was engaged to Spencer Kraig—one of the Cyclones' star players—Blue never used the fact to get special treatment.

Rowan took note. She had no plans to cash in on Nick's celebrity. But she knew some people might think she had latched onto him for his money and fame. She had been her own woman before they met, nothing had changed.

Noting the momentary decrease in the noise, Rowan used the lull to thank Blue.

"The surprise was a big hit. I couldn't have planted all those flowers without your help."

Blue not only let Rowan into Nick's house, but she also found a nursery that carried the plants Rowan wanted and arranged for their delivery.

"Keeping the secret from Spencer was the hard part. But he forgave me." Blue grinned. "Over and over again. Mm. I do love that man."

Chuckling, Rowan turned back to the game when she heard Nick's name announced. She didn't know a lot about baseball. The basics, sure. But she had never been interested in learning the subtleties. Of which, she realized, there were many.

The game was such a big part of Nick life. What if Rowan couldn't share at least a little of his passion? Of worse? What if the game bored her senseless?

Five minutes was all she needed. Boredom? Nope. Rowan loved every second. Though she had to admit, her favorite parts were when Nick had the ball.

Nick had made a play, diving to his right, popping back to his feet, and throwing the runner out at first with only a second to spare. Rowan's heart was still in her throat.

Nick stepped to the plate. Somehow, he picked her out of the crowd, his gaze catching hers. His grin widened. When he winked, the crowd went wild, necks craning trying to figure out who was the object of their superstar's affection.

Rowan knew. She wanted to stand on the seat and shout at the top of her lungs—that's my man. Instead, she watched as he took his stance, cocked the bat, and crushed the ball over the centerfield fence.

"What a way to start the season," Blue cried.

Raising her arms, Rowan jumped up and down, celebrating as Nick crossed home plate.

What a way to start a life.

COMING IN AUGUST
FOR ALL WE KNOW
ONE STRIKE AWAY BOOK THREE

AFTER THE RAIN
(One Pass Away Book One)

PROLOGUE

LOGAN. LOGAN. LOGAN.

Logan Price closed his eyes, taking it all in.

"Hear that, kid?" Starting quarterback Gaige Benson slapped him on the back. "Two games under your belt and you're a star. Now let's go out there and add super to the front of it."

The announcer for the team set them in motion down the tunnel with his familiar introduction.

"And now, let's hear it for your division champion *SEATTLE KNIGHTS.*"

The roar of the crowd. There was nothing like it. A packed stadium. Fans chanting his name. Few people would ever experience what it was like to take the field in a professional football game.

Logan Price had been working for this his entire life. He could still remember in exact detail the first game he ever saw. Too small to climb onto the stool in his father's bar by himself, his old man had lifted him onto the seat.

Stay and be quiet.

Not an easy order to follow for an active, inquisitive little boy. One look at the game and for once, Logan had no problem following his father's command. The old TV transported him to a foreign world filled with bright lights and shiny helmeted warriors. Logan didn't know what he was watching. He did know he wanted to be one of those men.

A Sunday afternoon in rural Oklahoma. *Lefty's Pub* was filled with after-church drinkers who figured they had done their duty to God and family. The rest of the day was their time. A beer. Or two.

Or six. Cronies who understood a man's need to unwind before the start of another workweek.

And football.

If the Friday night high school game was their true religion, the Sunday afternoon games were a close second. As Oklahoma boys, they hated anything Texas. The men of Denville gathered every week to root for whichever team was playing the Dallas Cowboys.

No matter how the games ended. Whether the crowd was happy or disgruntled. It meant more drinking. Hours later, husbands, boyfriends, and sons would stumble out, pile into beat-up trucks, and weave their way home to frustrated wives, girlfriends, and mothers.

As he grew older, Logan's view changed. He moved from the stool to behind the bar. And he promised himself one thing. He would never become one of those men. He wouldn't spend the week at a job he hated. His home wouldn't be a semi-wide trailer filled with hand-me-down furniture and a wife to whom he couldn't face going home.

His Sundays were going to be spent playing football, not watching it.

"Ready to take down this vaunted Arizona defense?" Gaige yelled at him, butting helmets.

Vaunted. Good word, Logan thought. His QB liked to use what his granny called highfalutin talk. Must have been that Ivy League education. He knew that Gaige Benson didn't grow up with a silver spoon in his mouth. He came from the mean streets of Brooklyn. He had the scars to prove it.

Like Logan, Gaige had vowed to get out of the life into which he was born. In the process, he polished himself up like a new penny. He took advantage of his full-ride scholarship to Yale. He didn't spend all his time on the football field. Fancy vocabulary. Fancy clothes. Fancy women. They were all part of the package Gaige purposefully fashioned for himself.

Seventeen years after clawing his way out of the tenement that he grew up in, very little of that borough-rat remained. Until game time. No one was tougher than Gaige Benson. Three-time league MVP. Considered one of the best ever to play the game. No one stood in his way when he was playing the game. He had the scars to prove it.

"Gather round."

Knights head coach Harry Coleman gathered the team close. He had to yell over the crowd, but he had the voice to do it. Booming was putting it mildly. The first time Logan heard it, he stood right beside the man. The ringing in his ears didn't go away for three days.

"Divisional game. If I have to say any more than that, you shouldn't be out here. Go kick some ass."

The defense took the field to start the game. Arizona had a rookie quarterback drafted in the second round from a small college in the Midwest. The only reason he was out there was because the regular starter suffered a concussion in last week's game and the regular backup had food poisoning. Thrown into action at the last minute, Logan swore he could see the guy's hands shaking before he took the first snap. When the ball went sailing between his legs, Logan shook his head.

The moment was too big for some people. For Logan, it wasn't big enough. He aimed for the biggest stage of all. The Super Bowl. It wasn't a matter of *if* he would get there, but when.

"Three and out." Gaige grinned, pulling on his helmet. "Come on, kid. Let's go show them how it's done."

Logan ran onto the field. *Kid.* He shook his head, grinning. From the first day of training camp, Gaige had hung that moniker on him. Ironic since he was almost twenty-five, a good two years older than most of the other rookies. However, he supposed when someone had been in the league as long as Gaige, all the new guys seemed like kids.

"We're starting on the ground," Gaige instructed them in the huddle. "Sweep out left. Basic. Got it?"

Lining up as he had a thousand other times, Logan checked the defense. He knew he was fast. One of the fastest in the game. What set him apart was his anticipation. He had the uncanny ability to read the guy covering him. He knew when to fake left or when to fake right. Stutter step or flat out, in your face, catch me if you can.

His speed got him out of Denville, Oklahoma. His brains and determination got him to the NFL.

The sounds of the game were as familiar to Logan as the back of his own hand. The call from scrimmage. Each quarterback had his own unique cadence. Gaige was a master of mixing his up. Study him all you want. Good luck figuring it out. His teammates knew. A signal just before they broke the huddle.

Pay attention, you were golden. Slack off even once? Gaige could ream a guy out with the best of them. And he had no problem doing it in the middle of the game.

An entire YouTube channel had been devoted to Gaige and his rants. They were as legendary as the man himself. With a ball in his hand, he was cool as ice. The rest of the time, watch out.

No one would ever accuse Logan of lacking focus. Today was no exception. They were driving down the field. First and ten from the Arizona twenty-yard line. He already had three carries of thirty-five yards. It was going to be a good day.

"Ready to take it in?" Gaige asked.

"Always."

"Then show them what you've got."

A quick snap later, Gaige handed the ball to Logan. The offensive line created a seam. Not a big one. Just big enough. Using the push of his powerful legs, Logan surged through. One more step. They wouldn't catch him. No one could.

Like everything connected with the game, Logan heard the snap of the bone with total clarity. The agony that surged through his body was so intense he almost passed out. In the next few minutes, he was going to wish he had.

"Get back." Logan heard Gaige through the haze of pain. "Goddamn it. Move the hell off."

The three-hundred-and-fifty-pound linebacker didn't get off by standing. He rolled. Crushing Logan's broken leg as he went. He would never know if the move had been deliberate. Now, it was the last thing on his mind. He only cared about two things. How bad was the injury and when would he be able to play again.

"Hold on, kid." Gaige took his hand. "They're bringing the stretcher."

The team doctor checked his eyes. Logan knew he was asked some questions. What they were and how he answered, he would never remember. By the time they carted him off the field, Logan knew the break was bad.

"Gaige." Logan reached for him.

"I'm here, kid."

"Is it over?"

"The game?" Gaige walked with him, his head bent toward Logan. "No. But I promise we're going to win the bastard."

They loaded him onto the open cart. They had him secured and the vehicle rolled away before Logan had his answer. He wasn't wondering about the game. It was his career.

To no one in particular, he whispered the question again.

"Is it over?"

CHAPTER ONE

LOGAN SAT UP in bed, his body covered with a fine coating of sweat.

He glanced at the clock. Three in the fucking morning. On the one night he managed to get to bed at a reasonable hour, he was plagued by the nightmare that had haunted his dreams for the past two years.

Running his hand through his long, damp hair, Logan fell back onto the mattress. His sheets were as wet as he was. With a grimace, he rolled onto the floor. Flexing his stiff knee, he stripped the bed, tossing everything onto a pile of dirty clothes he planned on taking to the laundromat on his day off.

There was an alternative. He could always take Linda Sue Hemmings up on her offer. She would do his laundry anytime. Payment. On-call stud service whenever her husband Darryl was out of town on business. As much as Logan hated folding socks, he decided the price was too high. He had lost a lot in the last few years. He still held onto his dignity. Just barely.

Still groggy, Logan shuffled to the bathroom. Flipping on the light, he grimaced at what the mirror reflected.

Too many late nights followed by not enough sleep. As patterns went, it wasn't a healthy one. Perpetually bloodshot eyes. Dark circles on his dark circles. He needed a haircut. Logan ran his hand over his face. Even more, he needed a shave.

He had to hand it to himself. When he let himself go, he went all the way. All he had to do was stop showering. If he wasn't worried about driving the customers away with his smell, he might have considered it.

The old plumbing rattled with protest when he turned on the faucet. It wasn't a bad place. There were worse. Logan splashed some cold water on his face. He didn't bother with a towel. It would dry soon enough on its own.

He had two choices.

Toss and turn for a couple of hours on the unmade bed – he really needed to get more than one set of sheets.

Or lose himself with an old friend.

Sleep wasn't coming which made the choice an easy one.

Logan pulled on a pair of old shorts, a faded t-shirt and sweatshirt that was too ratty to be called anything as fashionable as a hoodie. After lacing up his sneakers, he hit the road. When he was a kid, he ran for the fun of it. In high school and college, it strengthened his legs and improved his stamina. Now, the only thing it accomplished was getting him a reputation as that half-crazy Price boy. Running the deserted streets at all hours? Maybe his head had been permanently injured along with his leg.

Logan jogged past *Lefty's Pub*. The place where he spent most evenings tending bar. The day he left for college he swore to anyone who would listen that he had served his last beer. Eight years later, here he was, washing glasses and putting up with not so subtle jabs about how the mighty had fallen.

Coming back to Denville was more of an adjustment than Logan anticipated. He expected the cracks about his failed NFL career. Any kind of success tended to breed a certain amount of jealousy and resentment. There were those who reveled in his injury.

Logan Price always thought too much of himself. Denville wasn't good enough for the high school's star running back. He forgot all about us when he made it big.

The sound of his feet pounding on the unpaved side street couldn't keep the usual thoughts from creeping back. Some of what those people said was true. He had been full of himself. At seventeen, one wasn't written up in national magazines without it going to his head.

Logan never tried to hide his plans. A full-ride scholarship to the college of his choice. Then the pros. MVP awards. Super Bowl rings. The cocky attitude of a teenager wasn't any easier to take than if he had been an adult. Most of Denville embraced their golden boy.

AFTER ALL THESE YEARS
(One Pass Away Book Two)

PROLOGUE

SEAN McBRIDE WOKE up with a smile on his face. It happened a lot lately. And he thoroughly approved.

He stretched his long, athletic body. Some mornings every inch of him ached. Such was the life of a professional football player. Everything was about preparing for the game. Focus. Concentration. The goal was to be ready for game day.

He had to hold it together for sixty minutes. Pull out a win any way possible. Sacrifice his body to the football Gods and pray he walked away healthy enough to do it all again next week.

Sean dreaded the day after the game. The adrenaline had long ago worn off and he felt all of his thirty years. There were degrees of bad. Sometimes he shuffled to the shower, the aches and pains palpable, but mercifully bearable.

Then there were the bad days. After a day of three-hundred-pound defensive backs using him as their own personal punching bag, he didn't get out of bed—he crawled.

Bruised from top to bottom, his joints creaked and his muscles protested like screeching banshees. Those were the times he wondered why he did it. He could have been a doctor. Or a lawyer. He could have taken his father's advice and gone into the family business. No seventeen-year-old with dreams of glory in the NFL wanted to think about becoming a butcher. But damn. Cutting meat sounded good on those mornings.

This was a good Monday. His body felt lithe—limber. The bruises were there. That was part of his life. However, yesterday had been one of those rare games when every moment fell into place. From the kickoff to the final whistle, the outcome of the game was never in question.

Sean caught every ball thrown his way. He evaded the defense. Fast as the wind. Three touchdowns. One hundred and eighty-two total yards. A damn good day for any wide receiver. He would have had more if Coach Coleman hadn't taken him out of the game in the fourth quarter. With a big lead, there was no reason to risk injury when he wasn't needed.

The after-game celebration moved from the locker room to one of the team's favorite hangouts. Naturally the atmosphere was raucous. Cautiously so.

The Knights were having a stellar season. Ten wins, two losses. Sean and his friends had enough games under their belts to understand how quickly that could turn. Injuries tended to come in bunches. So far, they were healthy. However, that was bound to change. The hope was to get to the playoffs with all their major players on the roster.

After the game, they had a few drinks. Three was Sean's limit these days. A few years ago it was a different story. He would have closed the place down after a win. He and his bed partner of the moment would have moved on to someone's apartment, partying until dawn before going back to her place and fucking like demented rabbits. Then he would go home alone and catch a few hours sleep until it was time to grab a quick shower before heading to the Knights' headquarters to review film from the game.

Those days were over. Sean wasn't a kid anymore, high on his own press clippings and more testosterone than brains. Not that he had settled down completely. He could still party with the best of them. However, he chose his moments—ones that never took place during the season.

Women were another matter. Sean liked sex. Always had. If there were a God, he always would. While his bed partners weren't as varied, they were almost as frequent.

Sean knew players who abstained a few days before the game, saving their *juice*. He wasn't one of them. Sean had plenty of juice, thank you very much. Sex was necessary for a happy and healthy mind. For *his* happy and healthy mind.

A big plus to having sex at night was sex the next morning. It was one of his favorite things. A partner, warm and willing.

The perfect way to start the day.

Speaking of which. Smiling, Sean turned over. His hand reached out, expecting to find a soft, sweet woman. Instead, he found cold sheets. Sitting up, he looked around the room. Like the bed, empty. The bathroom door was open and the light off.

Not bothering to cover up, Sean jumped out of bed. Buck naked, he searched the house. She wasn't in the kitchen. Why would she be? She didn't cook, not even coffee. She was on a first-name basis with half the baristas in Seattle.

Was that it? Would she be back soon with two cups of steaming black caffeine and his favorite muffins? Sean was talking himself into that scenario when he saw the note.

He picked up the paper that had been propped against the lamp by the front door.

Sean.

Thank you for the past few weeks. After years of building it up in my mind, I was worried that it couldn't live up to my expectations. I should have known better. It was everything I had hoped for—and more.

We didn't make any promises. No strings were attached that need to be broken. After all these years, you can finally breathe easy. It's over. We are now friends without the expectation of benefits.

When we see each other, it will be as if it, we, never happened.

Sean read the note. Then read it again.

What the fuck? What was in those drinks?

Sean searched his memory for some kind of clue. The bar. His teammates. Then she was there. They laughed. Everything was smooth and easy. They seemed to be developing a rhythm. In his mind, they were together. Not a man and a woman—a couple.

It sounded good to him. He would have sworn she felt the same. He didn't want another woman. He wanted her. In his arms. In his life.

No expectations? Hell. He woke up with plenty of them, only to find out he was alone. Alone in bed. Alone. Period.

Sean scrubbed a hand over his face. He remembered the way she tasted. The way she melted into his arms. The curves of her luscious body pressed against his. Her sighs. His belief he would never get enough of her.

Crumpling the note into a ball, Sean tossed it across the room. Suddenly he felt every ache. His legs felt like lead. Slowly, he shuffled toward the bathroom. He needed a shower. Long and hot. Determined not to look at the bed, Sean's peripheral vision wouldn't let him off the hook that easily. It captured everything. The rumpled sheet. The pillow still holding the imprint of her head. A slash of red on the floor.

Frowning, Sean picked up the scrap of silk. So small he wondered why she had bothered. The image of her standing in nothing but her heels and the panties popped into his head. Unconsciously, his body tightened with desire.

Right, that was why.

Sean ran the smooth material over his cheek, feeling it catch on his morning stubble. He breathed deeply. He smelled vanilla and spice. Her essence. He would never forget it. As long as he lived, he would be able to close his eyes and conjure up her scent. Her taste.

His eyes popped open. *Friends? Nothing more? Bullshit*!

Keeping the panties in his hand, Sean headed for the shower. This wasn't over. Not by a long shot. It was just the beginning.

AFTER THE FIRE
(One Pass Away Book Three)

PROLOGUE

SHE HAD ONCE asked him if he believed in a higher power.

God? Buddha? Fairies dancing around a blazing fire late at night? Something. Anything bigger than us.

Gaige Benson hadn't known what to say. Not then. But as he stood in the empty open-air stadium—the stars lighting the evening sky—he knew the answer.

Football was his religion. The field he played on and the building surrounding it, his cathedral. If a higher power had a hand in it, then his answer was yes.

He believed.

Walking to the center of the field, Gaige took it all in. He found football at the age of thirteen. A boy who saw his future mapped out. Working in a factory. Drinking away his salary. Divorce. Doling out child support without maintaining a relationship with his children. A weekend father, who half the time didn't bother to show up.

The first time Gaige picked up a football, he felt a connection. The first time he threw it, it wobbled with the grace of a drunk leaving his favorite watering hole on a Saturday night. But it didn't matter. He threw the ball again. And again. Until he taught himself to make it spin in a perfect spiral.

At the time, Gaige didn't know his talent could be useful. Where he came from, Brooklyn kids didn't dream of bigger or better. Most of them didn't dream at all. Gaige was no different.

One day he was passing a playground when a football landed at his feet. The boys on the field yelled for him to toss it back. Without thinking, Gaige sent it sailing, a perfect strike. Then kept walking. He was wary of the man who ran after him. Strangers were the enemy—according to his father. They either wanted money or accused you of something you hadn't done.

Gaige took everything his father said with a big grain of salt. Don Benson didn't have a dime to his name. Why would anyone expect to get money from him? And if a man accused his father of something, chances were he was guilty.

But Gaige was a cautious boy. He fought when necessary and ran when he had no choice. The man trying to get his attention was big. His dark complexion didn't worry Gaige. In his experience, a man was either good or bad. The color of his skin had nothing to do with it.

It turned out that this man wasn't simply good. He was the best thing that ever happened to Gaige.

Terrance Aldridge coached the local Pop Warner football team. A boy with an arm like Gaige's shouldn't let his talent go to waste. Gaige listened. Play football? On a field? With other boys? Was such a thing possible? He didn't know if it were a scam—nor did he care. If there were the slightest chance, he would take it.

The only obstacle was getting a parent's permission. Terrance gave him the papers to be signed, telling Gaige to have his folks call him if they had any questions. Gaige didn't laugh aloud, but he wanted to. His mother never asked questions. Unless they were directed at his father. Wynona Benson hadn't made a move in fifteen years unless she received permission first.

His father was another matter. His word was law. Don Benson could do no wrong. If he drank too much and staggered home two days late, it was his right. If he backhanded his wife—just because—whose business was it? He earned the money. He made the rules. End of discussion.

Gaige hadn't asked his father because he knew what the answer would be. No! Not because he thought there was anything wrong with football. He watched it every Sunday—after laying down a bet that he never won. No, he wouldn't let Gaige play because he was a mean bastard who wanted everyone to be as miserable as he was.

Gaige got around it easily enough. He forged his father's signature. It wasn't the first time and it wouldn't be the last. There was no reason to think anyone would find out. His parents didn't care how he spent his days as long as the police didn't come knocking on the door.

He could steal. Lie. Cheat. Hell, his father wouldn't bat an eye at murder. *Do what you want as long as you don't get caught.* The mantra at the Benson house.

Gaige had no intention of his father finding out. He tried out for the team and made it. The money for equipment was another matter. Gaige didn't steal. Or cheat. Lying was a necessary evil. He would have done almost anything to play but it looked like his first and only dream would die before it had a chance.

Luckily, Terrance was able to dip into a discretionary fund to help boys like Gaige. It rankled to take charity. Especially when the other boys on the team had families to pay their way.

"Don't let it stop you, Gaige," Terrance told him. "Remember. And one day, when you have the means, pay it forward, son."

Twenty-five years later, Gaige hadn't forgotten that kindness and generosity. When he saw someone in need, he did something about it. Over the years, the *Gaige Benson Foundation* paid out millions of dollars to charities and individuals. He had filled the board with people he trusted and could count on to distribute the funds judiciously and without prejudice. The first man he had recruited was the man to whom Gaige owed everything—Terrance Aldridge. Friend. Father figure. Teacher.

"Hey, Gaige." Logan Price called out from high in the stands. "You coming? The guys are waiting to go to dinner."

"Five minutes."

Closing his eyes, Gaige breathed in the air. February in Texas. Tomorrow he would play in his first—and last Super Bowl. Win or lose, he was hanging up his cleats. He was thirty-eight years old. He had more money than he would ever need. He had won every award from Rookie of the Year to league MVP—four times.

This season he put everything on the line to get here—including the possibility that he had lost the only woman he had ever loved.

Gaige Benson was known for his razor-sharp focus. Any distractions off the field were left there as soon as the first whistle blew. It wouldn't be any different tomorrow. Nothing would get in the way.

His gaze drifted to the section where she would be sitting. If she showed up. Gaige planned on going out a winner. But what about the day after? Or the day after that? His future stretched out in front of him. He had plans in place. There were hundreds of options for him to consider.

Do you believe in a higher power?

Her voice and that question had haunted Gaige for almost sixteen years. If there were a God, he prayed the woman he loved would find it in her heart to forgive him. He had a lot of years left. He didn't want to spend them alone.

In his lifetime, Gaige Benson had dreamt of only two things. Playing football. And loving Violet Reed.

DREAMING WITH A BROKEN HEART
(Hollywood Legends Book One

PROLOGUE

THE ROOM WAS dark. Too dark for Garrett's liking. A little stuffy, a slight antiseptic smell with an overlay of sex. That's what you got from a cheap motel and furtive lovemaking. Odors and memories you'd just as soon forget.

The sounds from behind the closed bathroom door indicated his partner was trying to remove all traces of their recent activities. It shouldn't hurt. This wasn't the first time, and damn his weak resolve, it wouldn't be the last.

If he smoked, he would have something to do with his hands. Watching his father struggle with lung cancer put the fear of God in him and his brothers at an early age. All four of them had their vices; smoking wasn't one of them.

Get up. Get dressed. For once, be the first to leave. Even if he could find the balls to walk out on her, he couldn't leave her alone at this time of night. In this part of town.

God, it was like a furnace in here. Despite having the AC wall unit on high, Garrett knew it must be hotter in here than outside. The sheet riding low on his hips was too much. Damn modesty. The room was too dark to see anything; if she didn't like seeing his naked body, she could turn away. Garrett whipped off the coarse cotton material at the same moment the bathroom door opened.

"You don't have to go," Garrett said to the shadowed figure.

"Yes, I do."

She always made sure the light was off. Her silhouette showed a tall woman, thin. Too thin. Even by L.A. standards. She was gaining weight — slowly. Garrett could attest to that. He knew it was a struggle. One she fought every day.

Garrett felt the anger drain from his body — his heart melt. Her demands were not capricious whims. They weren't her attempt to gain the upper hand. Her goal was not to manipulate. She had her reasons. They were real. Legitimate.

"It's still early."

Garrett kept his voice low and even. Shouting didn't help. She never fought back. Retreat. That was her coping mechanism. The last time he blew up it was two weeks before she would take his calls.

"I..." she cleared her voice. "His flight gets in at midnight."

"Don't be there."

"You know how he gets."

Garrett knew all right. She was devoted to a man who treated her like crap, forgot her existence ninety percent of the time, yet expected her to be there when he decided to come home. His fists clenched the mattress. It was the only thing preventing him from grabbing her, begging her to stay. *For once, pick me.*

"I don't know when I can see you again."

I don't know if I ever want to see you again. Garrett thought the words. He would never verbalize them. She was his drug of choice. Weeks passed. The need for her grew. Outwardly, his life looked smooth as glass. Inside, the itch grew.

Garrett became an expert at compartmentalizing. His work never suffered. His family never suspected. No one had the slightest clue about what was raging inside of him. *She* knew. Because she shared his unbreakable habit. Enablers. That's what they were. It was sick. Sometimes, like tonight, he hated himself. He wished he could hate her. Then, maybe, he could walk away.

"I'll be out of town for the next month."

Garrett wished he could see her face. Was she sorry he'd be gone? Relieved? Would she miss him half as much as he was going to miss her?

"Take care."

Garrett waited a second, letting the motel room door close behind her. Jumping up, rushing to the window, he pulled back the thin, dingy curtain. He never walked her to the taxi. Even the minutest chance of them being seen was too much.

The ritual of watching until she was safely inside the vehicle, seat belt on, doors locked, was something he never ignored. Nothing bad would happen to her when he was around. It was when he wasn't there that trouble found her. One more frustration. It wasn't his place to protect her. Knowing that drove him crazy.

Garrett grabbed his jeans from a nearby chair, pulling them on. Unlike her, he wouldn't clean up before he left. He would carry the smell of her with him — let it fill the interior of his car. Tomorrow he would pretend it was still there.

Damn it. Enough. He deserved more than this. They both did. One month. When he got back, one way or another, things were going to change.

CHAPTER ONE

HOLLYWOOD. DREAMS FULFILLED. Dreams crushed. It happened every day. Wide-eyed kids still came hoping to be a star. More often than not, they went back home — a nobody. Iowa, Nebraska, Texas, Georgia. Insert state here. Small town, big city. It didn't matter. The movie industry seemed vast from the outside. In truth, it was the most insular of worlds. Making it took determination, perseverance, and a whole lot of luck. Talent was so far down the list it wasn't funny.

Connections. That was what got you through the door. If you had a recognizable name, the door swung wide, the smiles welcoming. If you couldn't pull your weight once you were inside, no one hesitated to kick you out. That famous name only got you so far. The rest was on your shoulders.

Sink or swim. No life preservers were thrown your way. If anything, you were fitted with cement shoes. The only thing this town loved more than a winner was the child of a Hollywood legend falling flat on his face.

Garrett Landis felt the weight of those expectations every time he stepped on a movie set. His father set the bar so high none of his sons was expected to reach his lofty heights. The fact that all four seemed well on their way to not only matching Caleb Landis' achievements, but surpassing them, caused quite a stir.

Resentment simmered under the surface of hearty backslapping and insincere ass kissing. Their father taught his boys many things. In this business, never turn your back on friend or foe. Treat everyone with respect, from the lowliest crew member to the head of the studio. The most important thing? In this business, trust no one — except brothers. Eight years after making his first low-budget independent film, Garrett followed those rules without question. The Gospel according to Caleb Landis. His father's words were his bible. His brothers were his rock.

Wyatt, the oldest, followed directly in their father's footsteps. He was a hard-ass, bottom-line producer. Nathaniel, Garrett's fraternal twin, was the daredevil of the bunch. He was the most in-demand stuntman in Hollywood. Baby brother Colton was blessed with movie star looks. His charisma leaped off the screen, pulling in even the most cynical audience member. Or so one critic wrote after seeing Colt's first movie. Individually, each Landis brother was formidable. Together, they dominated almost every branch of the industry.

"How can we be behind schedule when we haven't shot a single frame?"

"Welcome to the glamorous world of moviemaking."

Garrett grinned when he answered his assistant director, Hamish Floyd. This was their fourth collaboration. The first two made a nice profit. Number three broke box office records. Expectations for *Exile* went through the roof the second Garrett's name became attached. With Wyatt behind the scenes, the movie's success was practically guaranteed.

Garrett didn't believe in sure things. He worked hard on every project, no matter the size. Bigger budget, more potential headaches. That included a prima donna leading lady who couldn't get her ass on set at the designated hour. Garrett refused to start leaking money on day one.

"You want me to coax America's sweetheart of the week out of her trailer?"

"You'd never get past her PA," Garrett told Hamish. "Lynne Cornish thinks one hit movie and a few magazine covers give her the right to make her own rules. She's going to find out on this movie set, there is only one set of rules — mine."

"She has a contract."

"Wyatt's standard contract. She signed it. Her mistake if her lawyers didn't read the fine print."

Contracts were fluid. *Before* they were finalized. Each actor, depending on their box office leverage, could get their people to make demands, tweak the perks. The basics were non-negotiable. Under no circumstance, barring personal injury, a death in the family, or a genuine nervous breakdown, was an actor allowed to delay production. Once, you were warned. Twice, bye-bye. As far as Garrett's big brother was concerned, potential loss of a lead actor was the reason they paid huge insurance premiums. It hadn't happened to Garrett. Not yet. There was always a first time.

Tim Bodine, Lynne Cornish's PA, waylaid Garrett before he was halfway to her trailer.

"Lynne isn't feeling well."

"She was fine an hour ago."

When she was flirting with every man on the set. Apparently, Ms. Cornish could drag herself to any early breakfast if adoring men were present. She found out quickly that Garrett wasn't among them. Whether her sudden *illness* was a result of a hurt ego or plain laziness, he didn't give a damn. Starting right now, Lynne Cornish needed to know who was boss.

"Does she need a doctor?"

"Nooo." Tim drew out the word.

The PA's lack of concern only ratcheted up Garrett's annoyance.

"Five minutes."

"What?" Tim yelled at Garrett's retreating figure. When there was no response, the man hurried to catch up. "She can't make it in five minutes. Lynne doesn't think today will work for her. At all."

Garrett rounded on the smaller man. He topped him by at least eight inches. Tim was slight, Garrett muscular. Yet that wasn't what had the PA stepping back several feet. It was the look in Garrett's steely eyes.

This man exuded confidence. Strength, both physical and psychological, radiated from his core. You didn't mess with Garrett Landis. Not if you had half a brain.

"She was looking a little better when I left her trailer," Tim said, clearing his throat. "She wanted to speak with you. *Privately*."

Well, shit. Garrett didn't see that coming. Lynne made it clear, early on –she was interested. He made it equally clear he wasn't. End of story. They would have a friendly, professional relationship. Finding out his beautiful leading lady was angling for more didn't hold the thrill it once had. It made Garrett... tired. His personal life was full of enough turmoil — he didn't need the added drama of an on-set romance.

"I don't have the time, or inclination, Tim."

To Garrett's surprise, the PA blushed. In Hollywood, that ability was knocked out of a person fast.

"I can't guarantee anything."

"Then Lynne will be out of a job. How long do you think you'll last after that?"

Tim Bodine looked like a smart man. One capable of cajoling his uncooperative employer. Garrett didn't care what it took to get his star in front of the camera as long as it happened. Immediately.

"Five minutes?" Tim asked, a little panicked.

"I'll give you ten."

Garrett wondered if it was too late to get out of feature films. Animation. That sounded good. No location shoots. Voice-over actors happy to skip wardrobe fittings and hours in the makeup chair. A little direction on his part. Mostly setting the scene. One or two takes. Right now, it sounded like heaven.

"What's the word?" Hamish asked him.

"Bitch?"

"Any chance she'll be joining us in the near future?"

"Your guess is as good as mine."

Garrett looked around. They were ready to go. Cameras primed, leading man looking as impatient as Garrett felt. At least he'd lucked out with Paul McNally. He was a professional through and through. No power plays. No outlandish demands. There was no propositioning the director. Paul's first job was a small part in a Caleb Landis production. He was a great actor. More importantly, he was a friend. Garrett felt lucky to work with him.

"Once again, you've lived up to your reputation," Hamish said with admiration. "You really are a miracle worker."

Garrett looked over his shoulder. Lynne Cornish. In full costume and makeup. A little pouty. He could work with that. It complimented the scene.

"Tell them five."

"We're shooting in five minutes, people," Hamish called out Garrett's directions. "Pee now or forever hold it."

Garrett moved over to camera A, checking the shot. Perfect. This was his world. He knew what he was doing. No one questioned his authority or failed to jump at his command. Unlike his personal life, his professional life stayed on a clear path.

DREAMING WITH MY EYES WIDE OPEN
(Hollywood Legends Book Two)

PROLOGUE

NATE LANDIS NEVER thought much about the way he looked.

Women seemed to like his face. That was genetics. He was the son of Hollywood royalty. Alone, they turned heads. Together, they dazzled. It made sense that they would pass some of that on.

Nate took it in stride. He was strong. Healthy. His body was trained to do what he wanted it to do, under what could only be called extreme situations. He ate right, worked hard, and played harder.

At some point, his lifestyle would catch up with him. Age would take care of that. Right now, he was in his prime. If he wanted to scale a mountain, that's what he did. Jump from a plane? A piece of cake. Race car driving. Deep sea diving. You name it; Nate was the first one in line.

When he was three years old, his mother called him her little daredevil. Fearless, she swore he gave her wrinkles for worrying what he would get into next. Nate would always laugh, peering closely at Callie Flynn's flawless complexion. What wrinkles? In her fifties, she was, and would always be, one of the movie industry's great beauties. Nothing he or his brothers did could alter that.

As Nate stepped to the edge of the cliff, he didn't think about the two-hundred-foot drop. He'd jumped from higher than this. It was what he did. And he did it better than anyone else. For some reason, today he thought about his mother.

Callie never discouraged him from pursuing danger, even though Nate knew she wished he had chosen a safer way to make a living. She didn't say so, but he knew she worried about his safety. It didn't stop him — he seldom thought about it. Until today. As he waited for the director to signal the camera was rolling, for the first time Nate let himself worry about his mother's reaction if something happened to him.

He shook off the morbid thought. Now wasn't the time. He needed to focus. Ninety-nine percent of the time, if something went wrong, it was due to a loss of focus. Nate took a deep breath. He cleared his mind. Three flashes of light. That was his signal. He squared his shoulders, coiled his body. And jumped.

Nate Landis was a stuntman. Some might say it was his calling. If a director needed it done big and done right, that person called him. Nate loved his job.

He let his body relax as he sailed through the air. The count in his head was precise. If he pulled the ripcord too soon, the shot would be ruined. Too late, he risked ending up a pile of broken bones.

Nate planned every stunt. He worked out the timing, the logistics, and the angles. He never let anyone perform a stunt unless he tested it. Over and over again. He refused to rush. Anxious directors. Bottom-line producers. Some tried to push him into cutting corners.

Few things made Nate lose his temper. His brother Garrett claimed Nate had the longest, slowest burning fuse in history. But he had his hot buttons. Endangering himself and his crew was one of them. Last year, a director, trying to save time, ran a stunt when Nate was away from the set. Poorly conceived and executed, two stuntmen went to the hospital with second-degree burns.

Todd Winesap went to the hospital with a broken jaw and a tarnished reputation.

It took a lot to make Nate mad. But watch out when it happened.

Nate ran the count through his head. Eight, nine, ten. He gave the cord a firm, steady pull. Smooth as glass, the chute opened. Even so, he traveled at a high speed. The parachute was safety measure number one. Number two was the large, air-filled target waiting below.

Having done this stunt hundreds of times, Nate knew what to expect and how it should feel. And he knew when something was wrong.

The air bag, that Nate had personally supervised the placement of, wasn't where it was supposed to be. He didn't have the time to wonder how that had happened. If he didn't act fast, he wouldn't be around to beat the shit out of the asshole responsible.

Grabbing the guide strings, Nate pulled a hard right with all his considerable strength — and prayed.

CHAPTER ONE

HOLLYWOOD WAS AN unforgiving town with a long memory.

Drugs could be forgiven. Drunk driving. Spousal abuse. Those things could be forgiven. In the movie industry, your worth was measured by one thing — box office returns. Three strikes, you're out.

Early in his career, Caleb Landis knew the meaning of holding on by his fingertips. He was young, inexperienced, and hungry. That meant working all the angles. No one opened any doors for a dirt-poor would-be producer. That was fine with him. He had no problem barreling his way in. His take no prisoners attitude earned him respect. And enemies.

Hard work. Long hours. Sacrifice. Eventually, it paid off. Caleb's career spanned over four decades. He had money and power. The shelves of his office were lined with every award the industry could give him.

When a movie had the name Landis attached to it, the world knew they were getting quality.

Sitting back, Caleb looked around the table with pride. His family. That was his greatest accomplishment. The fame and money meant nothing compared to the joy of knowing the most important people in the world surrounded him. The people he loved. The people who loved him.

It all started and ended with his Callie.

Screen goddess to the world. To him, protector of his heart.

He had no doubt the first time he saw her. He knew she was the woman he wanted to spend his life with. She was the only woman he would ever love. Their life hadn't been the fairy tale some people made it out to be. They had their ups and downs. But through it all, one thing never changed. Their unshakable love.

His beautiful wife had given him four strong, healthy sons. Men a father could be proud of.

Wyatt was the oldest. Like Caleb, a producer. The difference was *he* trusted his gut. If a project felt right, he fought until he got it made. Wyatt was a thinker. His first concern was the bottom line. They had squared off more than once about artistry versus the almighty dollar.

The end was always the same. He and Wyatt were different enough that butting heads was inevitable. They had enough similarities to put those differences aside. The most important thing was the movie. Together they made art — and money.

Caleb's gaze moved to the other side of the table. The laugh he heard was a deeper version of his sweet Callie's. It made him smile. Colton. The youngest of his four boys. He was the only one to follow his mother's lead, stepping in front of the camera to make his mark. And what a mark it was going to be.

Colt had a face the camera loved. The first offer to put him in the movies came when he was only a year old. The offers kept coming. Callie didn't want any of her sons to be *child stars*. Caleb agreed.

Growing up was hard enough. In Beverly Hills, the temptations were magnified. Caleb and Callie did their best to give their children as normal a childhood as possible. Family dinners. Game night. Backyard barbecues. If that childhood included trips to Cannes and vacations on private yachts, so what? This was their version of normal. It wasn't perfect. But then, what was?

Colton was one of the biggest movie stars in the world. In public, that meant screaming fans and preferential treatment. At dinner with his family, he was expected to set the table and dry the dishes. It was true when he was ten. It was true now, even if his last movie *did* break box office records.

Then there was Garrett. Caleb sat back smiling when he heard his middle son complaining to his mother.

"What is the world coming to when a man's family takes sides against him?"

"First, Jade is your family. And ours." Callie patted Jade's hand. "Second. She's right. You're wrong. End of discussion."

"Hey." Garrett looked at the two women. His mother on his right. The love of his life on his left. There was no rock. No hard place. With a snap of his fingers, there would be a thousand men lined up to take his place. He was no fool. He knew he had it good. "I give up," he said, wisely conceding the point.

Dazzled by Jade's smile, Garrett melted. He tucked a lock of her long, silky red hair behind her ear. The unconsciously intimate gesture had his parents smiling with approval.

"A wise decision, son." Caleb nodded at Garrett with a wink. "When you realize your lady is the brains in the relationship, the sailing will be much smoother."

"Where are you on *Exile*?"

Garrett and Jade were just back from Vancouver where he had finished principal shooting on his current film. His last project had garnered him an Oscar nomination for best director. Caleb believed this one would win his son the statue.

"I'm in the studio next week. The soundtrack needs some tweaking, but the composer assures me it will be ready."

"It better be," Wyatt added. "The Los Angeles Philharmonic doesn't come cheap. You have them for a week. That's all the budget will allow. After that, I'll take it out of your salary."

"It's my own fault for working with family," Garrett sighed. "I could knock any other producer on his ass if he talked to me like that. Mommy would have a fit if I bruised her baby's face."

"Jade, you're marrying an idiot."

"Pardon my French in advance, Mom." Garrett gave Wyatt the finger, and then added, "Fuck you, Wyatt."

"Nice mouth, brother. You might think about washing it out with soap before kissing your woman." Out of Callie's sight, Wyatt flipped Garrett the bird.

"I just brushed. How about kissing me instead?"

"Nate!"

Callie was across the room in a flash. Instead of jumping into his arms, as was her custom, she held back. She knew the doctor said Nate's ribs were healed, but she was his mother. The thought of causing him the slightest pain was unthinkable.

"Where's your sling?"

"Gone for good. Thank God."

Nate's left arm was still in a cast. With little effort, he used his right to swing Callie in a circle. The comforting scent of roses and vanilla drifted around him. As always, it took him back to his childhood when she would tuck him in at night. Burying his face in her hair, he breathed deeply.

Mother. Love. Safety. From the time he was born, she had steered him with a gentle yet firm hand. There was a fine line between controlling and supportive. Callie Flynn showed her sons by example that a woman could thrill the world with her acting and still be the best mother anyone could ask for. Nate affectionately kissed the top of her head. What would he have done without this woman?

"We didn't think you were going to make it." Callie took his good hand, leading him to the table. "Sit. I'll get you a plate. I swear, since the accident you've wasted away to nothing."

Colt snorted in disbelief. "How can you tell? The man is a freaking brick wall."

"Callie's right." Jade smiled at Nate. "You look thinner."

"I knew the woman couldn't keep her eyes off me. Tell me you've finally realized you picked the wrong brother."

"One more word and I'll forget you're my twin." Garrett turned to Jade. "I always felt sorry for him. I got the looks, the brains, and the charm. And Nate got the...? What did Nate get?"

"The ability to kick your ass?" Nate flexed his impressive biceps. "And more women than even Colton could handle."

"Hey," Colt interjected. "That's my reputation as a man-whore you're besmirching. What would the tabloids say if word got out that my brother was getting more women than I was?"

"Don't listen to him, Colt." Garrett loved jabbing at his twin. Just as Nate loved returning the favor. The sport never grew old.

"He overcompensated for his shortcomings by living in the gym. I suppose some women find brawn over brains attractive."

"More than a few."

"Enough." Callie chuckled. She had heard this banter for years. "You," she said to Nate, "stop talking — eat. And you," she looked at Garrett. "Leave your brother in peace for five minutes."

Thanking her with a smile, Nate took the plate from his mother. It overflowed with roast beef, mashed potatoes, fresh green beans, all drowned in rich, brown gravy. Adding three fresh baked rolls from the basket on the table, Nate was a happy man.

The truth was, since the accident on the movie set last month, he hadn't been himself. It would be different if he could work. Keeping busy was the best way to calm his mind and body. Unfortunately, the injuries he had sustained kept him sidelined.

Too much time on his hands. Too much time to think about what had gone wrong. The botched stunt could have ended in tragedy. Thanks to his quick reflexes, physical strength, and determination not to end up in a heap of mangled bones, Nate walked away with a few cracked ribs and a broken arm. The only reason he stayed the night in the hospital was to appease his mother. The doctor assured her Nate didn't have a concussion. Callie didn't want to take any chances. One night of observation was a small price to pay for his mother's peace of mind.

It didn't hurt that his nurse was a curvy brunette with warm, soft hands.

"I know that smile." Wyatt shook his head. "Which conquest are you thinking about now?"

"You wouldn't give me such a hard time if you were getting laid more often." Remembering where he was, Nate gave his mother a repentant grin. "Sorry."

"Your brother's love life is his own business," Callie said firmly.

"Thank you." Wyatt gave Nate a *take that* glare.

"Though…"

"Ah, crap." Wyatt's head fell forward, his chin hitting his chest.

"Come on, Wyatt," Garrett laughed with delight. "Every man lives to have his mother discuss his sex life."

DREAMING OF YOUR LOVE
(Hollywood Legends Book Three

PROLOGUE

LIGHTS FLASHED FROM every direction. It blinded and dazzled all at once.

Screams drowned out every other sound. This was Los Angeles. Busy streets in every direction. Jet patterns overhead. The excited—in some cases rabid—fans that surrounded the roped-off red carpet made it seem like nothing existed but them and the bright lights.

It shouldn't have been a pleasant experience. Alighting from the over-the-top luxury of a Rolls Royce into chaos and mayhem? No normal human being would willingly seek out such an experience.

However, Colton Landis was not a normal human being. He was an actor.

Colt turned his world-famous megawatt smile on the crowd, eliciting another deafening burst of heartfelt screams.

"We need to get inside, Colt. The movie starts in ten minutes."

"Relax, Deb."

Colt's publicist had been with him for five years. Deb Kline knew how to spin a press release like nobody else. They saw eye to eye on most things. Except how much he should expose himself to his fans. If she had her way, he would zip from point A to point B as quickly as humanly possible.

In this case, point A was the limo, and point B was Grauman's Chinese Theater.

"I'll relax when you are safely inside. Have you forgotten Dallas already?"

"Dallas was an anomaly."

Colt continued to wave and smile. Deb wanted him to curb his accessibility. She had always been cautious, but after a fan somehow breached security during a press conference to announce his next movie, she was particularly leery of events like this one.

"Colt."

"Don't go over there, Colt."

Deb knew the second Colt observed the waving autograph books, her words fell on deaf ears. He believed in giving his fans what they wanted. It was one of the things that made Colton Landis a huge movie star. He genuinely loved his fans. He loved meeting them, speaking with them, having his picture taken with them. Most of her clients searched for any reason to avoid these moments. Not Colt. He didn't have a public persona and a private one. What you saw was what you got—twenty-four hours a day, seven days a week.

Colt made her job as a publicist a dream. Keeping him safe was a nightmare.

He refused to have a bodyguard. Part of it was ego—and he had plenty of that. Many of his parts portrayed him as a big, macho, tough guy. How would it look if he had a bigger, more macho, tough guy constantly shadowing him? Not great for his reputation. He would look weak. And in Hollywood, perception was everything.

It was a valid argument. Not so valid? Colt believed that, for the most part, his fans were harmless. Not that he was a naïve Pollyanna. There was no need for Deb to point out the entertainment world's tragic examples of the heinous acts obsessive fans could commit.

Colt lived the life. He grew up watching his superstar mother traverse that fine line between making herself accessible to fans and maintaining some much-needed privacy.

However, he didn't have a family to consider. No wife. No children. His life was his own. A bodyguard would mean he was giving in. Turning his life over to fear instead of embracing every single moment of his fairytale existence.

"Ten minutes."

Deb didn't know if Colt heard her over the screams. Nor did she care. She was getting him into that theater if it meant grabbing his ear and dragging him along like an errant five-year-old. And wouldn't that make a great picture in *People* magazine? Okay. No ears. *Ugh. This man was going to make her old before her time.*

Colt held a woman's phone at arm's length, including himself in a selfie of her and her three friends.

"I love you, Colton."

Colt couldn't single out the speaker. The cry came from every direction. He waved and called out, "I love you, too."

He signed a few more autographs, moving along the line. Deb was right. He needed to get inside. It wasn't fair to keep everyone waiting. Ten more, he promised himself. It killed him to see the expressions on the faces of the fans who were left out.

"Thanks. See you soon," Colt called out to the crowd.

Handing her signed book to a dreamy-eyed woman, Colt gave the crowd a final wave.

"Ready?" Deb tried to maintain the *stern teacher* expression she had spent twenty years cultivating.

Colt had a way of making her professional mask slip. Thank goodness she was old enough to be his youngish grandmother. While his charm was undeniable, her age and experience allowed her to put the sexual pull that radiated around him into perspective.

Until he turned his smile on her. Full blast.

"Am I that big of a pain in the ass?"

There it was. That naughty twinkle in his deep blue eyes that made the world swoon. On screen, it was irresistible. Paired with dark hair and a tall, muscular frame, was it any wonder the camera loved him?

Reluctantly, Deb returned his smile.

Colt was her client. He was also her friend. She knew he wasn't trying to be difficult. He was being himself. For a man who was adored by millions, catered to on a daily basis, and could buy and sell two or three third-world nations without raising a sweat,

Colton Landis was surprisingly down to Earth. And hard-headed. And opinionated.

On top of that? On occasions such as this one, a major pain in the ass.

Still, if she were honest, there wasn't a single thing about him that she would change. As movie stars went—hell, as human beings went—Colton Landis was a joy to be around. Not that she would ever tell him that. The last thing he needed was another person extolling his endless virtues. Colt hated that kind of treatment. One of the reasons they worked so well together was because Deb didn't kowtow.

Deb was about to hit him with one of the nifty sarcastic one-liners he loved, when a scream came from the crowd. Not a *we love you* cry, but one of terror. Before she could react, Deb saw a man jump over the velvet rope. He carried a knife.

Colt pushed her to the side, effectively putting himself between her and the attacker. *He isn't after me*, Deb wanted to protest. But everything happened so fast, she didn't have time.

In the blink of an eye, the man raised the knife and stabbed Colt.

IF I LOVED YOU
(Harper Falls Book One)

PROLOGUE

IT WAS SOMETHING out of a fairy tale.

Thousands of flickering lights dazzled her senses, almost as much as the tall, wickedly handsome man who so expertly danced her onto the shadowed balcony. The music that filtered from the nearby ballroom only added to the already magical atmosphere.

Women dreamed their whole lives of a moment like this — a prelude to a happily-ever-after ending. Ever so briefly, she let herself drift into that fantasy as if she was one of those women. For a moment, she let herself pretend that her childhood had been filled with the kind of whimsicality that allowed those fantasies to carry over into adulthood.

But no, she wasn't a romantic, hopeless or otherwise. She didn't want a prince to sweep her into his arms and carry her away on his faithful steed. She was more than capable of rescuing herself. She preferred it that way.

The stars were in the sky, not in her eyes.

"I'm glad you asked me to dance," her partner whispered, pulling her closer.

Suddenly, she was nervous. The champagne she downed earlier had completely worn off. No more floating on a cloud of false courage. If she was going to do this, she was going to have to do it on her own.

"Jack," she said. Damn, it was hard to sound seductive when your voice squeaked. "Jack." That was better, lower, and slightly husky. She'd read somewhere that guys liked husky voices.

"Rose."

"Yes?"

"Nothing, I just thought we were saying each other's names." He put his lips next to her ear. "I like the way you say mine."

"Jack." Good Lord, she had to stop repeating his name. "I need a favor, Jack. A big one." Or should she say, she hoped he *had* a big one. Rose groaned to herself. At least she hadn't said that aloud.

"I'll help if I can."

"You're the only one who *can* help." She took another deep breath. "I need you to take me home and screw my brains out."

FLOWERS FOR ZOE
HART OF ROCK AND ROLL BOOK FOUR

PROLOGUE

FOUR YEARS OLD. Zoe Hart was a big girl now. She could dress herself—mostly. Get her own bowl and cereal from the cupboard—with the help of a chair. And pour her own milk—the few spills that her brother Ryder quickly cleaned up didn't count. She was almost grown up. Unlike Suzy next door who was a whole year older, Zoe didn't need a nightlight, and she never wet the bed.

Pre-school was fun. Finger painting was the best because Zoe was allowed to make a mess. Ryder told her they couldn't make messes at home. She did her best—she *was* a big girl now. But sometimes she forgot. Her big brother would rush to put things right, keeping an eye on the front door. Then he would wipe away her tears—she didn't cry very often because only babies cried—holding her on his lap, telling her everything would be okay.

Ryder always made things right. He brushed Zoe's hair without pulling too hard and made the best peanut butter sandwiches ever. He knew how to tie her shoes and always held her hand when they left the apartment. He never scolded. She loved Ryder more than anything in the whole world—even her teddy bear.

It seemed like Zoe's friends were afraid of everything. Spiders. The dark. And something they called the boogeyman. She didn't know who that was, but she knew he wouldn't frighten her. Nothing scared Zoe. Except the Monster.

The music brought the Monster. Deep asleep, Zoe never heard it, but Ryder always did.

"Shh," he urged, waking her up with a gentle shake. Before she could complain, he would put a finger to Zoe's lips. "Hear that?"

Counting flowers on the wall, that don't bother me at all.

The sound was faint, but Zoe could hear the words through the thin apartment walls. When she was a little girl—a whole year ago when she was three—she thought the music sounded happy. Now that she was grown up, she had figured out that the song made Ryder sad. He was sad for a long time after it finally stopped playing. She might not understand the reasons, but Zoe knew one thing. If her big brother didn't like it, neither did she.

"Do you have your teddy?" Ryder would ask.

Zoe nodded, she always slept with teddy. Ryder would take her hand. He had her crawl under the bed, way in back to the farthest corner, before tucking a blanket around her.

"Remember the invisible game?" Ryder whispered. "You have to stay right here, Zoe. Curl up in a little ball, don't make a sound, hold on to teddy, and keep the blanket tight. The Monster can't see you if you follow the rules. He won't know you're here."

"I remember," Zoe whispered back. She knew it was part of the game. But she didn't like it. She didn't want to play by herself. "Stay with me."

"Shh." A loud thump from the other room made Ryder hurriedly look over his shoulder. "You know I'll be back."

"But—"

The bedroom door slammed open, making Zoe jump, the squeak she let out muffled by Ryder's hand.

"*I need my little boy.*" The Monster's voice was sing-songy, and though the words were slurred, they were unmistakable.

"I'll always come back for you, Zoe. Always. Now close your eyes. Please?"

Reluctantly, Zoe scrunched her eyes tight.

"There he is." Zoe knew she wasn't supposed to, but she couldn't help peeking. The Monster grabbed Ryder's arm, jerking him from under the bed. "Come keep Daddy company."

With a silent sob, Zoe shut her eyes. *Daddy.* She never thought of the Monster that way. He was rarely around. Ryder made certain Zoe had something to eat. They would play games or watch something on the television. After she brushed her teeth, her big brother would tuck her in, reading her a story. Zoe liked it when it was just the two of them.

On the few occasions when the Monster spent the evening in the apartment, Ryder made her stay in the bedroom, quietly playing by herself.

The song grew louder. Zoe pressed her hands to her ears, unable to block out the noise or the sound of Ryder crying out. She knew there would be boo boos on his arms in the morning. Dark spots he tried to hide under an old, ripped shirt that was way too big, the sleeves hanging past the ends of his fingers.

Why won't the Monster stop? Furiously, Zoe wiped the tears from her cheeks, clutching her teddy bear close. Humming a nonsensical tune, in her head she recited Ryder's words over and over, drifting into a deep but troubled sleep.

You are invisible. I'll always come back for you. You are invisible. I'll always come back for you. You are invisible. I'll always come back for you.

www.ingramcontent.com/pod-product-compliance
Lightning Source LLC
Chambersburg PA
CBHW061137170626
46809CB00003B/884